COOS COOPERATIVE

DISCARD

3 2881 0077

D0466667

AUCHIN- CLOSS, LOUIS East
Auchincloss, Louis
East Side story : a novel

COOS BAY PUBLIC LIBRARY

EAST SIDE STORY

Also by Louis Auchincloss

The Golden Calves
Fellow Passengers
The Lady of Situations
False Gods
Three Lives: Tales of Yesteryear
The Collected Stories of Louis Auchincloss
The Education of Oscar Fairfax
The Atonement and Other Stories
The Anniversary and Other Stories
Her Infinite Variety
Manhattan Monologues
The Scarlet Letters

NONFICTION

Reflections of a Jacobite
Pioneers and Caretakers
Motiveless Malignity
Edith Wharton
Richelieu
A Writer's Capital
Reading Henry James
Life, Law and Letters
Persons of Consequence:
Queen Victoria and Her Circle
False Dawn:
Women in the Age of the Sun King
The Vanderbilt Era
Love Without Wings
The Style's the Man
La Gloire: The Roman Empire
of Corneille and Racine
The Man Behind the Book
Theodore Roosevelt
Woodrow Wilson

LOUIS AUCHINCLOSS

EAST SIDE STORY

A NOVEL

Houghton Mifflin Company

BOSTON   NEW YORK

2004

COOS BAY PUBLIC LIBRARY

Copyright © 2004 by Louis Auchincloss

All rights reserved

For information about permission to reproduce selections from
this book, write to Permissions, Houghton Mifflin Company,
215 Park Avenue South, New York, New York 10003.

Visit our Web site: www.houghtonmifflinbooks.com.

Library of Congress Cataloging-in-Publication Data

Auchincloss, Louis.
East Side story : a novel / Louis Auchincloss.
p. cm.
ISBN 0-618-45244-3
1. Scottish Americans—Fiction. 2. Upper East Side (New York,
N.Y.)—Fiction. 3. Upper class families—Fiction. 4. New
York (N.Y.)—Fiction. 5. Newport (R.I.)—Fiction. 6. Rich
people—Fiction. 7. Socialites—Fiction. I. Title.

PS3501.U25E27 2004
813'.54—dc22   2004047499

Book design by Anne Chalmers
Typefaces: Jansen Text, Copperplate

Printed in the United States of America

MP 10 9 8 7 6 5 4 3 2 1

For
JUNE DYSON,
dear friend
and fellow trustee
through many happy years

CONTENTS

THE CARNOCHANS

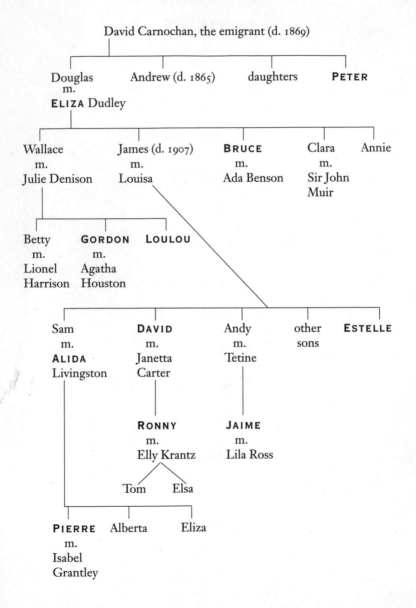

David Carnochan, the emigrant (d. 1869)

Douglas
m.
ELIZA Dudley   Andrew (d. 1865)   daughters   **PETER**

Wallace
m.
Julie Denison   James (d. 1907)
m.
Louisa   **BRUCE**
m.
Ada Benson   Clara
m.
Sir John
Muir   Annie

Betty
m.
Lionel
Harrison   **GORDON**
m.
Agatha
Houston   **LOULOU**

Sam
m.
ALIDA
Livingston   **DAVID**
m.
Janetta
Carter   Andy
m.
Tetine   other
sons   **ESTELLE**

RONNY
m.
Elly Krantz   **JAIME**
m.
Lila Ross

Tom   Elsa

PIERRE
m.
Isabel
Grantley   Alberta   Eliza

EAST SIDE STORY

1

PETER

To CELEBRATE, next New Year's Day of the year 1904, the seventy-fifth anniversary of our arrival on this side of the Atlantic, my great-nephew David urged me, as the only published author of the family, to write up a history of the Carnochans to be privately printed and distributed to the many descendants of my father, the original David, who, three quarters of a century ago, emigrated as a young man from Scotland to establish a branch of the family thread business in New York. When I pleaded age and illness as an excuse, he asked me at least to contribute a first chapter about my father, whom I, as the youngest of his offspring, was the sole survivor to remember, pointing out that as the patriarch had left no letters or journal, there would be nothing but account books with which to reconstruct his personality.

But would that be such a bad thing?

Father's obituary notices in 1869 were fulsome in their pompous tribute, but I always kept in a special file the funeral address of his Presbyterian pastor, which contained this gem:

> He was not a man of smooth words, a disguised flatterer, nor a person to seek even good ends by craft and indirectness. Making no pretensions to literary culture, though well instructed in all that belonged to his pro-

fession and his church, he dealt more in forcible reasons than in fair speeches, and this in business as in religion. It is just the sort of character which we should lament to see going out of date. Of any man it is sufficient eulogy to say that he so uses his powers as to be virtuously successful in his chosen calling. Such honor belongs to David Carnochan. The judgment of the commercial circle in this city, as uttered in the great centers of business in our emporium, is decisive on this point.

When I suggested to my great-nephew that he use this for his first chapter, he simply said: "Uncle Peter, you're making fun of me." Yet every word the pastor had written was true! The New York of that simpler day had at least not been hypocritical. It actually believed those things!

Well, I was not going to let myself sink into the role of crank, so I drafted for David a short, dry, factual account of my father's business and domestic life, which will constitute the innocuous preface to his little book. Don't most readers skip prefaces, anyway?

But as I wrote it, I found myself wondering if I shouldn't try my hand at a few pages on what Father was really like, at least as a father. And then I realized that any such portrait would be just as much a portrait of the son as the father, for each term implied the existence of the other. Well, why not? It would be the portrait of a relationship, and maybe that was as good a way as any to approach truth.

So here it is. David will never print it in his family book, but something tells me he will not throw it away. David is no fool.

We don't know much about our origins in Paisley. Paisley is an ancient town, set in the plain of the Cart rivers, seven miles west of Glasgow, in Renfrewshire, and a great thread manufacturing center. Some of the family used to take pride in the fact that David the emigrant came of a clan already established in business in the Old World rather than as an adventurous beggar or a refugee from religious persecution or even an ex-convict. But some of our less-reverent youngsters liked to circulate a story about my older brother Douglas — my father's true heir and prosperous business successor — when he returned to the homeland in quest of one of those family trees which (the mockers claimed) Edinburgh genealogists produced at so much a head for each Bruce, Stewart, or Wallace added, and happened to hire an ancient caddy (Scots had such then) at a Paisley golf course. "I am here, my man," Douglas is reputed to have informed the old boy in a lordly tone as they trudged across the green, "to trace my family origins. My name is Carnochan. Perhaps you have heard of it." "I have indeed!" was the caddy's enthusiastic rejoinder. "It's my name! And I do recall that my mither used to say one branch had crossed the ocean and done better!" Despite this suggestion of less than Olympian origin, Douglas returned to New York with a tree bristling with lords and ladies. He always denied the caddy story.

Today the fashion has changed, at least in the younger set, and people like to boast that they stem from sturdier stock, from outlaws and sheep stealers and pirates, but I suspect that the truth is that the Carnochans in the Old World were pretty much what they became in the New: good burghers with a sharp eye for a deal. You would not have found one of them risking a copper penny for Mary Stuart or Bonnie Prince Charlie.

The outline of Father's life that I gave to young David was, of course, factually accurate. Father was considered a success at each of the few things he undertook. He was a prosperous merchant in a town that boasted dozens of even more prosperous ones; he served a term as president of the American Dry Goods Association; he was a revered elder of the Fifth Avenue Presbyterian Church, and he enjoyed a seemingly tranquil marriage to the daughter of a fellow Paisley emigrant on whom he sired a multitude of children. I might here note, for whatever significance it may have, that all his many living descendants stem from only one of these, my brother Douglas. The rest died either childless or unwed.

What I have earlier written makes it pretty clear, I guess, that Father was a granite pillar of respectability. He lived simply but well in a big square red-brick house on Great Jones Street and a summer villa on Staten Island, entertaining frugally his carefully chosen few friends, mostly fellow Scots, and punctiliously attending divine services. He never cultivated the society of Gotham, where he would, in any case, have been considered too dour a guest; it was his son Douglas, whose wife, Eliza, was of ancient colonial stock, who went in for that. Father, needless to add, frowned severely on the frivolities of dancing and drinking and general hilarity. He had his own strict views of what such things led to.

But what I want to get at is what Father was to *me*, his youngest and physically frailest child. He was a tall, lean, gaunt man with large craggy features and thick unkempt gray hair — or is that simply the way I see him, looking back, without a trace of nostalgia, at those early years? No doubt I exaggerate his formidability. Neither of my brothers seemed to feel it as I did. And I admit there was a surprising serenity in his pale blue eyes, and that he never lifted a hand to any of us or even lost his temper, and that there was an air of mild benignity in what I could not help feeling was a basic exemption from the usual family attachments. No, he was not a bad man; there was no cruelty in his firmness, or malice, or even ego in his insistence on domestic obedience.

What was it about him, then, that filled me with such unutterable dismay?

What it was, I can now only suppose, was that he resolutely denied — with the blind faith of a latter-day John Knox — that there was anything but potential evil in all the things that to me made life worthwhile: in love and laughter and merry companionship, in sports and theater, and, worst of all, in art. In short: in pleasure. Life to David Carnochan was something simply to be got through by satisfying the fleshly appetites only with such aliments as were necessary to sustain it and only with so much coition as was needed to maintain it for God's glory on earth. And so he ran a business in thread to shield nudity not only from the cold but from temptation, and used his seed to increase the number of God's chosen. The deity who insisted on his own daily magnification could be counted on for compensation in a future life that was presumably *not* devoid of pleasure, though that pleasure would seem to consist primarily in the hallooing of anthems. When I watched Father, stentorianly out of tune, sturdily raising his voice in a hymn in church, I could not but wonder if this to him was the houri promised the deceased Islamite. I could never imagine him in bed with Mother. Was heaven to be a repetition of a Sunday service?

Of course, there are, and perhaps, alas, always will be, persons who hold such tenets, but Father's power, at least where I was concerned, was in making them seem more real than any other reality that I tried desperately to make out behind them. He simply stripped life of every aspect of color and charm that it might have possessed; he made an arid desert of every fancied oasis. In his flat voice, in the grating of his rare chuckle, in the slight elevation of his bushy eyebrows at any mention of a diversion, he made me wonder if the only feasible thing to do in the world he created was to die. His god may not have been my god, but I believed that his god not only existed but would probably get the better of any god I could conjure up to oppose him.

I did not, however, stand alone against him. I may not have had an ally in any of my siblings, but I had one, fortunately or not, as a reader of these notes may decide, in my mother. Mother's outward appearance was that of just such a wife as a man like Father might seem to need and want. She was large, plain, silent, thin-lipped, utterly conventional, an awesomely efficient matron and housekeeper. She appeared to have no difficulty with her spouse's way of life and gave no hint of not sharing his concept of God and what God expected. As a mother she was always patient with and mildly understanding of the whims and wiles of children, though it was sometimes possible to detect that her slightly tepid maternal feelings were in hidden conflict with a repressed exasperation. Except where the two younger of her three sons were concerned: Andrew and myself. Andrew, handsome, hearty, jovial, and charming, was her obvious favorite. He was everyone's favorite; even Father's, whose opaque glance showed almost a twinkle when Andrew smiled at him. The exception granted me was for a very different reason. From childhood I suffered from asthma.

My terrible attacks of breathlessness were allayed only by Mother's care and embraces. She had given life to my siblings, but I was the only one who seemed to need her to retain it. I think I may have represented to her the one thing in the whole Presbyterian world of her husband that she might call her very own, and she was determined to cling to me with a fierceness, always deep within her but hitherto untapped, before which even Father quailed. She raised a wall around my sickbed against which he would have battered in vain, had he not rather had the sense to wait for the day when I should emerge into more neutral territory.

It was thus that I grew up sheltered, so to speak, like a lion cub against a possibly dangerous sire. Or to use a less violent image, like the young Achilles reared amid the maidens, in my case my older sisters, to shield him from future battles. With the marked difference that Achilles managed still to grow up to be a warrior while I became the very reverse. At twenty, as a day student at Columbia College, I was thin and pale and drawn-looking. My attacks had almost ceased, but I made the most of those that still occurred, knowing that too much of a cure might cost me my exemption from the paternal rites of cold baths, vigorous walks on the hard city pavements, two-hour church services, and other soul-fortifying exercises. To me was permitted, in town, the luxury of long winter afternoons by the parlor fire with a treasury of romantic novels, and, in summer, the delight of not having to plunge into the sea but basking in the sun, daydreaming and watching the others bob in the water.

It was on the tender ears of such a nonparticipant in the bracing life that the angry tumult of pre-secession America fell. At first it sounded far from our quiet household. Father was of the school that found slavery sanctioned in the Bible and that felt, anyway, it was solely the business of the South; he joined my brother Douglas in holding that no compromise of the issue was too great to save a Union that was good for business. Andrew, on the other hand, was a fiery abolitionist and even dared to beard his father at the family board meeting with taunts about his tolerance of "Simon Legrees and women floggers." But the actual outbreak of war brought about a cautious lineup of the formerly peace-loving Carnochans on the side of "Honest Abe."

My brother Douglas led the way. Bluff and single-minded, he was already Father's right-hand man in the family business and was beginning to dominate his now aging parent. He had the gift of renewing his native heartiness in the wake of each new change in his point of view; he was able, I believe, quite literally to chase out of his conscious mind any memory of attachment to a superseded cause. New York had plenty of Southern sympathizers in its business community, and our family connection with Scotland might have inclined us at least to tolerate Britain's initial hostility to the Union side, but Douglas was a shrewd man in his predictions and he had surmised that the future lay with the North. Accordingly, no one was louder now in his denunciations of what were soon to be called "copperheads." Andrew, who was getting ready to enlist and who was well aware that his embattled older brother had no such military intentions, was more than willing to throw Douglas's past opinions in his face. I recall in particular one family dispute. Douglas, a recent member of the Union Club — his hand was already gripping the upper rings of the social ladder — was holding forth on the needed expulsion of certain members who, in his loudly voiced opinion, were no better than traitors.

Andrew went right for the jugular. "It seems to me, Douglas, that you take a pretty strong line for a man who only yesterday was supporting the Fugitive Slave Law."

"That was a simple question of law, Andy. A slave was private property, and strayed property had to be returned to its owner. My attitude did not for a minute imply that I was ever in favor of slavery. I respected the Constitution, that was all."

"You didn't think the law of God was superior to that of the Constitution?"

"Boys, boys," came Father's gravelly voice. "Will you kindly leave the name of the Almighty out of your political discussions. We have had no divine guidance as to which side, if either, He would favor in this unhappy conflict.

There are men of undoubted faith among our foes. We can only pray that what we are doing is God's will."

A short, respectful, but perfunctory silence followed the paternal admonition, but the brothers were soon at it again.

"Slavery was the price we paid for our Union," Douglas continued. "It was a bitter price, but we paid it. But now that the rebels have gone back on their word, we have every legal and moral right to free their slaves and force them back into the Union. They have torn up the Constitution. There is nothing inconsistent between my pre- and postwar thinking."

"Only between your pre- and postwar heart," Andrew sneered. "We remember how sweetly you used to cultivate all those rich planters who came North to spend their summers in Newport!"

But this was nothing compared to the bitterness between the two much later in the war when the draft was passed. Andrew, a twice-wounded army captain was fighting in Virginia when he got word from Father that Douglas, who had never left the family office, had purchased a substitute for $300. Father's letter mentioned this as if it had been the only thing that his much-needed assistant could do, but he may have anticipated something of his second son's reaction when he added a note of the connection between the thread business and the army's need of uniforms. But Andrew was not impressed. His stinging answer to Father's letter was that the family had been disgraced.

There had never been any question of my enlisting. I had felt an obligation to utter some murmurs about joining the colors, but Mother's indignant protests, backed by those of our kindly old family physician, Dr. Findlay, whom she had, so to speak, in her pocket, allowed me to retreat from glory behind my noticeably diminishing asthmatic attacks. The only slight shame that I felt was in the hearty endorsement of the maternal attitude taken by my war-minded brother Andrew, whose ever-generous nature ascribed to me a genuine disappointment at missing combat and who assured me, placing a friendly arm around my shoulders, that if I would be good about staying home, he would fight hard enough for two. I could not but blush at the thought of my own hidden relief at my nonenlistment, but I solaced myself with counting up how many of my contemporaries remained out of uniform and with the hope, soon to be dashed, that the war would be a short one.

The disasters that followed Bull Run darkened the next two years and ultimately necessitated the draft, which brought on the major decision of my life. For my health had gone as well as the war had gone badly; my asthma attacks had virtually ceased. It was evident that if I were to avoid military service, it would have to be through an official exemption, for I knew that I would rather die than submit my heroic brother Andrew, who had been severely wounded but had rejoined his regiment, to the humiliation of having *two* brothers who bought substitutes.

Of course, Mother and Dr. Findlay were vigorously of the opinion that there could be no question of the army's sending a sick "boy" (I was twenty) to perish on some freezing winter night in a Virginia campaign. If there was any question of my exemption not being promptly granted, they were prepared to appeal to the Secretary of the Army. But what attitude was *I* to take? For weeks I hovered miserably in indecision. And then something happened that induced me to request the exemption. I had another attack.

Was it that? How the question agonized me! Even now, decades later, it hurts me to write it. But I have long faced the truth. There *was* an element of the willed in it. I was so familiar with the nature of such attacks that it could not have been difficult for my psyche to simulate one, particularly if so much as the ghost of a former onslaught were to assail me. I made the most of my symptoms, and so convinced Dr. Findlay, who accompanied me to my examination by the draft board, that he lost his temper at one of its members who questioned his diagnosis. The board accorded me the requested status, but I saw in the expression of the doubting member that he, for one, had not been convinced, and I hated him, for I knew in my heart that he was right.

Anyway, it was done, and I pleased Father by telling him that I was now willing to enter Columbia Law School, from which I had so far been protected by Mother's fearing that the hard dry study of the law might not sit with my nervous disposition. Father, counting on his two older sons to succeed him in his business, thought it would be well for them to have a family lawyer, and although his hopes for me were slender, he thought that my effete taste for literature might be strengthened by a dose of the cod-liver oil of law.

But I had a different reason for choosing law. In a world at war the mood was masculine, and I had a nervous desire to merge myself as much as possible with a generation of young heroes, or at least not to stand out too harshly as not belonging to it. I think I was obsessed with the silly idea that lawyers were somehow more men than readers or writers, that I would, as a student of the profession, be more qualified to join in the brave chorus of "Glory, glory, alleluia!," that I would be, despite my shameful civilian garb, more a part of the general uplift, which could be very contagious. Was law to me a kind of protective coloration? But from what was I really protecting myself? From myself, of course. For I didn't really believe for a minute that anyone would see me as even remotely comparable to my gallantly fighting brother.

My defenses may have been artificial, and indeed, they

were not to last, but for a year they brought me the greatest, and perhaps the only real, happiness of my life. It was certainly not the law that brought this about. I attended the lectures and skimmed the cases, but without any real attention or without the least anticipation of ever being admitted to the bar. My big brown notebook was filled not with summaries of statutes and court decisions but with the scribbled manuscript of the romantic historical novel of the American Revolution that I was intent on composing, whose hero, of course, was a fervid Yankee and whose heroine a haughty Brit. When I opened its pages, the terrible Battle of the Wilderness would fade away into a gray distance.

But oh, the joy of that time, of those months, of those long, delectable afternoons when I was shut up in the dark, half-empty, overheated law school library, which excluded not only the war but my family: Father and Douglas and the sisters and even Mother, who in her daily tortured anxiety about Andrew had almost ceased to be concerned about my now quite sturdy health. I was alone, blessedly alone, accountable to no one, and I could hug to my heart my own little genius and cultivate the wild illusion that one day it might startle the literary world. For as I read over and over the seemingly mellifluous passages that flowed from my active pen, I treasured the notion that I was husbanding a talent of which future generations would have need, and that it would have been a sorry waste to let it perish with its possessor in the red dirt of Virginia. If I had done a wrong to myself and to my country in abstaining from battle, was I not making up for it in giving what I could to the future? The Carnochans would have produced more than just Father and Douglas; they would have produced me!

My dreams were shattered by the news of Andrew's death in the Wilderness Campaign, only months before Appomatox. Reading over the manuscript of my novel in the shadow of the shining monument that my agonized imagination immediately raised to his glory, I saw — unmistakably — what feeble stuff it was. And the gray shattered countenance of my mortally stricken mother, and even the new lines of sorrow on my father's craggy features, convinced me that it was, after all, a world of men which had little but a mild pity for and, at best, a mild tolerance of such weaklings as myself. I suffered what would later be called a nervous breakdown, quit law school, abandoned my novel, and moped at home. Mother was almost lost to me in the deep night of her mourning, and Father treated me with an almost kindly acceptance, which was intended to disguise, I had little doubt, an essential indifference to a son who was evidently to be of little further use to him or his business, but who, like his several unmarried daughters, was as permanent a part of his home as the chairs and tables and prints of biblical scenes. He never said a word about my draft exemption, but I suspected that he smelled the fraud. It was devastating, and it remained so until he died, which both he and Mother did, within months of each other, in the year 1869.

Their estates were divided evenly among their many offspring, and my share was just enough to maintain a decent bachelor's existence. Eventually I resumed my writing and produced the three light historical romances whose small but steady sale through the years has given me the faintest trickle of literary renown. It will soon enough dry up. And the brave Andrew is quite forgotten. It is only through Douglas and his posterity that we survive. That would not in the least have surprised my eldest brother.

Well, there it is. I leave this memorandum to young David in the mild hope that it may help him to understand the past. He is clever enough to glean what profit he can from its few pages without irritating the family by publishing them.

2

ELIZA

THE SUMMER OF 1905 was a high-water mark in the social and architectural history of Newport. The long line of birthday cake palazzos, seemingly products of a second Italian Renaissance, though one happily free of stilettos and poison, each standing proudly on a finely tended strip of green lawn as exiguous as its occupying edifice was huge, ran down Bellevue Avenue and the Cliff Walk in a glittering riot of marble never to be bettered. Maintenance was at its most perfect; there was not a stray leaf out of place. But there still survived an older Newport, an eighteenth- and early-nineteenth-century town that bordered on Narragansett Bay rather than the Atlantic, with smaller, soberer, chaster homes, among which, on modest Washington Street, stood the simple wooden frame, high-gabled residence of Mrs. Eliza Dudley Carnochan, widow of Douglas, whose porticoed front porch faced the water over a neat little lawn and garden.

Mrs. Carnochan was a small, plain, white-capped, black-garbed lady of nearly seventy, of the utmost respectability, whose large, drooping, but perceptive china blue eyes gazed not always benignly at what she evidently regarded as the tinselly aspects of such rich Johnny-come-latelies as the Vanderbilt clan. It was not that she scorned all the summer newcomers. But she picked and chose among them. She liked the staid, churchgoing Mrs. Alice Vanderbilt and called at the Breakers, but she avoided her imperious sister-in-law, Alva, and she would never have attended a party given by the flamboyant Mrs. Stuyvesant Fish. Nor did she ever forget that she hailed back to the pre-gilded age of a literary Newport, the summer home of Julia Ward Howe, of Thomas Higginson, of Longfellow, the Newport that had enchanted the young Henry James and whose meadows and rocky shores had been painted by John La Farge and Kensett. Eliza Carnochan numbered two colonial governors among her forebears. It was known that both her grandmothers had been Saltonstalls.

She was essentially satisfied with the role which she knew had been assigned to her by her friends, neighbors, and many visiting descendants. She was to be the steadying force in a changing world, a gentle reminder — never a comminatory one — of the necessity of preserving some minimum of standards in manners and morals. Like the elderly and benevolent late Queen Victoria, reigning over the pomp of her far-flung empire and softening the mailed fist of the Raj, so did Eliza Carnochan remind the barons of steel and oil that money was not and could not be everything. In New York, of course, Eliza's sober brownstone on West Fifty-seventh Street was dwarfed to nothing by the giant Vanderbilt copy of Blois on the Fifth Avenue corner, but in Newport, Washington Street was still recognized by the Breakers.

Eliza, however, was not altogether inwardly what her outer self suggested. This did not mean, of course, that she didn't firmly believe in decorum of manners, fidelity in marriage, decency in dress, and orderliness in one's daily tasks and pleasures. She knew that wildness in men and women had to be restrained. But she had a vivid sense of the rages that went on within the soul of man and an equally vivid sense of the hypocrisies used to conceal them. She knew, in short, the cost of discipline and could sympathize with the pains of those who had subjected themselves to it — or who had tried to and failed. She regarded herself in this respect as a victor, but she never forgot how easily the struggle might have been lost. She never allowed herself to put out of her mind what no one in the world had ever known or even suspected: that there had been a time in her young life, before she married Douglas Carnochan, when she would have agreed to any proposition that his brother Andrew might have put to her, however illicit. And she gave herself no credit for the fact that he never had, and had never even thought of doing so.

Her grandchildren visited her in the summer in turns, and she loved these visits, but she particularly relished those of David, one of her son James's six boys, who, still in his teens, was planning to write up the family history, on which he exhaustively consulted her. David was very clever and perceptive, sometimes uncomfortably so, for he did her the honor of treating her as a human being as well as an ancestress, and was bold enough to voice his suspicion when she was holding something back. Eliza was aware that there was a side to this young man that might ultimately lead him into false pride and disregard of intellectual inferiors, but she could still delight in his wit and openness.

David's great-uncle and Eliza's brother-in-law, bachelor Peter Carnochan, had just died, and among his effects had been the memorandum that David had earlier requested of him but never received. It was this memorandum that the two were now discussing on a veranda overlooking the bay.

"Was Uncle Peter's description of Great-grandpa Carnochan a true one?" David wanted to know. "Or was he simply inventing another character for one of his immortal tales?"

"*De mortuis,*" Eliza warned him. "You mustn't be sarcastic about your poor Uncle Peter's fiction. We can't all be Hawthornes. Let me answer your question this way. I recognize my father-in-law in Peter's sketch of him."

"You mean it's not the whole picture?"

"It's the whole picture of what he was to Peter. Peter had a motive for seeing his father as he depicted him."

"And that was?"

"To justify his own failure in life. There! I've said it. Perhaps I shouldn't have, but it's true, and I don't really think the truth, the real truth, can ever do much harm."

"Unless it's the greatest harm of all! Look where it leaves Uncle Peter."

"But, my dear boy, look what harm withholding the truth would do to the memory of your great-grandpa."

"He wasn't, then, a tyrant?"

"Certainly not. He was a strict disciplinarian to his children when they were growing up, but he never laid a hand on them. And after they were grown, he never interfered with them at all. He was always a great one for minding his own business. I found him an easy father-in-law to get on with."

"Was it perhaps because he didn't care that much about anyone?"

"That could have been a part of it," Eliza sturdily admitted.

"Or did he think those who didn't mind him would go to hell, and that was punishment enough?"

"No, David, he thought no such thing! I don't believe he ever speculated on the hereafter. The here and now was good enough for him. He did his duty, and that was that."

"What did he think of his sons, Peter and Grandpa, both not fighting in the war?"

"He never spoke of it. At least I never heard him do so. I doubt that he thought it was any of his business. Peter was the one who fussed over the ethics of his claim for exemption. He lacked the fortitude to accept the weakness in his own disposition, and he let it ruin his life."

"You mean he couldn't face his own cowardice?"

"You're very free with your terms, David."

"Perhaps I'm learning them from you. How did Grandpa feel about buying a substitute to fight for him?"

"Oh, he was totally different from Peter. He felt that it was his duty to stay in a business that helped produce uniforms for the soldiers."

"And, besides, he became rich while his brother Andrew was lying dead in the Wilderness!"

"David, be quiet!" Eliza rapped on the table by her big basket chair. Things were getting out of hand. "You must have more respect for the dead. Particularly your own grandfather!"

"Oh, Grandma, don't be like that, please! You're the one member of the family I feel I can really talk to."

Eliza was a bit ashamed of how quickly this placated her. "Let us talk of these things, then, my dear, without stamping our post-mortem moral judgments on them."

"Very well. How would *you* have felt had you been an able-bodied, well-to-do young man, even in a war-supporting business and even with a family? Would *you* have paid some poor devil to fight for you, perhaps die for you?"

"But I wasn't such a man, David! You're being ridiculous."

"Am I? Answer me, Grandma! I dare you."

After a pause, she heard her own reply surprisingly ring out. "No, I'd never have bought a substitute."

"Ah, you see!"

"I see only what concerns myself. It doesn't mean I condemn others. It certainly doesn't mean I condemn my husband."

"No, but it shows whom you really admire. It was Uncle Andrew, wasn't it? The slain Siegfried?"

"We all admired Andrew, certainly. Who would not have?"

"Dad says you were all in love with him! The whole family!"

"David, if you're going to go sailing, you'd better go now."

He left the porch reluctantly to amble down the pathway to the dock where the small family sailboat was moored. Eliza was relieved to be away from his penetrating stare. It was not that she had the least fear of disclosing matters so long and firmly locked in her heart, but she hated to have clumsy feet treading so near her secret garden.

Settling back in her chair and allowing her gaze to roam over the bay, she had no need to be faced with the ancient photograph over the mantel in the front parlor to have it fixed in a mind which it never altogether deserted. It showed, sometime in 1863, a group of half a dozen Union officers of different rank and age in relaxed poses, some sitting, some standing, but all aware of the camera, on the stout-pillared portico of the Lee mansion in Arlington, presumably commandeered as an army officers' club. It was somehow to be detected that all were veterans of combat; they had an air of gruff confidence, even a touch of something akin to defiance. Standing more stiffly than the others to the left, one hand on his hip, with almost a scowl on his dark handsome countenance, was the obvious junior of the gathering, and his inclusion seemed to mark the special regard in which his elders held him. His gravity of expression might have been attributable to the grim sights to which his youth had already been exposed, but it was easy to infer how rapidly his near scowl would change into a charming grin should a pretty woman obtrude upon the scene. The setting, however, was too darkly masculine for any such possibility.

Eliza had known Andrew Carnochan first in the summer of 1859, when his father, David, the emigrant, had moved his summer home from Staten Island to Newport at the behest of his eldest son, Douglas, who considered it a better address for business purposes. The Carnochans had rented a cottage near that of the Dudleys in Washington Street, and the children of the two families had rapidly become friends. Douglas, sober, serious, and direct in his manners and approaches, had constituted himself a beau of Eliza, and Andrew, whose good looks and exuberant friendliness had made him the darling of the summer community, had fallen violently in love with the one girl in Newport whose family didn't want him. The snobbish Amorys from Boston sniffed at the "haberdashery" Carnochans and took the position that their lovely Lily had already committed herself too unreservedly to the young Lowell of their choice to now dispose of her affections elsewhere. Besides, Andrew's loudly proclaimed abolitionism was wormwood to the hot-tempered gentleman he sought as a father-in-law.

Lily Amory's dazzling beauty was not partnered with a character of equal quality; she was not one to defy a bossy father. She tearfully consulted Eliza, her best friend and cousin (the Dudleys had long left Boston for Providence, but Eliza's mother had been an Amory), as to how to handle her situation, and Eliza soon found herself the confidante of both Lily and Andrew. Andrew was too modest and too preoccupied with his own passion ever to suspect that his long, private talks with Eliza could arouse any emotion beyond friendship in his consultant. Was she not by way of being his brother Douglas's girl? What nice young woman would want to create trouble between two brothers?

Nor did the silently stricken Eliza at all wish any such thing, though there were moments when she almost wished that the Amorys would persist in their pigheaded opposition so that she might continue these delightful sessions. But she was too honest not finally to let the supposedly lovelorn Andrew know that his victory was an assured thing.

"I understand that there's a romantic side to you, Andrew, that makes you want to equate your problem with that of Romeo and Juliet. Star-crossed lovers. But candor compels me to inform you that you only have to wait, and not too long at that. The Amorys basically know they're licked. Lily may be in a tizzy over their opposition — I even think she rather enjoys tizzies — but in the last analysis she's never going to give you up."

"Oh, you mustn't say she enjoys it, Eliza. You should have seen her last night in tears. Floods of tears!"

"Like spring showers. To make the sunlight, when it reappears, even brighter."

The Amorys, as Eliza predicted, at length did come around, and the engagement was eventually announced, but as it almost coincided with the bombardment of Fort Sumter, and Andrew had already enlisted, Lily's father insisted that the wedding wait until the end of hostilities. He had no wish to see his daughter a war widow, and thus it came about that she never was one. After the elapse of a proper period following Andrew's death in battle, Lily married her old Lowell beau, who was himself a war hero.

Eliza had married Douglas Carnochan even before the engagement of Andrew and Lily was announced. She had clearly seen that she was exactly the bride Douglas wanted, socially, physically, and temperamentally, and that he was just the husband she would need if she married at all: steady, faithful, even-tempered, and of a cool and dispassionate disposition that would neither feel nor require a great love. They would be the respected and respectable members of a sober and serious community and raise a large family in which she might have the luck to find another Andrew. She was convinced that she would never again fall in love, and looking back now over the decades, she confirmed how right she had been. She had made the most of her life and not wasted it in futile regrets. She had loved her five children — Annie, Bruce, Clara, James, and Wallace — particularly the gentle Clara, who had returned to Scotland to wed the thread tycoon, Sir John Muir, and died there of breast cancer. But she had not had another Andrew. Had she ever really expected it? Could the trespassing cuckoo bird that had deposited that golden egg in a nest of Carnochans be expected to do it twice?

Her plain and middle-aged maiden daughter, Annie, of blameless character, blameless and blank, now came out of the house to remind her that her ex-son-in-law, Sir John, was coming for tea. Ex, because he had remarried after Clara's death, though his second wife was also now deceased.

"How could I forget it, Annie? You know what he's coming for, don't you?"

"To tell you he's going to be married? Yes, that's the rumor. To the red-haired governess of some Philadelphia family. Imagine! The old goat! What will he do in heaven, if he ever gets there, with three wives to claim him?"

Eliza knew that people had to be saying that Annie was a saint to stay home to look after her aging mother. People had to be saying that because people *did* say such things.

But certainly Annie's extreme religiosity was a cross for her mother to bear. Eliza paused to prepare herself for a mild retort. "But, Annie darling, there's supposed to be no giving in marriage there."

"But the wives will still be there, won't they?"

"Perhaps they will no longer mind."

Sir John came on the dot of his expected hour and took his seat stiffly on the porch by his former mother-in-law. He was a portly, pink-faced, balding hunk of a man, affable enough, and, for all his wealth and baronetcy, inordinately proud of the humble origin that his business genius had allowed him to transcend. He had always admired and liked Eliza, two of whose sons acted as his American agents.

"We hear exciting news of you, John," Eliza began. "Is it true that you're to be congratulated?"

"Quite true, dear Mother Carnochan. At least that I am to be. There may be some question if the bride is. She is twenty-five years my junior."

"That's nothing where love is concerned."

"Well, there, my dear lady, you may be begging the question. Let me tell you how we met. I was in Philadelphia on business and dining alone in the very good restaurant of my hotel, when I observed a lovely lady with red hair sitting at a table across the room with two quiet and well-dressed children and a nice-looking couple who seemed to be their parents. I had the notion that the red-haired lady was in some kind of governess position with the children, for she supervised their eating and their table manners. Obviously, she had a way with them, and obviously, she enjoyed the full confidence of the parents. You could tell by the way they smiled at her. You may laugh, Mother Carnochan, but I was immensely struck by my young woman. I asked the head-waiter, who knew everybody, it seemed, and he reported the name of the man, a member of a distinguished Main Line family, and informed me that my redhead was a Mademoiselle Hortense Duval, the French governess of his children. I asked the headwaiter to deliver my card to the gentleman with my written request to be introduced to Miss Duval and the assurance that my intentions were strictly honorable. I watched the gentleman read my note, hand it to his governess, who read it and calmly nodded. Her employer then laughed, turned, and waved at me in the friendliest way to come and join his table. Which of course I promptly did. Miss Duval was utterly charming in what many women might have thought the oddest of encounters, and two days later I proposed to her."

"And she accepted."

"As a good French girl without a penny to her name or anyone to look after her naturally would. Obviously, to her it was a miracle. A baronet and a fortune appearing like Cinderella's golden coach! Love, however, is another matter. You may say there's no fool like an old fool, but I still know something about the French. A bargain to them is a serious thing. Hortense may take me for better, but she also takes me for worse. If I should lose my last shilling, she'd turn my castle into a hotel, run it to the queen's taste, and support me to the end. It would almost be worth going bust to see that happen. And my cynical friends proved wrong!"

"I have no doubt you're justified in that faith. And I'm sure that my Clara would have given you her blessing."

Sir John laughed, but he was obviously moved. "Clara would have wanted me to be happy, yes, but perhaps not *this* happy. Bless you, anyway, dear Mother Carnochan, for saying what so few would say — in other words, just the right thing. I'll tell my children, who, I regret to say, have taken a much less charitable view of my matrimonial plans. But they deeply respect their grandmother and will listen to her words."

"Unless they think I'm gaga."

Eliza sat alone after he had left, turning over his news in her mind with mild amusement and considerable sympathy. She wondered if the red-headed Hortense was not a bit like herself. She had to force herself to smile when Annie interrupted her quiet reflections and prepare herself for her daughter's inevitable fulminations.

"I'm sorry, Mother, but I really didn't want to sit and hear John boast of his romantic triumphs. Really! As if it were such a glorious thing to be taken in by an obvious gold digger!"

"Hardly an obvious one, my dear. I should say; if anything, a rather subtle one."

"These men! They can't bear to be alone, even for a few weeks or months."

"Why should they, if they don't have to be?"

"Because marriage is not a state to be entered into without mutual love. And a great love, too. Like yours and Father's!"

Eliza mused for a moment. "Is that really what you feel about marriage, my dear? That it can only be based on a great love?"

"Of course. Don't you agree?"

"I don't know if it has to be so great. If some fine, honest man should offer you a good home and the prospect of a family, would you feel obliged to turn him down because he hadn't set you on fire?"

"Well, it so happens that I see my duty here at home and that I'm proud and happy to remain here and perform it."

"I deeply appreciate that, my dear, but I should never

wish to stand in the way of your having your own home and family."

"You needn't worry about that, Mother."

And indeed, Eliza saw that she needn't. That fine, honest man was not going to come along, no matter how much Annie and Annie's mother might pine for him. Annie had built into her mind the heroic picture of a woman who had sacrificed any prospect of her own domestic bliss on the altar of her duty to an aging parent. To take that from her and leave her with the bleak alternative of having been condemned to old maidhood by a neglectful sex would be the last cruelty. Eliza saw that yet another role in life had been assigned to her to enact: that of the selfish old mother who hoards one child to be her nurse and companion in the so-called sunset of life. She could only hope it would be the last one.

3

BRUCE

ONE FINE SPRING EVENING in 1892 Bruce Carnochan
was striding east on Fifty-seventh Street toward Fifth Avenue, boasting neither top hat nor cloak (both faultless but
left at home), yet even more resplendent (or so he dared to
assume) in white tie and tails, with a scarlet carnation in his
buttonhole, as if to advertise to the humbler world of the by-
ways that he was dining *en ville* with the partner, however
lesser a one, of the richest man in the world. For wasn't that
what people claimed for Mr. Rockefeller? Of course, there
were all those Indian maharajas, but Bruce shook his head
impatiently, as if to disclaim their eligibility. Wasn't their
wealth all in jewels, and probably bad ones at that?

The weather was benign; only the gentlest breeze
brushed his clear pale forehead and large fine nose, nor did
it muss the sleek black hair so carefully parted in the exact
middle of his scalp, despite the legend that the late President
Grant had taken a dislike to Ambassador Motley for no
other reason. But then Grant, though the greatest of gener-
als (oh, yes, Bruce gave him his full due), had never been
quite a gentleman, had he? Where would he have been,
broke and nearly disgraced, dying of throat cancer, if the
late lamented Mr. W. H. Vanderbilt (God rest his generous
soul!) had not come to his aid?

Bruce, healthy and essentially trim (though he would
have to mind his tummy — yes, yes), and only twenty-eight,

nodded approvingly as he passed the giant pink improvement on the château of Blois that Mr. V.'s eldest son had reared on the avenue and turned south toward the even more glorious abode of Willie K. Bruce felt zestfully at home in the wonderful city, at least in this part of it; he liked to think of Fifth Avenue as the apex of civilization, a new Rome, but a freer and gladder one unstained by the blood of gladiators or of Christians mauled by big cats in an arena full of yowling wops. Oh, yes, of course, he was aware of the smart sophisticated little set, including the misguided Kitty Atwater — God help the poor stubborn girl — who referred to the beautiful architecture of Richard Morris Hunt as "the derivative and ostentatious palazzos of the new goldbugs," but he stoutly maintained that the great avenue was fully as fine as anything the Italian Renaissance had produced, and that the interiors of the new structures, illuminated by electricity and freshened by plumbing, were more edifying than marble interiors stained by the memory of the victims of Borgia poison or Riario daggers.

Did he not have reason to feel exalted? Only that morning his brother and partner, Wallace, had announced that each of them might expect this year that his share of the net profits of Carnochan Brothers, American agents of the Scottish thread king, Sir John Muir, would amount to $20,000! His mother was always after him to find a bride, and how many lovelies would not gape at a figure like that? Even Kitty Atwater might not turn her nose up at such an offer, intent though she was supposed to be on her search for a man who could give her all the things among which she lived but none of which she owned. For Kitty, as Bruce kept telling himself with a snort, hadn't a dime to her name, for all her habit of sponging off the objects of her scorn!

Yet Kitty, despite her evident pleasure in chatting and gossiping with him at parties, was inclined to downgrade him in her supposed compliments. When she referred to him as a "dandy" or "a boulevardier," the terms showed a bit of bite behind her always charming smile. Kitty, of all people! Talk about pots and kettles! And the worst part of it was that she echoed (though without being aware of it, as she hardly knew them) his two older brothers. The Carnochans had never been ones to restrain themselves in playing their favorite game of "The trouble with you." They had not left any of their sometimes brutal candor in Ayreshire. The slightest pretension, the least effort to ally oneself with anything that introduced a bit of color and gaiety into a world of grayness was promptly labeled what his mother, scorning the mitigating Gallic pronunciation, called "blazzy." And any such attitude on the part of a younger brother like Bruce, however much loved as a member of the sacred clan (even though they were lowlanders!), was considered essentially incompatible with the financial ability that the Scots needed on this side of the Atlantic to prove how different they were from the Irish. Even Wallace did not deem Bruce his equal, or near equal, in the office.

But could he not console himself, indeed pride himself, on being the one member of the family who knew what this New York of the nineties was really all about, who understood and appreciated how much its puff and its glitter were basic parts of it? Mightn't he one day write a memoir that would rival Cellini's? Which reminded him: he should start that diary he was always postponing.

As he turned west on Fifty-first Street to visit his favorite bar on Sixth Avenue for the preprandial gin cocktail and oysters which had become a treasured habit, he felt the mild sway of guilt that such a break from Scottish rigor still briefly entailed. And with it came the perennial, always lurking suspicion that in his exalted moments, such as strolling down Fifth Avenue was apt to give him, he was inclined to attribute overexalted motives to his inner thoughts and judgments. To be strictly honest now — and a son of Eliza Dudley Carnochan should know just what honesty was — had he been strictly fair in attributing a mercenary goal to Kitty's husband-hunting? What could any girl in their society do but husband-hunt, and should one expect her to seek a poor one? No, not at all, and hadn't he now to face the horrid suspicion that he was looking for his own excuse to exclude from the candidates for the hand of Bruce Carnochan a girl with no money? How about that? Hadn't he dreamt of wedding a Vanderbilt? Or even a Gould? No, never a Gould — one could step too low.

Pulling himself together now, he assured himself that he was too poor for a Vanderbilt and very likely too poor to wed a girl of Kitty's expectations, and that he should stop beating himself and look for a sweet girl who would be content with his $20,000 per annum, and perhaps bring him a little something of her own, so that together they might have a shingle house in Newport next to the one that his brother Wallace and his wife, Julie, had built?

His heart had regained all its buoyancy as he entered the great dark paneled bar and took his place at the long, oaken counter facing a huge mirror and a Bougereau canvas of naked laughing nymphs dangerously teasing a randy satyr. He signaled Paddy for his usual. If the truest joy lay in anticipation, what was better than his sense of the forthcoming gin in an iced glass and the prospect of a sumptuous dinner in Gotham?

"Good evening, my dear Bruce. Do we have the good fortune of dining at the same place? Are you going to the Stoddards'?"

It was Abel Fisher, in similar attire, who had taken the adjoining stool. Also a bachelor, though older, perhaps forty, with a pink boyish face and thick prematurely snowy hair, he was a well-known diner out and man about town whose encyclopedic knowledge of society gossip always impressed Bruce.

"I'm afraid not. I dine with the Bensons."

"Old Ezra's? Really? I didn't know you were an habitué there."

"I'm hardly that. This will be my first time. What may I expect? You, who know all."

"Well, nothing that need alarm you. They're a new type in town, so rich they don't honestly much care about society. It's true of several of the Standard Oil partners. The old guard that was ready to snub them were so surprised to find themselves the ones snubbed that now they cultivate them."

"But the Bensons have bought a mansion, Abel!"

Abel's shrug showed how little this impressed him. "They bought the Buckinghurst morgue when old Buckinghurst went broke. Ezra needed rooms for his big brood. He probably got his secretary to pick the house for him, just telling her to get the kind of thing Rockefeller partners got. You know how he made his pile, don't you? By a lucky loan to young John D. when the latter was just starting out. He was paid back in stock, which he's hung on to like a leech. You're on to a good thing there, my boy. The daughters may be on the plain side, but the man who marries one will find his ass in a tub of butter!"

Bruce was a bit disgusted by Abel's crudeness, but he was careful not to show it. He had no wish to stem the flow of his information. "I don't know the Benson girls. Kitty Atwater is spending part of the winter with them, and she's the one who invited me tonight."

"Kitty? Really? So she's on to them already. Ezra Jr. had

better watch his step." Abel suddenly pulled himself up. "I beg your pardon, old boy. Is Kitty perhaps something special to you?"

"Oh, no, just a friend. Or perhaps you might say, a friendly acquaintance. I think she's trying to expand the Bensons' social circle."

"Well, they've picked the right gal to do it. Kitty knows everybody. It's odd she hasn't caught herself a mate by now. She must be getting on, perhaps thirty? I guess the trouble is the heirs think she's after their money."

"Why should they think that, any more than with another girl?"

"Because she's poor and lives on the rich. It's a pity she has no parents to guide her."

"But she has a mother!" Bruce exclaimed, astonished at such a gap in the other's knowledge.

"Yes, but a complete nincompoop who makes no secret of the fact that she's on the prowl for a fortune for her not so *jeune, jeune fille à marier.* A clever mama would never show that, and she would train Kitty to hold that too critical tongue of hers. The sons of tycoons are mostly asses who don't care for wit. They want to be dumbly adored. Kitty's far from dumb, and she doesn't adore."

"No, she certainly doesn't do that," Bruce agreed. "But why does she have to marry a rich man?"

"Because that's the world her old ass of a widowed mother has brought her up in. Ever since her father killed himself after losing his shirt in the panic of '73. Sponging is a curious art. You wouldn't think that Mrs. Atwater would be an appealing subject of charity, yet she has been just that to several bloated dowagers. It proves that the crudest flattery can sometimes do the trick. And Mother Atwater is always ready to fill an opera box or help with a house party or chaperone young girls on a trip to Europe, and Kitty has tagged along, seeing through it all and hating it and expressing her mind too freely. But the rich life can become addictive. It's like the opera. *On s'ennuie mais on y revient."*

"And you think she may have her eye on Ezra Jr.?"

"She could be the making of him, but he's too dumb to see it. The girls, however, aren't dumb. Flora and Ada. How about Ada for you, my boy? She may not be Helen of Troy, but she's smart and she's true blue."

Bruce stared at his change of tone. "How can you be so sure of that?"

Abel looked to see if anyone was within hearing and lowered his voice. "Because I was one of the first to cultivate the Bensons. You know me and how I scan the newcomers to see who's going to make the grade. Well, I don't tell people this, but you and I have always hit it off, so I'll trust you with it. I proposed to Flora and was turned down flat. Indeed, I was put in my place."

"But why?" To Bruce, Abel had always seemed something of a catch, particularly to the new rich. "Why wasn't she complimented?"

"Because she thought me mercenary. And of course, she was dead right. Naturally, I was after her chips. But where she was wrong was in not realizing that I'd have made her a good husband, better, anyway, than the more convincing hypocrite who will ultimately marry her. For all I really wanted was to retire to the broken-down family estate in Virginia with someone who could afford to keep the old place going. We'd have had just the kind of tranquil rural life she'd have loved. Because I'm not altogether what people think me. Yes, even you, Bruce. I have my price, but the buyer would get her money's worth."

"Couldn't you have told her that?"

Abel shook his head firmly. "She'd have thought it only a snare. Girls like her and Ada, well educated, intelligent but morally rigid, don't admit qualifications to their blacks and whites. If you're mercenary, you're all bad. And, of course, some of us are. But I'd be an ass if I didn't appreciate the good points even in those who downgrade me. I study the world. And, believe me, my friend, those two Benson girls have the real stuff in them."

"Meaning that the man who marries one will have to be truly in love?"

"Or make her think so." Abel gave his friend a sly look. "You might be just the man to put on such an act, my boy. And once you'd done it, you'd believe in it yourself! So it might work out all around!"

Bruce twinged at the other's mocking laugh and lightly shook off the hand that grasped his shoulder in an effort to mitigate the irony. "I must be off now," he insisted, though he hadn't finished his drink. "You say you're going to the Stoddards'?"

"Yes, for my sins. You know what they say about Tom Kidder's odd death? That it couldn't have been suicide, for he'd dined the night before with the Stoddards, and why, to anyone who had *that* behind him, wouldn't the future have seemed bright?"

"Why do you go, then?"

"She's a cousin of Mother's. *Noblesse oblige.*"

Bruce reflected uneasily on the substance of their colloquy on his brief walk to his hosts. The husband of Ada Benson would certainly make a bigger splash in the pool of Gotham than any other male Carnochan. But that was idle speculation. He now reviewed word by word everything Abel had said about Kitty. It had been gratifying to hear as sharp an observer as Abel praise her wit and cleverness. It helped to justify the increasing hold that this irritating and intriguing young woman had taken on his fancies and fantasies. And perhaps it was just as well that he should learn that she was too busy promoting her own material future to listen to any crazy proposal that her charms might elicit from the likes of Bruce Carnochan! For even with his promised twenty g's, an unendowed wife would put him in the lower ranks of his rising family. Should not a proper gentleman stay out of the lady's chosen way of advancing herself? Was it not simple charity?

Arriving at the wide marble French façade of the Bensons', whose big glass double doors under a gilded marquee separated two pairs of vast rectangular windows, he paused and, consulting his watch, noted that he was ten minutes early and decided to take a tour around the block. Kitty again filled up the sudden vacuum of his mind.

He thought back on their first meeting. It had been at a Sunday lunch party on Sixteenth Street, given by old Ward McAllister, Mrs. Astor's dressy and garrulous majordomo, the veteran expert on manners and decorum, the exquisite gourmet and wine taster, who had taken upon his tottering shoulders the self-imposed task of reorganizing New York society into a simulacrum of European aristocracy. His star at this point had waned; to the men and younger women he had become something of a joke, but some of the so-called dowagers (whether or not they had a husband), still powers in the land, admired him, and his favor could bring some desired invitations. He was known to cultivate strapping young "blue bloods," and Bruce was not above flattering himself that he might be included in such a category. As the old boy, glossy-whiskered and colorfully clad, had approached to grasp his hand in both of his, he had made Bruce think of a septuagenarian beau in a parlor comedy. Now he poured out his welcome and his confidences in Bruce's listening ear.

"Always glad to see you, my dear fellow. Fresh as a daisy on a Sunday morning and not, like too many of your age group, sleeping off your Saturday-night excesses. I've put you at a table next to a protégée of mine, Miss Kitty Atwater. Smart as the proverbial whip, charming, and of good old Knickerbocker stock, doncherno. And with character, too, plenty of character. She's the only unmarried maiden to whom I've given a separate listing in my 400. I'm not speaking, of course, of rich old maids, of whom, *entre nous*, we have our fill. Enough, indeed, to challenge the notion that our city is worldly. In Paris every last one of them would be married, even crazy as a loon. But my poor girl is poor, poor as that equally proverbial little clerical rodent. What I'd like you to do is spread the word around among some of the gilded young bucks you see, the *jeunesse dorée*, doncherno, that a wife with a noodle can be as much help to a man in society as a dumb one with a pot of gold. Indeed, even more so. And tell 'em that comes from one who *knows*."

Miss Atwater had fulfilled her host's description. She was on the small size, but well shaped and with a pretty, heart-shaped countenance and large alert brown eyes, and she radiated a pleasant air of involvement with each new thing that met them. She was seated on her host's right, with Bruce on her other side, and as the lady on his right failed to appear (another note of the casual way that society was now treating McAllister), the talk at lunch in the first part of the meal was largely among the three of them.

She talked to Bruce as easily as if he had been an acquaintance of long standing, and she made no distinction in her manner between him and their host. He and McAllister were equally her audience, presumably gentlemen of goodwill. She held forth amusingly about the undue length of the ordinary fashionable New York dinner party and the martyrdom of the guest who is planted between two persons of no conversation.

"He might recite poetry to himself. In his mind, of

course." McAllister recalled an instance. "I had a friend who knew great chunks of 'Marmion' by heart. While the lady at his side droned on about her wonderful children and grand-children, he would be the escaped and recaptured nun who is about to be buried alive. 'Yet dread me, from my living tomb, / Ye vassal slaves of bloody Rome!'"

"But I have a better idea, Mr. McAllister!" Kitty ex-claimed. "And you, as the arbiter elegantiarum of our mod-ern Rome, should be the one to initiate it. How about creat-ing a bore insurance company? The members, in return for a modest premium, would receive a secret list of all the notorious bores in Manhattan society. Then, if you found yourself seated next to one, you would call the company the next day and collect the sum with which that particular bore pays off and be able to buy yourself an etching or watercolor or what you please."

McAllister seemed much taken with the idea. "Bravo! But mightn't there be those who would hint to their hostess beforehand that they'd like to be next to some bore of high return? People do cheat, doncherno."

"Oh, our members would have to be persons of probity, of course. They would form a highly exclusive group."

Bruce wondered uncomfortably if he might not have found his name on Miss Atwater's list of bores. "Supposing a bore applies for a policy in your company?" he asked her. "Could he recover by sitting in his own seat?"

"Oh, there'd be no applications," she assured him. "Membership would be only by invitation. And kept strictly confidential."

No, her friendly smile seemed to offer him reassurance that she did not deem him a bore, and she even looked pleased when, after the meal, he had offered to escort her up the avenue to the Bensons', where she was staying. They continued their pleasant chat as they walked, until at last she said something he didn't like at all. She had reverted to their old topic of bore insurance and now volunteered the notion that their recent host, despite his apparent amusement at the concept, was disqualified to hold a policy, as he had created the very society which had engendered the epidemic of boredom.

"But that should make him president!" Bruce protested.

"Well, then there's an even better reason for barring him."

"And what, pray, is that?"

"Why, the simple fact that he's the most crashing old bore of the lot!" she cried with a spurt of laughter. Bruce was shocked. Could any really nice girl speak so callously of an old gentleman who had condescended — yes, condescended — to call her his protégée? But he found nonetheless that she remained very much on his mind when he went to bed that night, and his sleep was restless.

He had found other things, too, in the days that followed. When his mother offered him two seats in an opera box loaned her for the night by one of her grand friends, he invited Miss Atwater, and she not only came but explained to him in the entr'acte some interesting points about *Siegfried* that helped him for the first time to appreciate Wagner. And she did it charmingly, he had to admit, never seeming to reproach his ignorance. And then he took her to an exhibit of Holbein drawings at the Metropolitan Museum, where she proved equally congenial and instructive company. She seemed to like him, or at least to put up with him easily. He wondered if she didn't attribute a greater intelligence than he possessed to his silences as he took in her lively prattle. When he did speak, she listened carefully, and her responding comments seemed in their interpretation of his thoughts to give them a defter touch.

But there was another aspect to her responses that at

once chilled him and relieved him. She did not once, by so much as a tremor in her tone or a downward glance, seem to note or acknowledge the least hint of a suit for her affections in his sudden attentions. If he was constantly on the watch about committing himself in his relationships with the opposite sex — and he was fully aware that he was — he seemed to have nothing to fear where Kitty was concerned. If this was relaxing — and it was — he was delightfully at his ease with her — it was also a bit mortifying. Who did she think she was, that the likes of Bruce Carnochan wasn't good enough for her? He was tempted to tell her about the anticipated twenty g's.

The great hall of the Benson palazzo, into which, after his walk around the block, he now entered, might have been harmlessly if conventionally grand without the huge stucco putti attached to the pilasters with the supposed function of holding up the capitals, a style disastrously borrowed from Bavarian baroque. Bruce, spreading his hands to indicate to the approaching footman that he had nothing to remove, proceeded up the curving marble stairwell, reminding himself of what his bar friend Abel Fisher had said of his host's indifference to interior design.

The family and a few guests were somewhat dourly gathered in a rigidly correct French eighteenth-century parlor with Fragonard panels that portrayed a life of swings and kisses and gaiety that Mr. Benson, a portly, silent tower of crusty self-assurance, would never have tolerated in his home. Everyone nodded discreetly at Bruce as his host, one firm hand gripping his elbow, took him about the chamber; Kitty, standing somehow independently by the fireplace, simply smiled at him. The Benson children, unlike their progenitor, were on the short side, with square bland faces and small staring eyes; they bore an almost comic resemblance to each other. Yet they were somehow obviously de-

cent folk. They even made Bruce feel that it might be superficial of him to miss the charm that was lacking. But miss it
he did.

The gentlemen outnumbered the ladies in the dining
room, and Bruce, who had a largely silent man on his left,
held an uninterrupted discourse with his other neighbor,
Ada Benson, who was Kitty's particular friend in the household. She was the shortest and smallest and plainest of the
tribe, but she was also sensible, definite, and very articulate.
She was clearly devoted to Kitty, and she merely nodded,
without smiling, when he described the bore insurance
company as an example of her wit. But then she added this
comment:

"I daresay you'd get a fat check in the morning for having been stuck with me." Her tone was not rueful, but simply dry, and she pressed on, ignoring his flurried protesta-
tion. "But Kitty is actually much kinder than that idea of
hers might make you think. We had some Western cousins
here last week who would have fitted into Kitty's despised
category, but you can't imagine how nice and helpful she was
with them. Mummy calls her an artist in making people feel
at home and bringing out the best in them."

Bruce wondered immediately if that was what Kitty did
with him. And he worried that Miss Benson might think
him superficial for having primarily noted a sharper side of
her friend's nature. But he soon discovered that he need
have no such concern. Ada did not bother to make judgments in matters that to her had little significance, and now
she proceeded, obviously briefed on his trade by Kitty, to ask
him about the thread business.

"We buy from the Scots," he explained, "and we sell to
the Jews, and on the slim profit that such a deal allows us, we
endeavor to subsist."

This evoked Miss Benson's first smile. It was a small

one. "Kitty said you had a sense of humor. And that despite your strict Presbyterian background."

"I'm afraid I've a good deal lapsed from that strictness. Does Kitty object to Presbyterians?"

"Oh, no, I don't think she objects to any religion."

"Isn't that apt to mean one doesn't care for any?"

"It's hard to tell what Kitty really cares about. She's very tolerant and very deep. But she's good."

"And that's all that really matters, is it?"

Ada's hint of a frown seemed to debate whether his tone was sarcastic or sincere. "Is it to you, Mr. Carnochan?"

"It is."

At that moment he was imagining what it would be like to be in bed with Ada Benson. The man who had married her for her money would now have to earn it. Could he do it? Well, why not, with the aid of fantasies of his own? He recalled his first college visit to what he liked to call a *mauvais lieu* and how he had barely managed to overcome his shyness and disgust. Yet he had! Oh, yes, he had! Mating was no great shakes. He visualized Ada slipping out of her nightie and revealing her small breasts and rounded tummy and considerable rear end. He supposed her less shy than passive, supinely offering what she had to offer to his shrunken and cold nether parts, confident that she could translate his awkwardly spilled seed into a rosy little Benson. But the money would be there forever and ever!

"You are silent, Mr. Carnochan. Are you thinking of something?"

"Yes." But his duplicity simply amused him now. "I was thinking there's more goodness in our poor old world than the cynics allow."

"Perhaps. But not much more, I'm afraid."

He repressed a start. Had she read his mind? But what a mad idea! "Are you a cynic, Miss Benson?"

"I hope not. But there are moments when it's hard not to be."

Had she already had the bitterness of suspecting that some professed and even preferred suitor was only after a dowry? Very likely. She was not only observant but a friend of Kitty's. She would not be naïve.

After dinner he was allowed to sit by Kitty in the long parlor. Across from them hung a huge splendid portrait, unmistakably a Sargent, of Mrs. Benson. Unlike her offspring she was tall and angular, with raven black hair and a long oval face that was barred from beauty by a nose too large and a chin too square. The painter had tried to remedy this by making her regal, clad in striking scarlet and seated in a fauteuil with gilded golden arms, erect, proud, almost disdainful. Bruce commented that it was still a remarkable work of art.

"Yes," Kitty admitted, "but it's not really at all Mrs. Benson, who's basically a simple, home-loving woman."

"I suppose he painted what he thought she wanted to look like. And he took for granted that was what the society he painted wanted. He's like Hoppner and Reynolds and Lawrence, and just as good as they were, too. Only they painted an era more than they did their models. The ladies had to be showy and blowy and grand to look at."

"And that's why none of those painters were of the first rank," Kitty pointed out, almost eagerly. "The very first, I mean. Like Holbein and Velázquez and Goya, where you get both the era *and* the model. The tenseness of the Tudor court, where men were willing to risk their heads for a few years of power. Or the decadence of the royal house in Madrid."

"And what would a greater painter than Sargent have shown?"

"The tinsel. The phony glitter. Fifth Avenue in fancy

dress as dukes and duchesses under the urban rule of Irish bosses. And the Stars and Stripes fluttering faintly in the ill wind."

"Of course, we have some real dukes and duchesses now. Perhaps you would say they're the phoniest of all!"

"Thanks for saying it for me!" she exclaimed, with a little snort of laughter. "You know, Bruce, when we first met, I was afraid I was going to find you a bit on the stuffy side. But you're not. And now I feel I can talk to you. And, oh, my friend, do I need someone to talk to! There's dear Ada, of course, but she's inclined to be literal, and I can't say to her the things about her family and their friends that I'm thinking. Certainly not while I'm her houseguest! And my other girlfriends are all such terrible gossips and not to be trusted with anything remotely like a secret. There's Mama, naturally, but the poor darling hasn't a spark of imagination, and she finds everything on Fifth Avenue too, too divine."

"What do you want to talk about?"

"Bless you for coming right to the point. Myself, of course. What else does anyone really want to talk about?"

"Then talk. Please talk. You do, and I won't."

She hesitated, like one at the end of a diving board on a cold day. "Oh well, why not? Ada told me this morning that her brother Ezra is engaged. To the daughter of one of her father's partners. Ellie Jennings. Isn't it obscene? Shouldn't this new Sherman law, or whatever it is, be invoked to prevent it?"

"Is this a blow to your heart?" He ventured this because he was suddenly and exuberantly convinced that it wasn't. "Or to your pride?"

She laughed. "Well put. But to neither, really. There has been nothing between Ezra and me but the kind of tomfoolery young men feel socially obliged to engage in. But to be fully candid — and what else is the point of my talking?

— yes, pride *does* have a part in it. For why else should it so irritate me to think of all the people who will be saying: 'Poor Kitty. She's missed out on another goldbug. Perhaps she'd better learn to play her cards more subtly.'"

"I've never heard anyone say anything like that about you," he averred stoutly.

"Thank you, my friend, but your nose is just a mite longer. The trouble with the reputation I'm developing is not that it's deserved but that it can come to be. Living among the rich and seeing how badly they do it, it's impossible not to speculate on how much better one would do it oneself, given half the chance. And that kind of speculation can lead to your beginning to pick and choose a mate, at least in your imagination, among the young male goldbugs. The mate who might most adequately fund your mental experiments. Add to that a desperate desire to get out of your rut and the first thing you know, you've become a gold digger!"

"But you're not that."

"Not yet, anyway."

"Keep an eye on me, then."

He smiled as he gave her a long look. But she didn't smile back. Nor was there even a faint hint of flirtatiousness in her drawn expression. They had to drop the subject as Ezra Jr. and Miss Jennings came over to join them, and Kitty became at once as cheerful and welcoming as if she had made the match.

SOME WEEKS LATER, on a Sunday evening, he was sitting with his mother in the library, he with an opened but unread novel of Marion Crawford in his lap, and she with her eternal needlework. With the black satin that she had consistently worn since her husband's death and her white widow's cap, she might have seemed a milder Queen Victoria whose benevolent blue eyes occasionally took in the silent figure of her youngest child.

"If *Saracinesca* doesn't amuse you, my dear, you must have something on your mind. Didn't you tell me it was something of a thriller?"

"Oh, yes, it's that. It's just that I'm not in much of a reading mood tonight."

"You should have something more attractive to come home to than an old mother bent over her needlework and a sister who's gone to her Bible class."

"Oh, Ma, not that wedding theme again! Do you really want to be all alone in this house?"

"I have Annie. She's rarely away, as you know. She goes out all too little, poor dear. And one child is surely enough for any old parent to keep at home. Not that I wouldn't welcome some nice young man who might take a shine to Annie, but she doesn't seem very much that way inclined. But you, on the contrary, have a whole world of young lovelies to pick from. You have only to choose."

"Ma, you exaggerate as always my attractions. I'm a very small butterfly in the world I flutter about in. Not many of your 'lovelies,' as you call them, are seeking to add me to their collection with a pin through my abdomen."

"That's because you won't see, my dear."

"Whom won't I see? Name one."

His mother was prompt and definite in her reply. "Kitty Atwater."

Startled, he let his book fall to the floor. "Mother! What makes you think there's anything between me and Kitty Atwater?"

"The fact that you never mention her. And that I know you've been seeing her. Annie told me."

"Annie's a gossip. An old maid gossip."

"She's no such thing. Why shouldn't she mention that

you've been seeing a bright, pretty girl like Kitty? Of course, I've only met her a couple of times, but she strikes me as perfectly charming, and I hear good things about her. I know she has a fool of a mother, but the poor girl can't help that, and no one's suggesting that you marry Mrs. Atwater."

"You're only suggesting that I marry her daughter. And what makes you think there's the slightest likelihood of my being accepted by a young lady surrounded by the richest young bloods in town?"

"If she's so surrounded, why hasn't she married one?"

"That's a fair question, I admit. But, Mother, the fact that she hasn't landed a rich one doesn't mean she'll accept a poor one."

"You're far from poor, my lad."

"But it's a question of degree. You know that, Ma. You couldn't compare this house, for example, with the Vanderbilt pile at the corner."

"Why should I want to? This is a very fine house. And we were around town when the Vanderbilts were nothing. And that was not so long ago, either. Your father used to say that people were always a good deal richer or a good deal poorer than one thought. That one never got it just right. Well, in the same way we may get their goals wrong. We're only too apt to suppose that a poor girl living in a rich society is looking for a cash box. But it may not be the *only* thing she's looking for. Miss Atwater, I'm told, is a very smart young woman. If that's so, she's plenty smart enough to know there's such a thing as happiness in the world. And such a thing as love!"

"But Kitty's not in love with me, Ma!"

"Have you ever asked her?"

"Why, of course not. What a question!"

"Ask her, then. After first telling her, of course, what *your* feelings are."

"Oh, Ma!"

"Well, there you are. Think about it!"

And think about it he certainly did. Indeed, he thought of little else in the next days and nights. And the more he dwelt on the idea, on the mere possibility of what she had said, the more his whole being was suffused with a kind of creeping joy. The curtains of his future, which he likened in his mind to the great golden ones of the new opera house, were slowly rising, not on a social setting where he was only a timid bystander hoping to pass muster artfully dressed up as an attendant lord, but on the interior of a happily snug home where a man, an impossibly real man, was actually loving and being loved by a beautiful woman with raven black hair and adoring eyes. Did his wise old mother actually know the world better than he did, for all his social gadding? It *could* be so!

He began to calculate how he and Kitty could live on his income. Wouldn't he have as much as his brother Wallace? And hadn't Wallace constructed a large shingle summer villa in Newport? Of course, Julie had some money, but not all that much. They would certainly sell him a patch of their land there to build on, perhaps even give it to him. They would welcome him and Kitty as neighbors. Everyone would!

His fantasies took a suddenly concrete turn on a Sunday afternoon "at home" in the Benson mansion, when he and Kitty were sitting in a far corner of the parlor while the other guests were grouped around their hostess's tea table. This unusual chasm between them and the rest of their world gave him a sudden airy sense of independence.

"Would you ever consider marrying a man with only twenty thousand a year?" he heard himself put to her.

She was at once attentive, oh, very attentive! "Would that be all he had to offer?"

"Oh, no. He would be young, passably attractive, and very much in love."

Her attention was not mitigated by any relaxing smile. "Is this a proposal, Bruce?"

"It certainly would be if there were the slightest chance of its being accepted." In the silence that followed he reached to put a hand on hers. She glanced at the group down the room as she pulled her hand away. But she pulled it; she did not snatch it.

"You must have guessed that I love you," he added, perhaps a touch lamely.

"I've guessed that you think you do" was her guarded reply.

"Doesn't that come to the same thing?"

"I daresay it could."

"Could you possibly imagine your loving me?"

"I could imagine it, yes."

"But you don't know."

"There's no way I'm going to answer that now. There's no way I'm going to commit myself now. I'll be quite frank with you, Bruce. I'm not totally surprised by your offer. I could see you were leading up to it. And I deeply appreciate the honor of it. Truly. But it will need some very careful thought on my part."

"But that sounds so cool!"

"But that's the way it is, my friend. Do you withdraw? You're quite free to do so, and I promise you we'll remain as good friends as ever. I am the way I am. You must take it or leave it. All I can assure you is that I will be a very good and faithful wife to any man I decide to marry."

"That's good enough for me," he said stoutly. "My offer stands. You are free, but I am not."

"Though, in fact, you are," she assured him, smiling at last. "And now we'll leave it at that. Let us join the others."

The only reason Bruce found sleep that night was in his repeating to himself her assurance that he really was still free. For he had begun already to question his rashness. To love and marry a girl with love and no money was one thing, a perfectly feasible and even desirable thing. To love and marry a girl with no love and no money was quite another. But in any event, the morrow brought him catastrophe.

When he went to his office, he found Wallace waiting for him there, with an ashen countenance and a cable in his hand, which he silently handed over to his startled brother. It was from Sir John Muir, and it read: "You say you must choose your own partners. So be it. And, similarly, I must choose my own American agents. Please hand over all my business matters to Isaac Fletcher & Co. Our family relationships, I trust, will remain unaffected."

Sir John had recently proposed that his new American son-in-law, Frederick Ames, be taken in as a full partner in Carnochan Brothers, and Wallace and Bruce had, somewhat stiffly, declined.

"Could we backtrack?" Bruce gasped. "Do you think we could still get hold of Fred?"

Wallace shook his head gravely. "Not a chance. I heard yesterday that Fred had accepted a partnership in Fletcher. It's all sewed up. And you know Muir. He never changes his mind. I had no idea he'd take our refusal so hard. I thought he might understand that you and I would be reluctant to share a business that we've built up from nothing with a young and inexperienced fellow who's just had the luck to marry into the family. But I guess nothing that we can do can reduce the size of the swelled head that John's brand-new baronetcy has given him."

"But Muir Thread is three quarters of our business," Bruce moaned.

"Well, we must look for a substitute, that's all."

"It's all very well for you, Wally. You have Julie's money."

"And what do *you* need money for? You live free at Mother's, and you dine out every night at other people's houses. Buck up, old man! It's not the end of the world."

"It's the end of part of one. There are things you don't know, Wally!"

Bruce lost no time in doing what he now knew he had to do. He wanted to get it over with as quickly and painlessly as possible. He called at the Bensons' that very afternoon, asked to see Miss Atwater, and was received by her in a small antechamber next to the great hall.

"Could you even think of marrying a man with only five thousand a year?" he blurted out.

"Oh, my poor Bruce, what's happened?"

She listened attentively while he poured out the sad financial tale. But she took it in more as a friend whose sympathy and advice were to be sought than as a potential partner in woe. At last she said: "Of course, I see that this puts a definite hold on the discussion we had yesterday."

"A hold or a veto?"

"Don't you have to wait and see if your brother-in-law may change his mind?"

"But he never does."

"Well then, you must wait and see what new business opportunities show up."

Bruce shook his head firmly. "I'm afraid Muir was the chance of a lifetime. It was a great boon for me. The long and short of it, Kitty, is that I'm afraid I may never be an adequate earner. But I'll always have something, and when Mother goes, a bit more. You and I could make do on it."

Kitty's smile seemed meant to confirm the depth of her worldly knowledge. "I don't think we would ever be a happy couple just making do, Bruce. We might be pretty enough

flowers in the sunshine, but I'm afraid we'd droop sadly in
the shadows. I know myself too well, and I think I know you.
We're both spoiled brats, in a way. We might be hard to live
with on a beer income dreaming of champagne."

"Unless we were in love."

"Yes. Unless we were very much in love. More in love,
in fact, than either of us is apt to become."

"Oh, Kitty, you can be cold!"

"Or realistic. Choose your word."

He rose. "Goodbye, Kitty."

She rose as well and held out a friendly hand. "You
make it sound as if it were forever. Won't you come back?"

"What for?"

"Well, why not for Ada? She thinks the world of you.
And the sun will always shine for Ada."

In the months that followed, Wallace Carnochan engaged his not inconsiderable financial talents in promoting
various commercial enterprises, including a phosphate mine
in Georgia, and he invited his brother Bruce to take an interest in each, but Bruce would always shake his head and
mutter: "It's too soon, Wally. Pardon me, and give me another chance in a month or so. I just don't feel up to any new
business as yet." Wallace hoped that while he was engaged
with minor successes in risky ventures, his younger brother
would at least mind the old shop and take care of such little
thread business as remained after the defection of Muir, but
this soon melted away under Bruce's inertia, and the latter
took to spending his days moping about the family house
or walking his mother's poodles in Central Park. Eliza was
at first silently sympathetic, then admonitory, and at last
briskly critical.

"You must take hold of yourself, my boy, or you'll end
up in a sorry state. You're not the only young man who's

been crossed in love or failed in a business. When you're down, the only sensible thing to do is to get up."

But Bruce seemed unable to do this. He felt himself sliding into what threatened to become a chronic state of depression. He had had his first dazzling glimpse of what it might be like to have a "real life," founded on his own character and not on what he had tended to see as the image of a character devised to conceal the smallness and weakness of Bruce Carnochan from a critical but fortunately still gullible world. It was hard now to live with that glimpse snuffed out. A "real girl," by which he meant a girl whom *he* could really love, and not one he just made up to, and a "real business," like the one John Muir had offered to him and to Wallace and not just to Wallace, had now escaped him, and there was something about the sad finality of Kitty's parting smile that persuaded him it would never return. He was driven back to the status of calling-card dandy he had once not been ashamed to be, but which now seemed to deserve the scorn he had been so silly as to deem envy.

He was frankly recognized as a family problem. His brothers called to buck him up, to joke with him, finally to subject him to stern lectures. His sister Annie wept over him, which was even worse. The pastor of the Fifth Avenue Church came to remind him that the deity's patience might be exhausted by his behavior — or at least by his lack of behavior. Bruce, to give them some reassurance, or at least to keep them at bay, took pains with his clothes and appearance, so as to present an immaculate exterior over his inner troubled self, and spent his mornings in the library on the excuse that he was writing a novel. This fooled nobody but himself, and he was actually surprised to find that six weeks of plotting had produced only six pages. It was then that, with the avowed purpose of seeking material, he started going about in society again. And with the dinner parties something like a cure began to creep over his blue spirits.

He was surprised to receive a card from Mrs. Benson inviting him for dinner, as he had heard that Kitty was no longer staying there, but when he went and found himself sitting next to Ada, he suspected the handiwork of his former inamorata.

Ada informed him, when he inquired about Kitty, that she was well and had rejoined her mother in the latter's flat after Mrs. Atwater had returned from one of her chaperoning trips to Europe. But the big news was that Kitty was engaged to one Gilbert Palmer.

"A gentleman of means, no doubt," he remarked with unbecoming bitterness.

"Why do you say that? He's just been made a junior partner in the law firm that represents Daddy, and I suppose he'll do well there, as everyone says he's brilliant. But I know he had to work his way through college and law school. Do you assume that Kitty is interested only in riches?"

"Something like that."

"Because she wouldn't accept you?"

Bruce was startled, not only that she knew this, but that she should say it. "Oh, you've heard about that?"

"Of course, I have. Kitty's my best friend. Did it never occur to you that she might have thought that *she* was too poor for *you*? And not just that you were not rich enough for her?"

"You mean that she was afraid I mightn't be easy to live with if we were poor?"

"As you just said. Something like that."

He found himself wondering what it was about this flatly outspoken little woman that seemed to brush aside his incipient resentment as a foolish intrusion on their colloquy.

"I suppose many men mightn't be easy to live with under those circumstances" was his lame conclusion.

"How true. It's women who have to put up with such things."

"You won't."

"With poverty, perhaps not. The way things look now. But life has other hurdles. However, I think I can get over the ones I see at the moment. At least I can make a running jump."

He looked at her half in wonder. "You don't get angry? At life, I mean?"

"Oh, yes. But I keep it in. I only make a scene when I'm pretty sure it's the only way."

"I could learn a lot from you. Would you care to teach me?"

"If you'll teach me in return."

"What on earth could I teach *you*?"

"How to enjoy things more."

"Ah, but my faculty in that direction has taken a rude bump in recent months." Bruce here tried to look melancholy.

"Then teach me how it used to be."

And so began their curious friendship. Bruce became a regular visitor at the Benson "at homes" and a frequent occupier of a back seat in their opera box. When he sat in a corner of their parlor with Ada, nobody came to join them. The family had clearly decided, no doubt after one of their formidable conferences, to accept him as a suitable beau. After all, was he not utterly respectable, afflicted with no known vice, and of agreeable presence and manner? And, where money was concerned, there was surely no need of that. Besides, Ada's stature and plainness were not designed to make a catch that would awe the town. It was only realistic to face this, and the Bensons were nothing if not realistic.

Yet Ada was like Kitty in showing not the least hint of having anything like a match in mind. Any step in that direction would have to be made by him alone. She was always serious, factual, and rigidly truthful, and oddly enough, she did not bore him the way her siblings sometimes did. It might have been because he felt that she saw through him and didn't mind what she saw. He could be utterly frank and natural with Ada. He could discuss, it seemed, anything in the world but the possibility of their ever marrying each other. But this was a large, and increasingly larger, exception. It came almost to torture him.

It was Kitty who broke through his block. At a large dinner in honor of her and her fiancé, Palmer, given by the Bensons, she, despite her position as chief guest, took him aside after dinner for a quiet talk. He couldn't help wondering if it were not with the secret consent of Ada's mother and Mr. Palmer. Certainly the latter, whom Bruce had been somewhat chagrined to find absolutely charming, made no move to interrupt Bruce's *tête-à-tête* with his future bride. Kitty came straight to the point.

"Look, Bruce. I want you to listen carefully, for I have only a few minutes before I have to join the other guests. You must marry Ada. She's just what the doctor would order for you."

"That doesn't sound very romantic."

"It wasn't meant to sound romantic. I don't believe that romance is what you need, or even very much want. What I believe you really need is a firm base from which you could operate to amuse yourself and the world with your good taste, your collegiality, and your cordial and generous nature."

"That base being Ada's money."

"That base being Ada herself, as well as Ada's money. You and she together could entertain the world and travel over the world, and collect art and wonderful friends, and raise fine children who would love you . . ."

"And bore me."

"You don't mind that in children. Not in dear good children such as Ada's would be, even if they were as dull as the dullest Benson! You're basically a family man, my friend, and you'll love being the center of a warm, admiring clan."

"Admiring? But you're painting me as a superficial ass, Kitty!"

"Once you were rich you'd cease to be superficial. The dilettante becomes the art patron. The diner out, the foundation trustee. The party wag, the charming and witty host. What you don't appreciate in yourself, Bruce Carnochan, is that you have that rare gift of enjoying life, something your Scottish forebears knew nothing about. And people who enjoy life, really enjoy it, help others to. But, of course, like a cricket, you need a little sunshine. Well, Ada will provide all the sunshine you perish without!"

"But what sort of a friend are you being to Ada? What is there for her in marrying a man who's not in love with her? For you may as well know, if you don't already, that however much I may respect and like Ada, however much I might want to be in love with her, I'm not! So there you are, Kitty, and don't tell me that love doesn't matter, for I suspect you of being very much enamored of that bright attorney across the room!"

"Yes, I've been blessed, far more than I deserve. But I am being a good friend of Ada, for I know that *she* knows exactly what she wants and has a good idea of the man you are. She's not going to sit home waiting for a Romeo who won't come. She wants a decent man of kindly character who will be a pleasant companion in life, a good father, and a faithful husband. I've assured her that, once you were pledged, you'd never so much as look at another woman."

"It's not necessarily a compliment to a man to say that of him."

"I'm not trying to compliment you. I'm trying to make you appreciate yourself as you are. Half the unhappiness in the world comes from people trying to be someone else. Anyway, I've said enough. Probably too much. And there's Mrs. Benson giving me the eye. It's time to join the others."

The very next day he called at the Bensons' and took Ada for a stroll in Central Park. She accepted his temperately stated proposal without the least fuss, and on their return they were warmly congratulated by her mother and more formally so by her father. In the days following, arrangements were made quietly and efficiently and with a minimum of embarrassment to a fiancé of very disproportionate wealth. A large fortune was settled on Ada outright; her father said he had entire trust in her ability to handle wisely anything that was hers. Every Benson and Carnochan expressed what was obviously their sincere pleasure at the match.

And Kitty was right, very right. In the three decades that he survived his wedding, Bruce had every occasion to be reminded of this. Ada settled an income on him to satisfy his every want without his having to appeal to her, and he never overspent it or made any demands on the far larger sums that she kept under her own watchful control. For this he was respected and well liked by all the Bensons into whose midst he fitted neatly, almost, he sometimes feared, in a rare pre-marital mood, too neatly. Four healthy, affectionate, and normal children, two boys and two girls, were born to him and Ada, almost indistinguishable from their numerous first cousins on the maternal side. Bruce reflected that the Benson genes were strong indeed, but he saw less and less reason to regret this. None of his offspring ever indicated that they were even aware of the fact that their wealth came from only one parent. The money seemed to cover them all with the same dye.

He and Ada lived in four places; they had a Palladian villa in Newport, a French *hôtel* in New York City, a rambling stone mansion in Fairfield, Connecticut, from which town the Bensons had sprung and in which each loyally maintained a residence, and a shingle villa in Jekyll Island, Georgia. The year was divided in four quarters between these, involving four stately annual moves and the displacement of some thirty in help, the walling up of garden statues against the cold, the packing and unpacking of countless trunks, and the shipping of large family portraits which could not be left in empty parlors. All this was efficiently supervised by Bruce, who sometimes wondered if it were not a life trade in itself, but he also had time to assemble a distinguished collection of Hudson River landscapes and to act as an oft-consulted trustee of the two Metropolitans, the museum and the opera.

Oh, yes, it was a life and not a bad one. And he had made Ada happy; there was nothing phony about that. And he sometimes wondered if he had not, after all, become as "real" a man as he had sometimes imagined his brothers and brothers-in-law to be, in contrast to himself. His children were as much Bensons in looks and wealth as any of their cousins of the Benson name, and totally accepted as such in society, and had he not created them?

4

GORDON

BY THE YEAR 1900 the Carnochans had established themselves on a firm middle rung of the New York social ladder. Of the second generation from emigrator David only Douglas's widow, Eliza, survived, in quiet and sober respectability, in her brownstone on Fifty-seventh Street, which she shared with her maiden daughter, Annie, but her other children had made rather more of a splash. Bruce's French *hôtel* was a familiar sight to tourists who gaped at the long row of mansions on Fifth Avenue, and the annual visits of Sir James Muir, Clara's widower, were duly noted in the evening journals, though a city that could now claim two duchesses could hardly be much impressed by a mere baronet, even a rich one. Still, it was something.

But the members of the third generation, now middle-aged, who were most visible, particularly in the world of business affairs, were the brothers Wallace and James. Wallace, who had largely redeemed himself from the collapse of his thread business in some half dozen other enterprises, was a stout, gruff gentleman whose rare and supposedly well-conceived pronouncements on stock market trends carried conviction to many, and James, a long, lean, also often silent lawyer with a large and loyal clientele, were close friends as well as brothers. They had built adjoining matching brownstones in the same street as their mother's and filled them with the academic art of the period: cavaliers boisterously drinking in taverns, cardinals playing chess in gilded interiors, and gladiators pleading for their lives to a stony Caesar. In the early fall and spring their numerous progeny played noisy games up and down the chocolate stoops.

Both brothers had made appropriate matches: Wallace with Julie Denison, hearty member of a hearty, sports-loving, card-playing Brooklyn clan, and James with Louisa, the strong-minded and strong-willed daughter of a minor railroad tycoon. But the great difference between the two couples, at least in the eyes of one rueful observer, was that James and Louisa boasted six sturdy sons and Wallace and Julie only one.

Gordon, that sole male, was the rueful observer. He had not always been the sole. He had had a twin, Michael, not identical, but bigger, stronger, and more loudly yelling. Yet for all his apparent physical superiority, Michael had succumbed to the diphtheria that had attacked the twins when they were six, leaving a violently stricken mother who was only mildly consoled by the survival of Gordon and the presence of his two sisters. Julie's passionate favoritism had been no secret to the household; she had adored little Michael beyond anyone else, including her husband, and though she made periodic efforts to conceal this from the others after the boy's death, for she had a good enough heart and some sense of duty, she never wholly succeeded. Gordon, a puny child, at least in his early years, grew up with a keen sense that, in the eyes of Fifty-seventh Street at least, the wrong twin had survived, and that for some mysterious reason he was the cause of it.

It didn't always help that next door was the home that his mother must have really wanted: the nursery of six young males, a vigorous brood that would guarantee the future of the Carnochans. Fortunately, however, the closest rapport existed between the two establishments. Gordon's two sisters were in constant chattering and giggling relationship with Estelle, the single daughter of the other house, and Estelle's brothers included Gordon in all their games and sports with the same joshing put-on reluctance that they used with each other. Gordon saw it as a kind of desperate solution to his problem to lose himself in a merger with other Carnochans.

It was thus that he became the silent, curious, wide-eyed lad who was both a part and not a part of the tumultuous cousinhood, filling to overflowing the dark interiors of the twin brownstones, tumbling in and out of the narrow halls, steep stairwells, and square parlors crammed with big black knobbly furniture and hung with unlit paintings and prints. And there were not only the multitudinous cousins but all the neighborhood friends, the Browning School classmates, the neat little next-door girls, so surprisingly bold and shrill, who swarmed up and down the high stoops and played hopscotch under the eyes of Irish nursemaids in nearby Central Park. It seemed to Gordon a world dominated by Carnochans, a cheerful, sometimes too cheerful world, secure, if with smothered doubts, in its own continuing prosperity, and defiant, if a bit edgily so, of the alien population of the slums that so closely bordered it — oh, yes, he had seen these! — and of the menacing bums and beggars who sometimes invaded the park and even had the gall to fall into drunken slumber on the benches until a cop aroused them with his stick.

Just enough of the ancestral Presbyterianism survived in the heritage of his father and Uncle James to alert Gordon to the realization that sin might still penetrate even to the heart of all the jollity and goodwill. His mother, a Brooklyn Denison of pure English forebears without a taint of John Knox, was a square-faced, down-to-earth, worldly-wise woman who had little use for the moral severities of the old kirk and faced ethical choices with a broad practicality. She loved parties and card games and gossip and stylish dress, and took the world pretty much as it was, feeling sure that a society that favored such congenial souls as the Denisons must have enough good in it to get by. She ruled her husband more by his recognition of her efficiency and good sense than by any self-assertion, but when he was seized by one of his rare but violent fits of anger, she always promptly gave way. Gordon knew, from bitter experience, that the child who had had the bad luck to arouse the paternal ire, even if not at fault, could not count on Mama's support. The shrug with which she abandoned the victim to his father showed how few, if any, were the issues over which she felt called upon to make a scene. Certainly a child was not one of them. Julie knew it was a man's world, but it was still one where a clever woman could get anything she needed if she played her cards right. And cards were her strong point. As for Gordon, wasn't he, too, a male? He could jolly well learn how to cope with his own often unreasonable sex.

To Gordon the paternal rages, however happily rare, were illuminating as to the persistent existence of a darker reality behind the brighter appearance of daily life. Papa's temper was like a thinly smoking Vesuvius over a seemingly benign Pompeii. A large portly gentleman with a protruding pot and strong stubborn features that had once been handsome, Wallace Carnochan had gruff kindly manners and a charming courtesy, even in addressing his children, toward whom he usually maintained an attitude of mildly detached benevolence. Indeed, he appeared to manifest this detachment for many things besides his offspring; no one knew just what preoccupied him in those long, silent sessions in his study, where he was supposed to be poring over business reports or reading his beloved Gibbon or Macaulay. Sometimes Gordon or his sisters, standing outside the closed door, would hear the clink of a decanter against a glass, but the clinker never betrayed the least symptom of inebriation. His favorite sport was fishing in the Maine woods, but this, of course, was just another form of isolation. The only advice that he ever gave to Gordon when the latter was about to matriculate at Yale was a terse "Just remember that you're a gentleman and the son of a gentleman."

Wallace had one ugly burst of temper that particularly affected his son. Of Uncle James's sons, David Carnochan and his "Irish twin" Andy (they were born just under a year apart) were closest to Gordon. David, the undisputed leader of the trio — Andy was only his plump and amiable, dirty-talking sidekick — had the big nose of the Carnochans, craftily innocent blue eyes, and a long, equine face capable of a serene air of attention as the masque of a cleverly manipulative brain. It was generally conceded in the family that David, even more than his older or younger siblings, was the one to "keep an eye on." He had the look of a boy who would go far.

When David and Gordon were eleven and ten, Gordon found himself greatly coveting a toy of David's, the small replica of a steam yacht sent him for Christmas by rich Uncle John Muir in Glasgow. It had been a more expensive gift than any others sent from across the sea, for David had already shown a premature perspicacity in making up to the baronet on his annual visit to New York, but he had already tired of the toy, as he was quickly apt to do with new possessions, and was now himself casting an acquisitive eye on the prize of Gordon's collection, the model of a Madison Avenue streetcar. A swap was soon effected, but two days later Gordon's new yacht fell apart. It had been previously smashed in a fall from its table and cleverly glued together by its former owner.

Instead of facing his cousin indignantly with the charge of fraud, Gordon sought desperately in his mind to excuse him. He could not bear to think that a friend and cousin would treat him so shabbily. It was suddenly vital to him that David should remain what he had always taken him to be. And might not the transaction simply be a lesson in American business as it was daily transacted? Was that not what his father meant by the *caveat emptor* he always quoted to his mother when she went shopping? David had never told him that the vessel was damaged, but hadn't it been Gordon's duty to inspect it? So he remained silent, knowing that David would certainly never mention it or even ask to see the broken toy when he came to visit.

But this was not the end of the story. Sir John arrived on his annual visit to inspect his American markets, and David's father told his sons to have all their gifts from the baronet ready to be prominently seen if the great man chose to ascend to the nursery. David protested that he could not find the vital toy, but, under pressure, admitted to seeing it in Gordon's home. He implied that Gordon must have swiped it, and denied any knowledge of a trade. Never, he insisted loudly, would he have voluntarily parted with a gift from his beloved uncle. The ruined toy was retrieved and expensively restored for the unlikely event of a Scottish inspection, but Gordon, whose frantic explanation was disbelieved by both his father and his Uncle James, was branded as a liar and a thief.

A terrible scene ensued in Wallace Carnochan's dark study, where father and son faced each other standing, one pale and trembling, the other red-faced and of a sudden grotesqueness.

"You're worse than a robber! Even a gentleman fallen from grace might sink to that. But a liar, and to his own flesh and blood — no gentleman could stoop so low. It's one thing if a man owns up to having filched some piece of trash that has caught his fancy, but to deny to his own kin is something I never thought I'd have to face in a son of mine!"

"But, Daddy," Gordon cried, with tears of dismay, "I didn't take it. I . . ."

"Hold your tongue, sirrah! Haven't I heard the whole story from my brother? Has your mother a word to say for you? Just learn this. The next time anything like this happens, you're going to get the whipping of your life. And from this right arm!"

Terrifyingly, he raised his right arm and shook it at his shaking son. He had never whipped Gordon, nor did he ever thereafter. He didn't even possess a whip, so far as his son knew. Yet the mere threat seemed to shatter forever the complacent brownstone world that had so long and so precariously sheltered the younger Carnochans. Gone was the pleasant joking realism of Gordon's mother, so alien to these sultry comminations. Had not his father implied that she had washed her hands of the whole business? Oh, yes, she was not one to risk a hat, a dress, or a soul in such foul weather. The bright Episcopalian skies of the Denisons rolled back before the storm clouds of a Scottish Presbyterian doom. The Carnochan god had only been hidden away. He was back, and there would always be the danger that he would come again.

But the injustice was too great; Gordon had to make one further appeal. He went to his mother's bedroom one morning, after his father had left for the office. She was sitting at her dressing table, brushing her hair for the day, a time when she did not like to be disturbed by children, but when she took in how pale and grim he looked, she relented.

"What is it, Gordon?" But when he stood before her,

still speechless, it took only a moment for her impatience to rise. "Come on, child. Out with it."

He then told her the whole story of the broken toy. She listened with a growing concern that he desperately hoped might be on his account, but he soon found otherwise.

"Well, I certainly agree that David Carnochan has treated you badly. I'm shocked, really. But what can we do about it now, dear? Isn't that water pretty well under the bridge? Anyway, you've learned to keep a sharp eye on your cousin in any future swaps. If there are any. Which I strongly advise against."

"But won't you tell Daddy I'm not a thief and a liar?"

Surprisingly, his mother reflected on this for some moments. There appeared to be difficulties he had not suspected. "The trouble with that is that your father will go to your uncle, and your uncle will go to David, and David, of course, will stick to his story. And the chances are that your uncle will side with David, and he and your father will both lose their Carnochan tempers, and we'll have a shattering family row. No, I think we'd better let the whole matter drop, which it already has."

"But, Mummy, Daddy will always think of me as someone wicked!"

"Pooh. You don't know your father. When something unpleasant is over for him, it's over. He never thinks of it again. I'm sure he's put the whole thing out of his mind already."

"Oh, please, Mummy, I can't bear to have him think those things of me!"

"Don't be silly, child. I've told you he won't."

"Mummy!" And he started to sob.

This was a mistake. Julie Carnochan could not abide what she considered excessive emotional displays in her offspring. "That will do, Gordon. Go and get ready for school. You must learn that the family always comes first in these matters. I do not want a row between your father and your uncle. And that's that."

Gordon had to admit that his mother seemed to have been right about his father's easy dismissal of the unpleasant. The following Sunday, at a family lunch, Wallace Carnochan behaved to him as if nothing at all had happened. His mother was as brisk and smiling as ever, and even his sisters, Betty and Loulou, older and younger than Gordon, usually so smirking and teasing, uttered no word on the baleful subject. There was no way he could further defend himself, as no one in the family cared to be reminded of what he was supposed to have done. The unspeakable incident was closed.

That the family, both families, had dismissed the matter was far from meaning that Gordon did. He could not seem to help brooding about it. Did a thing have to be one's fault to be held against one by some mysterious fate that kept its own secret records? Might not even a sin, however falsely attributed to him, if never corrected in the hidden score book, achieve a kind of reality? He began to feel an actual guilt over this thing which he had not done, as if accusation and conviction were one and the same. He had heard about original sin in sermons. Was it not something that man had inherited rather than committed? Did one need much more than that to be damned?

And then David had the gall to bring up the matter himself. "Sorry to have let you down that way, Gordie," he told him casually. "But I'd have got the very dickens from my old man if he'd learned I'd swapped anything Uncle John had given me. He can use a birch, too, and we all know that your father never would. Uncle Wallace is all talk, no do, when it comes to discipline. That's true, isn't it? That he never touches you? So you see, it was better all around for you to take the blame. But I'll owe you one, fella."

Gordon wanted to protest that he had been vilified with a crime while David would have been found guilty of a mere indiscretion, but something made him pause. Was David a mere factor in the mysterious morality of the world, essentially acting as fate obliged him to act, as helpless as Gordon himself? David, of course, was a true Carnochan, every inch of him. And his father, Uncle James, was even more of one, having sired six sons as opposed to Wallace's one. Gordon could only conclude that he would do better to accept David's excuse, lame as it was, and hope that the blanket of family solidarity, out of the coverage of which he seemed to be slipping, would continue to shelter him.

But it was not easy to adjust himself to a life where the tepidity of parental affection, which he attributed to their seeing him as the usurper of his deceased brother's lost place, was somehow further justified by the fracas he had brought about, however involuntarily, over the broken toy. He became increasingly despondent, and his marks at school dropped, soon alarmingly. His mother, at last truly concerned, took him out of Browning and had him privately tutored for some months.

This resulted in his being sent to Chelton School in the second form rather than the first, so that when he arrived at that handsome, red-bricked, green-lawned Palladian compound, an hour's drive west of Boston, that strictly Protestant Church boarding academy for boys of respectable upper-middle-class origin, he found himself a "new kid," while David and Andy, having been entered the year before, though in the same class, were "old kids" and possessed of all the privileges pertaining to their status.

Gordon had hoped that David would be his friend and

helpful guide in this new life, but he found that his cousin conformed strictly to the school code and kept himself coolly aloof. Andy, as was to be expected, followed his brother's suit. Gordon accepted this, as he accepted without question all the school traditions. Freed, at least temporarily from the emotional frustrations of his family life, he was relieved to find that he could cope with the lessons and games at school and even make some new friends. He had grown in size and was beginning to be not bad-looking; he was quiet, modest, and inoffensive, and the other new kids accepted him.

In his second year at Chelton, now an "old kid," he received overtures from David to renew their friendship. David explained that his coolness of the year before had been only in conformance with school prejudice. But it was evident to Gordon that David had noted that his cousin was now well enough liked in their form to be an acceptable friend. But there it was again, the chance to be approved by the all-powerful family, to seek its shelter from the gales of black chance. And besides, there were distinct advantages to being under the aegis of his clever cousin. David was a politician to the core of his being; he was almost surely going to be one of the prefects of the school, and he knew how to ingratiate himself with those who would smooth his upward way. And then it was also true that no boy at Chelton was funnier or wittier or better company than David Carnochan when he chose; nobody was more fun to be with, so long as he got his way.

David made no secret of his ambitions or how they were to be implemented. He explained frankly to Gordon and to his always loyal brother Andy his project to forge the three of them into a tight social unit to promote themselves: "There's nothing so powerful as a well-organized team. It works in football. It can work in every side of school life. We can be like the Three Musketeers. All for one and one for all. So long as we stick together and back each other up in everything, we can become a force in the form."

Gordon, while perfectly realizing that David fully intended to be the leading musketeer, was gratified to feel that he was at last a full member of the family, almost as if he were now a seventh son of Uncle James and not just the unwelcome survivor of Wallace and Julie's twins. And furthermore, he could see nothing but good in David's plans for the three of them. If these plans were primarily concerned with the glory of David — one could never get away from that — they also involved the achievement of school goals that were perfectly laudable. David wanted to be senior prefect of the school, yes, but he also wanted Andy to be president of the Dramatic Society and Gordon to be editor of the school literary magazine. What was wrong with any of that?

As they worked together toward their goals, Gordon began to find a new peace and satisfaction in identifying himself with the spirit and idealism of Chelton. It was as if the clouds of his early life had been rolled back and he had become an integral and accepted part of an institution dedicated to the raising of fine pure young men to the service of God and man. And he owed it to David! It was through David that he had come to share the radiant vision of the inspiring headmaster!

The Reverend Silas Nickerson was a big, hearty, deep-voiced minister of forty-odd years who had founded his very fashionable academy only twenty years before with the blessing and financial backing of Boston's first families, to all of whom he was related. He professed to be what was then called an ardent Christologist of the school of Bishop Phillips Brooks, and his daily joy in the felt presence of a never-absent Jesus was instantly contagious to a boy like Gordon, who had been passionately wanting such a solution to his adjustment to life. The dark Carnochan Presbyterianism evaporated before the glory of Nickerson's enthusiasm. David and Andy, Gordon could not help but observe, failed to share his feeling in this respect, but they accepted religion as a formal aspect of the life they would one day be expected to lead, and David was heard to observe respectfully that the headmaster was held in high regard by many of the great of the land, including President Theodore Roosevelt himself. David never downgraded Gordon's faith. He simply ignored it.

Their final year at school crowned David's efforts, not with the success he craved, but with a fair simulacrum of it. He was not elected the senior but one of the six prefects; Andy did not make president of the Dramatic Society, but he was a member and played Falstaff creditably in the school play; and Gordon became an editor but not editor in chief of the magazine. It was a good-enough show.

James and Wallace Carnochan had gone to Yale, and to Yale their sons were sent. Gordon and his cousins did many things as a trio in New Haven, but in sophomore year Gordon, who had a greater interest in literature than his cousins, drew slightly apart from them by trying out for the *Yale Literary Magazine*, known as the *Lit*. It was in the cramped offices of that publication that he met Philip Key.

Key was a long, thin, young man with a long, thin face, a small, mean, oval chin, and opaque eyes that re-emphasized the distrust and disapproval of his fixed expression. He was a New Yorker, but of a different background from Gordon's; his father ran a bar in Chelsea, and Philip Key, politically, espoused radical views. But his stories in the *Lit* were both imaginative and thought-provoking, far more mature and sophisticated than any others in the magazine, and actually showed promise of a significant literary future. Gordon well knew how greatly these surpassed his own poor efforts, but it was nonetheless disagreeable to have this flung in his face by his merciless new friend. He used the term "friend" to describe his tenuous relationship with the ever-sardonic Key, though it never received a reciprocal use by the latter, who seemed to have no need for intimate companionship. Gordon had decided to suffer Key's constant jibes as the price of a literary education that he was beginning to see might be wider — or at least different — from what was offered in the classroom, as exemplified by the roseate lectures of Professor William Lyon Phelps. And Key tolerated Gordon as his only available audience.

Given the draft of one of Gordon's short stories and asked his opinion, Key drawled: "In *La Bohème* the manuscript of Rodolfo's tragedy was at least useful as fuel for the stove to keep him warm. But as there is just enough heat in this dreary attic of our beloved *Lit*, we needn't put a match to your masterpiece, Carnochan."

With a stubborn faith in the salubrious effect of humiliation, Gordon persisted in visiting Key in his bare but untidy room, where he was received with the grudging welcome of a hermit who needs at least one ear in which to vent his contempt for the outside world and who noted that his caller was always the bearer of a packet of beer.

Gordon's spine tingled with a mingled dismay and excitement as his new mentor savaged the reputations so inflated by the enthusiastic Billy Phelps. A Browning worshipper who had not hesitated to rank *The Ring and the Book* with *Paradise Lost*, Gordon gaped to hear the sainted Pompilia reduced to a flirting adulteress.

"Who the hell did Browning think he was kidding?" Key sneered. "He tells you again and again that he got it all from an old volume about the trial he picked up in a bookstall. He insists that he's telling the gospel truth. But he isn't. Unfortunately for him, scholars have unearthed that book and read it. They've seen that Pompilia was a sad little bird who was abused by a brute of a husband and fled the nest with a priestly lover by whom she had a bastard child. That's not a bad story in itself. But what does Browning do with it? A fatuous Victorian, he makes Pompilia inhumanly pure, so pure, in fact, that if she were alive she'd be a psychopath!"

Under Key's guidance Gordon began to read Whitman, Emily Dickinson, Baudelaire, and Verlaine. His world was beginning to expand. But just as he was speculating on the possibility of inviting Key to spend some days with him in the forthcoming summer in Bar Harbor, counting on the perhaps irresistible friendliness of such an invitation to induce his guide to mitigate the rigor of his spoken judgments in the presence of his parents, Key, who had hitherto been one of the obscurer members of his Yale class, attained a sudden and undesirable notoriety with the publication of the last story that the *Lit* would accept from his pen.

In it the protagonist, who has led a sinful life, repudiating in his every thought and act the teachings of Christianity, dies, only to discover that those teachings have all been true. There *is* an afterlife; there is a God; mercy is accorded and all is forgiven. The angels trumpet the glory of the Almighty in the golden streets of a new Jerusalem, and the Trinity is worshipped by an exuberant chorus of the saved forever. Forever and ever and ever! "I must be in heaven!" the new arrival exclaims joyfully. "Oh, no," a little voice whispers in his ear. "You're in the other place."

David Carnochan, who had kept a suspicious eye on his cousin's new friendship but who knew better than to encourage something by too harshly discountenancing it, now saw his chance to sever Gordon from this unwholesome association. "You see, Gordie, this Key fellow just won't do. He's not our sort. Andy and I have not wanted to talk to you about this before, because we assumed you'd catch on in time to what a meatball the guy really is. And then nobody of any consequence in our class knew how much you were seeing him. But now that he's become infamous as a radical and an atheist, it won't do you any good to be seen palling around with him."

"What harm can it do me, David? What have I got to lose?"

"It can blow your chances for Bulldog, that's what it can do."

"But what chance do I have for Bulldog, anyway?"

They were sitting in David's room. He rose now and closed the door to the hallway. Returning, he looked very grave and serious.

"I have it on very good authority that you and I and Andy may all three be tapped for Bulldog."

Well, this *was* something to pull Gordon up. Bulldog was one of the Yale senior secret societies, generally considered second only in distinction to Skull and Bones, each limited to fifteen members who were selected in the spring on "Tap Day," when the junior class assembled on the campus to await the blow, or "tap," on the shoulder from a society member circulating among them and to hear the shouted "Go to your room" for the initiation. The selection process was carried out with the greatest secrecy, but Gordon well knew that his cousin was capable of ferreting out the darkest concealments.

David watched Gordon carefully as he let his startling news sink in. "Bulldog is not apt to tap a man who is cozy with the likes of Key, and if they pluck one Carnochan, the contamination may spread to the other two. This is serious, Gordie. Andy and I are counting on you not to do anything to hurt our chances."

This argument was irresistible. Gordon could have forfeited his opportunity for admission to Bulldog — he had no particular feeling for or against the senior societies about which, in his new literary preoccupations, he had given little thought — but the idea that he might stand in the way of cousins who had played so dominant a role in his life was simply unthinkable. Bulldog, he knew well, was something that not only David and Andy cared passionately about but that the Carnochans of the generation earlier would consider a desirable tribal enhancement. And as for the family member who botched it . . . well, there would indeed be weeping and gnashing of teeth.

"You can count on me, Davie," he muttered, and left the room before he had the humiliation of being thanked for the task of dropping an inconvenient friend.

He decided that the way to handle Philip Key was to tell him frankly the dilemma in which fate had cast him. He hoped that even Philip might understand the pressure that had been brought to bear on him and agree that a friendship suspended for some term was not too great a price to pay for family loyalty and solidarity. He was careful to make it entirely clear that he himself knew just how vile it would ordinarily be to slight one friend for the social advantage of another, and that he was depending on Philip's intelligent detachment to understand the particular circumstances that made Gordon's action imperative. But Philip's silence as he listened was ominous, as was his malicious half smile.

"But it's not just for the sake of your cousins that you propose to give me the sack," he observed at last. "Are you not yourself expecting to be tapped by this august institution?"

"Well, David says I may be, yes. But you know I don't give a damn about those things. If I joined, it would only be because the family would take on so if I didn't. It's not a matter worth upsetting them about."

"You're gobbling the cake you're keeping, my onetime

friend. Disgustingly, too, I might add. You want Bulldog's and my approval of your dropping me! Your greed is unimaginable!"

"Philip, what would you do in my case?"

"In your case? How could I have the gall even to conceive of my humble self wearing the tartan of the Carnochans? But you needn't be concerned over my missing your little visits. You were born to be your cousins' toady, and you might just as well get on with it. I even doubt you have the character *not* to be a toady. As they say about inevitable rape, relax and enjoy it."

Gordon turned away from him, in part relieved that Philip's nastiness softened some of his own guilt feeling. It was unreasonable, after all, for Philip not to see that life could offer some hard choices, and that it wasn't always cut-and-dried which way to take. On second thought, however, he found himself wondering if life really did have choices. Wasn't it fairly plain that the way for him to go was a Carnochan way? Was he really qualified for any other? Did he really *want* any other?

He and David and Andy were all tapped for Bulldog, and everyone was delighted, even his usually indifferent father, who seemed to sense a dim revival of his own Yale days so many years before. Uncle James and Uncle Bruce, however, were more visibly enthusiastic. Never before had a senior society taken in three new members of the same family.

His senior year brought another honor to Gordon. He was named class poet. He did not send a draft of his poem to Philip Key. He knew only too well that the latter would label it sentimental drivel, and that, indeed, was just what it was.

David had planned that both Andy and Gordon should go with him to Harvard Law School, and Gordon, who now fully realized that his literary talents were not such as to sustain a writing or even a journalistic career — if he owed anything to Philip Key, he owed him at least that — was willing enough to compromise on a career which still made a primary use of words, for however different a purpose. Even David, however, could do nothing to overcome Andy's decided lack of capacity for law, and the latter was destined for New York and a firm of stockbrokers.

Alone now, so to speak, with David, for they shared rooms in Cambridge, Gordon had much occasion to reflect, with his self-impressed passivity, on the forceful role that his cousin seemed increasingly to be playing in his life. David struck him at times as a leader looking for loyal troops to support him in a battle for ends he had not yet determined but which time was bound to make clear. With his long, bony face and lean, bony figure, his high, balding dome and eyes that could turn in a second from a winning friendliness to an icy disapproval, David seemed to be training his agile intellect to subject other men to his pressures, and he appeared to sense intuitively whom he could bully into submission and to whom it was more politic to kowtow. David was intensely clannish, even for a Scot; he viewed the Carnochans, and in particular his brothers and cousins, as a force to be united in a general push to become a major league in the football games of life. And just where would Gordon fit in? Oh, that was obvious enough. He would be the utterly trustworthy second in command, or executive officer, an aide whose primary value would lie in his unwavering loyalty.

Oh, yes, Gordon saw all this; he was not a fool, nor would he have been much use to David had he been one. But he also saw that he needed David. David could cope with the world, especially the Carnochan world, with which Gordon found it often difficult to cope. His father was remote and unpredictable, his mother intent on leading her own life, if cautious not to trespass too heavily on her husband's guarded territory. His sisters were giggly and silly, obsessed at this time with boys. The practical maternal philosophy of the family had no place for the moral doubts and questionings of what to them was a more or less neurotic son and brother who could be expected to answer them himself, and he turned in the end to David for the benefits of a relationship that he liked to think of as symbiotic. If David supplied him with confidence in his own ability to survive as a member of David's team, did he not help David by acting as a sounding board for his plans and projects and a consolation in his inevitable if temporary setbacks?

But it continued to trouble Gordon that David's failure to share any of the idealism that had inspired Gordon at Chelton seemed, when they progressed from Yale to law school, increasingly to divide them. At school and at college the atmosphere in the sometimes excited discussions, political, ethical, or literary, among the friends was apt to be imbued with a shared desire, if not expectation, for a better world to which the disputants might hope to make some modest contribution. But in law school, in all the heated general discussions that he and David shared with fellow students, David was apt to focus, not on the growth of the law as a material factor in the improvement of society, not on how best to interpret the Constitution to deal with changing times and conditions, but on how to achieve a client's purpose in the teeth of a seemingly prohibitive statute. David appeared to see law as something to get around and a lawyer's function as how to advise him to do it. And a good many of their classmates seemed to agree with him.

It was a woman, of course, who, at last, and at least temporarily, released Gordon from the pervasive influence of his cousin. He met Agatha Houston at a Sunday lunch party given by his mother during a Christmas vacation when he had come down from law school in Cambridge. Julie

Carnochan and Agatha's mother were old friends, and Agatha's father, Dr. Houston, who was also present at the lunch, was the well-known throat doctor to some of the great singers at the Metropolitan Opera in what was coming to be known as the golden age of song. His name was associated with such shining ones as Fremstad, Nordica, and Eames. Agatha, however, reflected none of this glamour. She was pert, bright, and pretty, with large brown eyes, but she made an immediate point of being matter-of-fact and down-to-earth.

"If you had experienced the temperaments of some of Daddy's patients as I have," she told Gordon after he had spoken of his envy of her opportunities to meet the great divas, "you would be less anxious to hear them anywhere except on the stage, where they belong. It's just as well to keep on the other side of the footlights. They preserve the illusion, and that's what they're for."

"You never wanted to be a singer yourself?"

"Well, I didn't have a voice, which settled the question. But yes, I might have liked to, when I was in my teens. I used to fancy myself singing the 'Liebestod' to an audience too rapt even to applaud. I saw the curtain descend in a reverent silence more gratifying than the loudest cheers. But I've graduated from that. I live in the real world now. I hope it's better, but I'm not always sure. How about you? Do you dream of yourself as formidably clad in black robes, sitting up there on the Supreme Court bench, explaining the Constitution to admiring counsel?"

"How did you know?"

"Well, maybe you'll make it, then. I sometimes wonder if daydreaming is not the road to success. Does being preoccupied with hurdles really help?"

"You should know. They seem to interest you."

"And look at me. I'm nowhere!"

Gordon indeed looked at her. It was true, then, he felt with a sudden leap of his heart, that one could love at first sight! And the very first weekend after his return to Cambridge he came back down to New York to call on her at her family's brownstone, only two blocks from his. It soon became a habitual thing.

He was enchanted by her openness and candor. She was devoid of the coy flirtatiousness of so many of the girls of his acquaintance, who were only too well aware that the only game they were allowed to play was the marriage game. Agatha did not hesitate to let him know that she liked him very much indeed and saw no reason that either of them should be bothered or concerned with where their friendship might be heading. Let the future take care of itself! If marriage, why not? Neither family would object. If no marriage, was that such a tragedy?

He took her to the theater; he took her for long walks in Central Park. They were both twenty-two; they were free. Gordon found himself telling her all kinds of things he had never told anyone else, including his old fear that his mother, perhaps not even consciously, blamed him for surviving his twin brother.

"Of course, you don't know that," she warned him. "To be absolutely fair, you have to admit it's only a supposition on your part. But suppose it's true. It may not be a thing your mother can help. She's never said anything about it, has she?"

"Oh, never. Of course not."

"Well, give her credit for that. She's probably tried to be as good a mother as she was capable of being. I'm an only child, as you know. My mother was not allowed to have another baby after my very difficult cesarean birth. I've always been aware how bitterly disappointed my father was that I wasn't a boy. As a little girl I used to resent that terribly. But I got over it. And you can, too, Gordon. It's not easy, but you can."

He found such exchanges exhilarating. It was as if this wonderful girl was hewing him out of a marble rock of family solidarity and turning him into something that was at least the statue of a man. One Sunday night, arriving back in Cambridge at the rooms he shared with David, he decided that the time had come to tell his cousin that he was planning to propose to Agatha and that he had reason to believe that he would be accepted.

David, of course, was aware that Gordon had been seeing Agatha, whom he knew, though not well, but Gordon had not chosen to let his cousin know how far things had gone, being afraid that David might make some snotty remark about there being better social fish to fry than the Houstons, who, however respectable, were not notable in the fashionable world. He suspected that he would not be able to control his wrath if David should do so, and their friendship might be gravely marred.

But he had grossly underestimated David's capacity to deal with any novel situation. His cousin had fully appreciated the depth of his involvement with the girl and clearly recognized that it was something that had to be accepted. And when David made up his mind to accept something, he knew how to do it right.

"And do you know what, Gordie?" he cried, as he jumped up to embrace his cousin. "She's just the girl for you. She'll even be the making of you!"

AN UNEXPECTEDLY LARGE allowance promised the young couple by Agatha's enthusiastic father made possible their marriage right after Gordon and David's graduation from law school, and David was best man at the wedding. But the cousins did not go to work for the same law firm,

Brown & Livermore, as they had originally planned and as that firm had offered. At the last moment Gordon had decided to accept another offer, one proffered by an equally distinguished firm, Perry, Whitehead & Cox. It had been the result of a tense parley he had had with his bride-to-be, shortly before their union. She had been firmer than he had ever seen her.

"The Perry firm has one great advantage," she had insisted.

"And what is that?"

"David's not in it."

"Darling? What's wrong with David?"

"Nothing. Except for you."

"For *me*?"

"Yes. Not for anyone else. Or at least not for anyone else I care about. Only for you."

"You don't like David?"

"I don't like him at all. But that's not the point. I'm not going to be a bossy wife, Gordon, but in this one thing you must yield to me. This one thing I insist on. Don't go into the same firm with David."

"Darling, what's come over you? Have you gone crazy?"

"Let's put it that I have. But I won't marry you if you don't give in to me in this one instance."

Well, what could he say to that?

5

ESTELLE

ESTELLE CARNOCHAN, David's sister, the youngest of the seven children of James and Louisa, was their only daughter, and being pretty, blond, and very bright, she was the family pet. Her perennially delicate health — the early signs of tuberculosis — only added to the domestic affection. She was the particular favorite of her father, a charming and witty man, only intermittently faithful to his large, formidable, and adoring spouse, and after his premature death at forty-six, in 1907, Estelle had obligingly assumed the role of primary emotional support to her widowed mother, whom all New York regarded as a heroine, left as she was with all those sons to launch in the world. Why a heroine? Estelle sometimes asked this question of the shrewd little observer whom she artfully concealed behind an impassive front. Was Louisa Carnochan not possessed of robust health, an exuberant disposition, and a comfortable inheritance from a father who had bought farmland in northern Manhattan for nothing? But New York liked heroines, and Louisa enjoyed the role quite as much as her audience enjoyed attributing it to her.

Estelle may have been willing to play her part as acolyte to this grand figure of sorrow, and to act as confidante to rowdy brothers who seemed, for all their bravado, to need more pats on the back than might have been expected from their boasts, but she was determined that she was going to have a life of her own and never sink into the position so often then expected of the youngest born of a large family: the patient companion of a never-dying parent. Particularly if that youngest was afflicted with the symptoms of a dread disease.

She defied her mother's protests by insisting on attending Barnard College, although she had to submit to the humiliation of being accompanied on her daily trips uptown by an Irish maidservant, whose odd presence in the back of the classroom she explained to her new and more liberated friends as that of a cousin who desired to audit the courses. And when she had her first beau, a former Harvard Law School classmate of her brother David, whom she had met on his visit to her family's summer place on the Cape, she thought she might have found an independent base for a vision of life outside her family and her frail lungs.

Bronson Hale was a Bostonian to the core of his being. His dark and rather solemn good looks were accompanied by a gravity of demeanor that might have chilled had it not been accompanied by the warmth of his evident sincerity. The Hales were kin to half the Brahmins of his native city, but his high-mindedness eschewed the least tint of social snobbery. He seemed to feel a kindred soul in Estelle, and she found herself wondering if she had perhaps met the man who could answer all the questions that her brothers could not.

Not that he asked those questions. It was the answers that he seemed ready to provide. Bronson Hale did not openly challenge the values of a society that Estelle tended to find restricted and money-grubbing, nor did he query the existence of a beneficent creator somewhere in the heavens, nor did he even criticize the code of dress and deportment laid down by the social leaders of New York or Boston. But he believed in a constantly progressing society; he had faith that mankind was improving with each century and that our ills of today would one day be shed in a world more perfect. But he also believed that a man must be always at work to bring about this better state, and he had no smugness in regard to his own minor part in the task which, however minuscule, would be all that a hardworking and idealistic lawyer could contribute. Oh, it was clear that he meant every word that he uttered!

Estelle was impressed by his earnestness, so unlike that of his more cynical friend, her brother David, but she was a bit troubled by his obvious feeling that the Hales and their like in his hometown were a good deal closer to the future ideal state than any of their more material opposite numbers in Manhattan. She chaffed him on this.

"You know, Bronson, everyone in my world doesn't see the first families of Beacon Street and Commonwealth Avenue quite as you do. It is not uncommon to hear them accused of narrow minds and ancestor worship. We've even heard of a family on the 'hub' that refers to the great Queen Elizabeth as Cousin Bessie Tudor."

"And that's perfectly fair," he admitted. "There are such, and I'm not proud of them. But I maintain there's an idealism under the layer of snobbery and stuffiness in Boston that's unlike anything else I've seen in America. Take our record in the Civil War. What city sprang to arms to eliminate slavery as quickly and as widely as Boston? In New York you had the draft riots."

"The Irish did that."

"Do you think we didn't have our Irish?"

She had to laugh. "It's funny, you know, that you and David should be such good friends. He doesn't think at all as you do. David looks at the world as something to conquer. You see it as something to improve. But I suppose you should be complimented by his interest in you. It means he's spotted you as a comer. David is already selecting the friends with whom he will share his triumph."

"I don't see myself in any such grand role. If I ever accomplish anything in this life, it will be because someone like you believes in me."

They had been seeing each other for some weeks now. He had come down to New York on several weekends to call on her despite the heavy demands of his law practice. Of course, she knew that it meant something, and she found that something exciting, though she tried not to exaggerate it. For he had uttered no word — not a syllable — until this last statement, to indicate the birth of the least romantic feeling on his part. And yet the warmth of his tone and the intensity of his dark stare seemed to belie any imputation of indifference.

Did he know something? Had he been told something? Oh, God, she thought. She had to know.

"Has my mother said anything to you?" she demanded. "Or David?" They were sitting in the rarely inhabited stiff little front parlor that was used by any family member who wished to receive a guest alone. "About me, I mean. My health."

As his dark brow seemed to darken and she glimpsed the immediate pain in his eyes, she caught her breath at her sudden sense of how sharply his looks attracted her. Could she really be falling in love? But of course she could!

"Your health?" His tone was barely audible.

"Yes. My lungs."

For another long moment he was gravely silent. "Your mother told me it was not good for you to get excited."

"She was warning you!"

"Warning me of what?"

"That I wasn't marriageable!"

"Nothing could make you unmarriageable" was his firm reply. "Nothing in this world, Estelle."

"Not even death!" she exclaimed defiantly.

"Nothing," he repeated. But he did not repudiate her term.

"I don't want to be married out of pity."

"I could never have the gall to pity you."

She felt that she could almost hear the crack of her breaking heart. Were the doors of life to slam shut just as they seemed about to open? She was too undone to do more than ask him to excuse her and rush upstairs to bury her head in the pillows of her bed.

That night she suffered her first massive hemorrhage.

THERE WAS NEVER any real hope after this. When she was released from the hospital, it was only to return to a chaise-longue existence in her well-heated third-floor bedroom. There were books and visitors to relieve the dreariness of such a life, but her only true consolation was in her correspondence with the faithful Bronson. He had wanted to leave his law firm and move to New York to be available for as many visits as her doctor allowed, but she was resolute that he should do nothing to hurt his legal career. She was going to fashion the end of her existence in her own way, and in this determination she would not be gainsaid. She made this very clear in the first letter that initiated their weekly interchange.

Dear Bronson,

Not the least of the hardships to which the dying are subject is the visitation of their loved ones. The poor darlings, God bless them, may feel every impulse to condole and console, but their primary sensation is nonetheless one of embarrassment in the presence of the unspeakable and a guilty gratitude that it is not yet their fate. They never dare to mention the one topic that most nearly concerns their affected friend — no, that is strictly forbidden. And so their conversation, as with all chatter when the mind is otherwise preoccupied, is hollow and dull when it is not actually painful. Even some of our nearest and dearest have a genius for saying the wrong thing.

And yet one yearns to talk of one's own demise. Which is why I have conceived this idea of a correspondence with the one soul I feel understands me, and who happens to be the man who might have become more than a friend had I been healthier and had our mutual interest continued to grow. You see? I can say that now. What need have I anymore for maidenly restraint? Of course, I cannot know what might have developed between us, nor can you. Certainly couples have been happily wed who started less congenially than you and I. Some might even claim that we have already enjoyed the sweetest part of a relationship between a man and a woman: the early dawn of what might mature into a great love. But it does not matter now except to demonstrate my freedom to say whatever is on my mind. What I need is someone to whom I can open my heart in writing, and I choose writing as the blessed veil to cloak the inevitable embarrassments of face-to-face communication.

Will your Emersonian transcendentalism allow of that, dear Bronson? An exchange of keen minds rather than vulnerable hearts? I know you are too honest to undertake something in which you do not believe, simply to placate an ill woman. However delightfully you may be one, don't in this case be a Boston gentleman!

And Bronson replied:

Yes, dearest Estelle, I accept your offer. But far from not being a Boston gentleman, I will endeavor to be one of the truest. Every word that I write to you will be as sincere a reflection of my thoughts as I can make it. There may be motives that lie beneath that are hidden from me — we have read of recent Viennese explorations into the unconscious — and therefore must remain hidden to you, nor can I promise you that I shall unveil every passing thought or fantasy that may flit across my mind. There may be such, of which we have no control, that I refuse to dignify with my pen. No mind should be totally free of the censor of decency. But what I inscribe here will be true.

To begin with, yes indeed, dear heart, I had dared to hope that our friendship might ripen into something more binding. But I am not going to belabor our correspondence with anguished sentiment — I know you have not embarked on a *Sonnets from the Portuguese*. I am steeling myself to face what you must face, not with as clear an eye and brave a heart, for I am much your inferior in such, but with as much clarity and courage as I can muster.

I will not say that had you been blessed with stronger health, all would have been plain sailing between us. I had my doubts as to whether you would ever be fully happy in Boston or I away from it. Not only is my law practice almost immovably grounded here, but so, it seems, is my stubborn soul. I could have moved anywhere rather than have lost you, but I would always have felt "New Englandly," and that might have created a difficulty for both of us. One that we would have surmounted, but there it would have been. I have always believed that there was a fundamental nobility of character under all the constantly satirized traits of old Boston. There! At least I have got that off my chest.

You might, of course, have come to see the best in the "hub," as you call it, as I do, but I fear that your sharp eye would have always seen the common caricature of the Brahmin type in those of my friends and relatives who adhere more closely to it than I dare to hope I do. But I only make the point to introduce another: the point of your much more fundamental variance from the principles of my family background, by which I mean (oh, I can hear your "Here we go!") the absence in you of any brand of Christian faith. It is here that I see the strength in even the weakest and silliest of my tribe, and I desperately stretch out a hand to offer to your reluctant self even a drop of the divine consolation that they receive. You may wince at my choice of words. I stick to them.

You believe strongly, I know, in the difference between right and wrong, and no one has been more resolute than yourself in your determination to be on the side of the former. When I have asked you what impels you to choose to do the unselfish rather than the selfish thing, your reply has always been the same: "Because I don't wish to be the kind of person who would do the other." On that distinction hang all your law and your prophets. It is a matter, one might almost conclude, of taste, of turning away from sin as one would from an unpleasant odor. What need of a god has a person of strong enough nostrils?

But if right and wrong have any meaning, any true existence other than as mere figments of your imagination, there must exist somewhere, somehow, a standard that defines the difference between them — a moral sense in the universe. Can one not make out a dawning of this even in beasts? The lion that kills the cubs of its mate to bring her back into heat to satisfy his lust is obviously devoid of it, but the African wild dog, which kills only the precise number of its litters needed to keep the pack within the limits of the available food supply, and forcibly feeds any reluctant puppies, shows the beginning of a social conscience, the faint origin of a moral standard. And if such a standard exists, even outside the ken of mortals, is it not feasible to suppose there is a purpose in creation? And if there be any purpose at all, is it not irresistible to infer that this life, with its manifold injustices, its bizarre distribution of comedy and tragedy, is not all?

That is all I urge upon you. I do not suggest that you embrace any creed or adopt any ritual. I do not open the gates of a new Jerusalem whose streets are paved with gold and echo the anthems of angels; I do not even offer you a resurrection of the body or a reunion with loved ones. I only ask you to open your mind to the possibility that this is not the end.

I yearn to see you, but as long as you restrict me to the meager epistolary consolation of a Horace Walpole or a Madame de Sévigné, I obey.

Estelle replied:

Of course, my dear, you're too intelligent not to see that where an ultimate purpose is concerned, you're begging the question. You feel there *must* be purpose in the universe. I see no reason that compels me to agree. Like Pascal, *je vois ces effroyables espaces de l'univers qui m'enferment,* but I lack his abiding consolation. Nor do I really think I have much needed it. By fastening my thoughts on this terrestrial globe and concentrating on how to make such life as we have a bit pleasanter for myself and those in my immediate vicinity, I seem to have managed to get by — at least until now.

I readily concede that my range of vision has been very limited. Indeed, it has been largely confined to the story of the Carnochans. What have they accomplished to make life more agreeable since they braved the Atlantic waves to establish a branch of their thread business on the shores of a new world? And what have I done to aid them?

Well, I seem to see their accomplishment as largely negative, but that is something. As you rightly point out, I myself have been mostly motivated by the desire *not* to be a certain kind of person. The Carnochans, at least in America, have been guilty of no felonies, no public improprieties, no incitements to disorder, no grotesque outbursts of scandalous behavior. They have been law-abiding, tax-paying, pacific members of the community, minding their own business and minding it well enough. If the whole world behaved so, would it not be a peaceable kingdom? Perhaps. But the Carnochans never reached out very far; they never regarded themselves as their brother's keeper. Or perhaps as keepers only of one as close as a brother. And, for all my criticism of them, have I? I may not have been the kind of person I didn't want to be, but have I been anyone else?

My mother, as any mother would be, is proud of her six sons, who are all on their way to making some sort of mark in the world. She sees them as vigorous, manly, and, I fear — for she admires this — aggressive, and she attributes what she deems their tough hides to the rugged lowland Scottish farmers from whom we presumably descend. But actually the Carnochans seem to have been already rather watered-down stock by the time they arrived in New York. They had just enough energy to perch on the seaport where they landed and never moved an inch farther west. Our original immigrant, David, had nine children, but all of his many living descendants owe their being to only one of them: his son Douglas. The other eight died without issue; six of them, all daughters, never even married. I remember when I was doing a volunteer temporary job in the library of the Seamen's Church Institute finding an old daguerreotype of a very plain lady over the caption *Miss Phoebe Carnochan*, on the back of which some rude sailor had scribbled the words "Why I went to sea." No, our vigor, if such it be, must stem from the colonial aristocrats in the family tree of my grandmother Carnochan, born a Dudley of your beloved hometown, who was able to say — and I'm sure frequently did — "*Both* my grandmothers were Saltonstalls." I sometimes even wonder if my mother, who is the soul of consideration and love to her ailing daughter, isn't puzzled by the contradiction, in a family so apparently strong, of a member as frail as myself.

Do you know what I think is the secret of the "moral" success of such American so-called upper-class families as the Carnochans, and even the sacred Hales of Boston? It's that they never for a moment admit, either to themselves or to anyone else, that they are not the "nicest" people on the globe. They shy away from the brutal candor of their British opposite numbers, who scorn to hide their open snobbery, and they deplore the French and German aristocrats, who actually glory in it. No American mother would ever admit that her children had married for any reason but a sincere and abiding love, nor would her children dare to deny it. Friendships, they insist, are formed on the basis of mutual affection and admiration; business is always conducted for the greater development of the nation's God-given resources, and death contains, as in the old hymn, "welcome for the sinner and more graces for the good." There have to be moments, of course, when even the rosiest Pollyanna has doubts about all this, but so long as the flag is kept unfurled to flutter in the breezes of fatuity, such darker periods can be kept under control.

Well, does it really matter what gets them through this life so long as they get through it? I don't know. Does it help people to face the void? What is it in me but a hollow pride that makes me rear up and cry, "I won't be taken in! I face the truth and defy it!" And where does it get me? I still can't make up my mind not to be, not to exist. I still shrink before that door through which such countless numbers have passed before me. I'm like the blind woman in the Watts painting, plucking the last string of the shattered harp of hope. And I'm ashamed of it.

I used to go to church. I even went through a rather intense religious period when I was sixteen. But the idea of an everlasting life — a never-ending banquet, as a stupid visiting minister to our church once appallingly described it — filled me with a greater terror than the concept of extinction, and when our regular preacher tried to assure me that there would be no time in a future life, I found it unimaginable.

To which Bronson replied:

Of course, you're right about being only in a small part a Carnochan. You're no more a blood member of that clan than you are of the families of your mother and her parents and of your paternal grandmother. Indeed, as we travel down the family tree, the blood of our cognomen shrinks to a mere trickle of our life stream. But I was interested to learn that you have Dudley and Saltonstall forebears, for so have I, and I embrace anything that brings us closer. I feel, I fear, I share a bit of my own parents' ancestor worship; to be linked to an honorable past has seemed to me a way of adding a touch of dignity and order to the chaos of modern life, but I cannot be unaware that an undetected fault on the part of an unsuspected many-greats-grandmother could lop off the finest limbs of a haughty tree. Not that I suspect any of those revered puritan ladies of having a lover on the sly — heaven forbid! But the past contains wide tracts of undiscovered country. All we can be sure of is that we are ourselves.

And perhaps of something else. That a man and a woman can form a relationship that is something more than themselves, a thing of beauty, a thing, I dare to suppose, that has its own existence. Oh, I'm talking nonsense, and I promised you that I wouldn't belabor our epistolary communication with such outbursts, but oh, my dear one, it is very hard.

But I pull myself up. I will be good. How about this? At the time of your first diagnosis, you expressed to me the wish that, if things should turn out as darkly as predicted for you, I should nonetheless, after a due interval, marry and raise a family. Very well. I will undertake to do that. I will seal you up in a watertight compartment of my heart into which no wife or child of mine shall ever enter. But that compartment will not be either a reproach or a cloud to them; it will simply not exist for them. It will exist for me and me alone. This will take will-power, but I shall have the willpower. I shall have learned it from you.

The above is to show you my willingness to comply with even your sternest instructions. But you have not forbidden me to abandon all hope. Your nice cousin Gordon told me that a famous specialist, a Dr. Bretton, had seen you and spoken of the possible beneficent effects for you of a winter in southern Italy. Estelle, is that true? Why didn't you tell me? And what in God's name is keeping you here?

Look. Your brothers are all occupied with their lives and families as they should be. In Italy you would have help — ser-vants are cheap and plentiful there — as well as nurses and per-haps your mother to care for you. But you would need a man to cope with the household, the currency, the shopping, the tak-ing you on drives, the checking on doctors, and all the myriad little odd jobs living abroad entails. I speak some Italian — enough to get along, anyway, and I could easily become more fluent — and I have a sufficient private income to support my-self. It would be my pride and joy to take an indefinite leave of absence from my firm and go to Italy as your majordomo or courier, or whatever it pleased you to call it. And I could stay there for a year or two years, or as long as it took you to get well. Nor would you have to worry about the propriety of it; I would of course not occupy your villa or even visit it except to perform my duties.

What are we waiting for? Let's go!

What follows is Estelle's last letter.

I did not write you, dearest Bron, of Dr. Bretton's brief opti-mism because the day after he had expressed it I had a severe hemorrhage that almost carried me off, and after a consultation with my regular attendant, dear old Dr. Wren, he regretfully changed his opinion. It seems I am past even Neapolitan mira-cles. But oh, dear man, what a joy and a lift it gave me to know that you were willing to jump off the ladder to the legal fame which I *know* is your destiny to devote to my welfare a great span of your working time that might well be fatal to your career. You may remember how you and I once talked of the great J. P. Morgan (whom, with his partners, the Carnochans worship as the twelve apostles), who abandoned his career as a young man to take his ailing first bride to Egypt for her recovery. Of course, she died before it was too late for him to resume it, but he didn't know that at the time, and you and I agreed that he showed a love of which no other contemporary American tycoon would have been capable. Can you imagine Gould or Rockefeller doing any such thing? And now I can boast that I have inspired an equal devotion! It makes me on the one hand bitterly regret the fate that keeps us from sharing a golden partnership, but on the other, it gives me a glorious consolation to think that I have not lived without a great happiness.

Bless you, my beloved. I can die in peace. Well, anyway, in a kind of peace. I think I can make do with it. And I owe it all to you.

BRONSON SURVIVED ESTELLE for half a century. He became the senior partner of a major Boston law firm, a renowned lecturer at the Harvard Law School, and the author of a classic textbook on the law of contracts. A wise and grave gentleman of the old school, he was respected and esteemed by all who knew him, though many found him too formal of manner and difficult to approach. His marriage of forty years to an amiable and noble-minded woman, a Cabot, seemed serenely smooth, and it was blessed with three fine children. He was reputed never to have mentioned his first love, but everyone knew his story.

6

GORDON 2

GORDON CARNOCHAN did not remain long separated from his cousin David in the practice of law. After only a few years in the Perry, Whitehead firm, interrupted by a brief service in 1918 in officers' training camp brought to a sudden close by the Armistice, he was faced with the dazzling offer of a partnership in David's firm, which was in the process of being reorganized, largely by David himself, due to the near-simultaneous deaths of its two senior partners in 1920. David had prevailed on Adam Carter, one of the leading legal lights and statesmen of the era — and whose daughter Janetta David had wed — to take over the administration of the distinguished but now leaderless Brown & Livermore, and David himself, of course, was to be a junior partner in the new firm. He had also been authorized by Mr. Carter to offer an equal position to his cousin Gordon, who had a fine record in his own firm but who had not yet been promoted to partnership there.

"We'll be at least two of the old musketeers!" David exclaimed, with something of his old Yale enthusiasm. "And when old father Carter goes to his well-deserved reward, we two, if we play our cards right, should be able to rule the roost."

It was certainly a tempting offer. Carter had a fine reputation, and the new firm had every look of future success.

The partners in Gordon's old firm might have applauded his work, but they had been stingy and slow in promoting their juniors. Agatha had her doubts about the project, but she was happily engaged now with two children and a job she loved, teaching at a private girls' school, and she thought Gordon had shown sufficient independence of his family to be free of domination from any of them. So the offer was accepted.

At a later period in his life Gordon looked back on the years 1920 to 1933 as the golden ones. The children were growing up healthy and happy; Agatha was content with her job, and he was finding keen satisfaction running the lucrative bond department of the firm, which had made him quite as much a voice in its management as David with his corporations. The cousins had worked together harmoniously, and it was beginning to look as if David's prediction would come true. There was talk among the partners now of renaming the firm and including both the Carnochans in the new title. He and David were not only musketeers; they were almost rivals!

But in 1933 his life seemed to darken. It was not so much the Great Depression, which had seized the nation, and which his firm had survived, though it formed an appropriate background. It was more a kind of disillusionment and apathy. It started with an incident that David at least would have regarded as trivial.

Gordon had adopted a private hobby of preparing a history of the firm, and one morning he uncovered a document in Mr. Carter's private files, which had been freely turned over to him, that deeply upset him. He told Agatha of it that night; he said it might have changed his whole attitude toward the firm. She was surprised.

"As bad as all that?" she queried. "I suppose you can

give up the history. How many people know you're writing it, anyway?"

"Oh, plenty. But nobody gives a damn about it, anyway."

"And to tell the truth, neither would they give much of a damn about this memo that's got you so upset."

What he had shown Agatha was an appalling memorandum exposing the curious dichotomy between the public and private morals of the great Adam Carter, the revered deity of the firm. Agatha, however, in her usual practical way, had taken the matter less dramatically. She suggested it was not so unusual.

"Well, that's just it!" he exclaimed. "That's what really gets me. It's their world. Has it always been their world? It's what has haunted me, isn't it? That I'm a braying ass in an ass's paradise?"

"But that memo is an old one, my poor dear. You know that things were different then. That lots of matters were tolerated then that are frowned on today."

"They weren't as different as all that. If they had been, people wouldn't have taken such pains to hide them. Do you think for a minute that if I offered to print that memo in my history, the whole firm wouldn't shriek no?"

"No, I daresay they would. But don't they hope your history will be a kind of advertisement of their legal expertise? If you're boosting Lifebuoy soap, you won't concede that it ever sinks."

"But that's just what's wrong, Aggie. You've put your finger on it. They don't want a history. They want a panegyric. And you know how much I admired Adam Carter."

"Oh, dear heart, you don't have to tell *me* that."

"I'm sorry. Perhaps I overdid it. Perhaps I've always overdone this habit of seeing the best in people."

"It's an attractive quality. I've always admired it in you."

"But it can be a weakness, too. It might come from the fear of facing evil."

The author of the memorandum was none other than his cousin and partner, David, Adam Carter's son-in-law. When each of the firm members had been asked to write a tribute to Adam Carter to be included in a privately printed volume to be presented to him on his eightieth birthday, David, like a snickering evil godmother, had dropped on his father-in-law's desk this memorandum entitled "The Two Adam Carters." There had been no serious idea of its being incorporated in the tributary volume, but Carter, who had the rare quality of being able to enjoy a satire on himself, provided it was clever enough, had kept the paper among his private ones, which was where Gordon had come across it.

It described first Carter, the good citizen and conscientious public servant, a gentleman of the old school, upright in all his standards, a model of strict and punctilious behavior, tireless in his performance of duty in the high federal offices he from time to time undertook: as solicitor general and Secretary of the Interior of the United States and as ambassador to France. And then the author turned, as from a kind of Dr. Jekyll to a species of Mr. Hyde, to Carter the lawyer, who seemed to obliterate himself and his scruples in the interests of his great corporate clients, coldly justifying their every grab act and attempted monopoly in and out of the courts, seeming to see nothing in the least deleterious in an economy subject to the manipulations of Wall Street and the barons of rail, oil, and steel.

The particular genius of Adam Carter, according to the memorandum, was in his deft use of the holding company. Where there was to be any activity of doubtful legality, such as freight rebates to obliging customers, sweetheart deals to

eliminate competition, or cash payments to compliant legis-
lators, it would be done by a corporate entity far enough
down the chain of ownership to leave Carter's client free of
any legal responsibility. Indeed, Carter would not even represent the victim if it got into trouble. One of the greatest
tycoons in the gilded list of those represented by the firm, a
man notorious for his ruthlessness in building an empire of
rails, was able to boast truthfully that he had never broken a
single law.

And Gordon had to admit ruefully to himself that he
could imagine his late idol chuckling over this supposed
tribute to himself. For Carter the man was quite capable of
laughing at Carter the lawyer. Life to him might have been a
game where skill was everything.

"Isn't evil a rather strong term to describe what you saw
in that memo?" Agatha asked at last.

Gordon had no immediate answer to this; the question
seemed to justify the very existence of a dark creed that was
forever hidden in the unparted folds of the past. But he
turned away now from his loving wife as if she belonged,
always and irreducibly, to an irrelevant present. He was
plunged in the harsher reality of all that had gone before.

Nineteen thirty-three was to bring even worse news.
Gordon's father, Wallace, who had aged badly, had been
playing the bull stock market recklessly, even by the standards of the boom era, and with the crash on Wall Street he
lost three quarters of his capital. As this was followed by
no noticeable economies on his or Julie's part, the results
threatened to be dire indeed, and Gordon's sisters complained bitterly that, as his father's counsel, he should have
exercised greater control in restraining him. At the same
time, his firm was faced with the possibility of a liability for a
bond issue the state constitutional validity of which, sup-

ported by Gordon's opinion, had been challenged in court. The remnants of Wallace's fortune were ultimately saved, and he and his wife at last placed on a feasible budget, and the challenge to the bond issue was defeated in court, but the double crisis in Gordon's professional and private life had triggered off a black depression, and in 1934 he was obliged to seek a leave of absence from the firm.

His depression, like the national one, hit its lowest point in that dark winter, when Gordon, still unable to work, had been persuaded by the practical Agatha to cut their expenses by spending the year entirely in Maine. It was at this time that Gordon learned of a reorganization of the firm in which David had been raised to the rank of a "named" partner in the new title, Carter, Brown & Carnochan, and his own percentage of the profits severely cut. He had not been notified of this before the decision was made, according to a letter from David, as his leave of absence had suspended his vote in office decisions.

A return to New York was imperative, and two days later Gordon was back in his office, waiting for the call from Mr. Carter, with whom he had requested a fifteen-minute interview. It was promptly granted.

The great man was all sympathy. The high balding head, the long tapering nose, the pointed chin and small steely eyes of this slight but formidable statesman, the stillness of his fixed attention, all combined to receive his visitor as if the latter were the embassy of some great power. He treated all alike, confident in his ability to grant or deny whatever petition might be made of him, and to end, one way or another, any potential dispute.

"I'm glad that you've come to talk to me, Gordon," he began, seizing in his usual courtroom fashion the genial offensive. "Of course, it's about the knock in your percentage.

Let me assure you at once that it has nothing to do with the quality of your work, which is, and has always been, first class. You may not know it, my friend, but you and I have something in common. We are both artists. And that is something that is not always true of our fellow lawyers, even the best of them. It may not even be necessary for a successful practice of our profession. Indeed, some might say one was better off without it. It's an inner thing, a state of mind, really. The idea that you're creating something beautiful. Even if its beauty appears only to yourself. If I make a point in a brief or an oral argument, say, one that disposes of an opponent's contention, and does it sharply, conclusively, concisely, in just the right words, neither too many nor too few, I feel a delight in my heart that is like no other joy on earth. And I include the joys of sex and power and health and wealth. Oh, yes, I do! The artist knows an ecstasy in creation that no other man is given. And I believe you know that, Gordon."

Gordon did not know it. But the wonderful thing about Carter, he reflected, was that he was absolutely sincere in every pose that he adopted. While he adopted it. It was what made him a great trial lawyer.

"It may be easier," Gordon replied with a wry smile, "to see the artist in the great orator spellbinding an awed jury than in the drafter of a municipal bond indenture."

"Not at all. The whole thing is in the inner man. I see you planning the different tributaries into which the tolls of the great utilities must flow like the explorer of an unknown river, mapping out the uses to which the mighty flood must be put, so that all may be repaid or profit. Is that not to you a thing of beauty?"

"Anyway, I'm proud to share anything with you, sir." Gordon did not choose to employ, at so lofty a moment, the use of Carter's first name, and the latter's small smile seemed to recognize the distinction.

"Which brings me to the other point. Which less exalted folk might call the central point. The real central point to you and me, Gordon, will always be our work. Compensation is a different matter. My law work I'd do for a mere cost-of-living allowance. What the firm pays me over and above that I regard as my charge for the more pedestrian matter of administration. Indeed, left to myself, I might favor an even split among the partners. Still, we must consider pedestrian matters. We live in different times, my friend. Gentlemen like you and I can't expect to rule the roost. We have in our expanding partnership today new members who seek to match a man's compensation strictly with the revenue he brings in. Indeed, they will not admit any other criteria. And if that revenue is reduced, even by circumstances beyond the power of an individual partner to control, say by illness or family emergency, a corresponding docking of pay must ensue. I don't like it, Gordon, any more than you do. But facts are facts. But do not think that you were without advocates in our reorganization talks. There was one partner, Jack Lawrence, who took your part very strongly. He thought it was you and not your cousin who should be the Carnochan in the new firm name."

Gordon knew that he was beaten the moment the blame for his demotion in the firm was laid on the absence caused by his illness. He would not and could not discuss his depression with the senior partner; it was a subject too alien to the latter's iron mental health. He had wanted to discuss frankly the role that his cousin might have played in the matter, but now that he had learned that David had had to face the possibility, however remote, of actually being outranked in the firm by his humble self, he had all the confirmation needed of what he had already suspected. David in such a situation would have used every weapon he could get hold of. He wouldn't have been David otherwise. And when had David not been an integral part of his life?

He was touched, however, deeply touched, that the great Carter should have so confided in him, and even equated Gordon's attitude toward his practice with his own, but he was still not unaware that he was in the presence of a man who would never have tolerated the even split among partners of the firm's net that he professed to prefer and who, despite his claim of adapting himself to the greedy demands of younger firm members, would never, even in his seventies, surrender a penny of his lion's share of the profits. But Carter was a great man, and who was Gordon to compare himself with such? What had Carter been but his substitute god?

In his subsequent lunch with David, however, he felt himself on more equal ground. The framed, bearded worthies of deceased presidents of the Downtown Association looked gravely down at the table where they sipped a preparatory cocktail.

"I have heard a surprising thing, David. I have heard that my mental state has been the subject of executive discussion and that you seem not to have taken my side."

David, who had just raised his napkin to wipe his thin lips, threw it down on the table in a brave show of pique. "I really wonder if it wouldn't be wiser to hold our meetings in the presence of the entire firm. Or at least record them and circulate them to the partners. This way there are constant leaks and exaggerations, and the whole thing gets out of control."

"Then you did defend me?"

"I couldn't, Gordie. There were some who wanted your

share cut more than it was. There was even one who suggested it was time for you to retire altogether. It was I who gave them a more exact idea of just what your depression amounted to and how temporary a thing it was. I think I can say truly that without the interference of your good old pal and cousin, things would have gone a lot worse for you."

Gordon was silent for a long moment, and then reached a hand across the table to shake his cousin's. "Thank you, David. Thank you very much."

He had not believed David. At least not totally. But it seemed a final and conclusive answer to what the world was really like. He could only live with it.

7

ALIDA

ALIDA CARNOCHAN, wife of Samuel, David's brother and the eldest of the six sons of James and Louisa, had every reason to suppose in 1937, the year of her fiftieth birthday, that her life was as much a success as even the most optimistic woman, bred and wed as she was, could have hoped. Yet it was in that very year that the imps of the comic spirit had spied with glee her husband's susceptibility to the lure of the Society of Reborn Christians and her long-delayed trial began.

To understand Alida's predominance in the social world of New York one must first note that she was not only born a Hudson Valley Livingston but of a rich branch of that distinguished tree. As such, she took serenely for granted that no family in America — and few in Europe, for that matter — could claim a perch on a higher twig, and she could shrug her shoulders, with the indifference of pity, at the pathetic dynastic claims of the Carnochans. She had not married her big, strapping, loud-laughing, balding husband for his ancestry, but because he had literally, and despite her own not inconsiderable size, swept her off her feet. Not that she was indifferent to worldly considerations. Far from it. But she had been confident from the start that her aggressive mate would do well in any field he chose, and indeed he had, making a small fortune in investment banking. Nor had he been

the philistine that his outward appearance might errone-
ously have caused a first observer to assume. Sam, for all his
noisy love of male reunions and his passion for spectator
sports, had a keen eye for the best in hunting and fishing
prints, the most exquisite paintings and drawings of birds
and animals, and the most finely wrought of early swords
and guns. And above all, he was a kindly man of equable disposition, and he loved his Alida.

And so did her world. At least a good part of it. There
were always those who suspected that her air of self-assurance insufficiently masked her downgrading of themselves.
Her tall, rather bony figure and large-featured, plain physiognomy were familiar sights in her neighborhood, getting
in and out of her big shiny Cadillac town car or entering or
leaving the handsome red-brick Georgian house that was
one of a matching and abutting trio erected by her and two
of her brothers. Her dresses were oddly fashionable for one
who seemed so above fashion, and the thick wavy blond hair,
which the world thought dyed, was actually entirely natural,
even at her age. Alida was always a rule to herself.

She was the president of the Martha Washington
Women's Club, of the Tuesday Evening Club, of the Schuy-
ler Livingston Settlement House, and she served on the
boards of two private schools and of the two subscription
holiday dances that dominated the social lives of the
Knickerbocker young. All this marked her strong sense of
social and civic responsibility.

In 1917, when Sam as an army captain had been sent to
the front in France, she had left her three infant children in
the good care of her mother in Rhinebeck and torn her way
through red tape to go abroad as a nurse's aide. What she
had seen in military hospitals by the Marne had given her a
lasting horror of the chaos that lies in the wake of battles and

a deep respect for even the shallowest ribs that hold a society together. It intensified her childhood feeling that clothes and covers were apt to be better things than what they concealed, as her dresses sheltered a too lanky torso and helped her to compete more fairly with more beautiful girls. It was the weak who discarded appearances. The strong recognized weapons and seized them.

Alida was far from being an unreconstructed rightwinger, but she was always inclined to try to make do with the present situation, tending to regard change, even change for the better, as something to be watched lest it get out of hand. But when change was really needed, in her opinion, she was ready to push it. Some of her friends even thought that she at times went too far, as when she proposed a Jewish couple for membership in the Tuesday Evening Club. They were at first turned down, but her immediate and clearly serious threat to resign the presidency precipitated a hasty reconsideration by the admissions committee and a reversal of the decision. "You have to be firm to be taken seriously," she had told her supporters. "But don't get into a fight until you're pretty sure you can win. I wouldn't have proposed the Rosenbergs ten years ago. There's no point getting too far ahead of the times you live in. Today anti-Semitism is dead, or at least moribund."

Which was why she did so little for the cause of feminism. "Women have enough for the present," she would say. "The rest will come in due time. And what's more, it will come without a serious fight." The same argument she used when it came to blacks. "Their time has not yet come."

She did, however, on one occasion indulge in a bitter controversy which she almost lost. It was not a question of the time being right or wrong; her opponents claimed there was no question of timing involved. The elder of her two daughters, the lovely Alberta, the one who most closely resembled her mother in character, though less so, fortunately, in looks, attended a fashionable girls' boarding school in a Philadelphia suburb, Delamar Academy, named for its headmistress, where she roomed with one Molly Kane, whose family were neighbors of the Carnochans in Glenville, Long Island. Molly suffered from excessive modesty, so much so that she waited until the gymnasium shower room was empty before slipping in for a hasty cleaning. To cure her of this, a group conspired while she was in the shower to hide her clothes and then chase her naked, when she emerged, throughout the building past throngs of girls all hooting at her.

Alberta related this to her mother when the latter had come to the school for a parents' weekend. She had not herself been one of the conspirators, but she found the incident amusing. Alida did not.

"It might have given the poor girl a dangerous nervous shock," she protested.

"Well, she did take it pretty hard, I admit. But she shouldn't have been so prim about other girls seeing her starko."

"A natural modesty isn't a bad thing at all. I'm sure Miss Delamar must have been horrified if she heard about it. Have any of these nasty girls been punished?"

"Oh, Miss Delamar is supposed to have been tipped off. There was no teacher in the locker room that day."

"Well, Miss Delamar is going to get a piece of my mind this very afternoon! She'll find that she has no rubber stamp in the school board. I shall demand an apology to Molly and to her parents!"

Alida recognized the look that immediately clouded Alberta's features. It was the look of the daughter who realizes that she is no longer dealing with a parent but with a power of the outside world immune to the charm of even a favorite child. Alida had had occasion to see that look on the faces of her other children, and she did not deplore it. She was willing, when needed, to be feared by her family. To be feared was to be respected, and to be respected was to be obeyed.

"I think Miss Delamar meant well, Ma. After all, it was only a way of getting a silly girl over a silly hang-up. Everybody was nice to Molly afterward."

"Afterward may have been too late. Who knows what permanent damage may have been done to that girl? Stripped in public! Why it's like one of those old Academic paintings of a slave market where some poor lady captured by pirates is exposed to the leering gaze of purchasers!"

"But it was only in front of girls, Ma!"

"Girls can leer. Do you know what clothes are, Alberta? Clothes are civilization!"

Alida paused, noting a new and unwelcome expression of astonishment on her daughter's face. Had she gone too far? Was she opening, even by a crack, the door she kept so firmly sealed on her own inner being? The door that *everyone* should keep sealed? Clothes were not the only veil that protected civilization.

"Well, never mind," she concluded. "But I am certainly going to speak to Miss Delamar."

Walking that early spring afternoon down the pretty little lane that led from the campus to the headmistress's cottage, Alida recalled every minute of the episode in her childhood that had made the ordeal of Molly Kane so particularly vivid to her. It had occurred in Bar Harbor, where her family had a vacation house, in the summer of 1902. She had been on a hike with her parents and two brothers up one of the hills, and they had picnicked by a tarn in the forest and had had the rare excitement of startling a drinking bull moose which had crashed away from the intruders through the brush. The day had been an unexpected scorcher, and her mother had suggested a plunge in the water before eating.

"But we have no bathing suits," Alida had protested.

Mrs. Livingston prided herself as being above the inhibitions of the vulgar. Her progenitors, she insisted, had always been leaders and not followers of fashion. It may have been a natural desire to put a smug and sometimes impertinent fifteen-year-old in her place that made her now take a step beyond her usual pale.

"Here we are alone with nature!" she exclaimed, flinging her arms toward the sky. "Why should we be ashamed of the bodies the good Lord gave us? It was not He but Adam and Eve that provided the fig leaves. Let us like King Lear cry, 'Off, off, you lendings!' Don't you agree, Robert?"

And calmly, slowly, deliberately, as though he were in his own dressing room at home, Robert Livingston proceeded to disrobe. His sons enthusiastically followed him and were soon splashing in the water like boys in a Thomas Eakins painting.

"Come on, Alida," her mother called to her cowering daughter. "Join us, dear. There's nothing like the feel of cool water against your bare skin."

"No, no!" And when one of her brothers, horridly bare, leapt from the water to make a merry move to yank down the front of her dress, she slapped his hand away with a shriek of actual terror.

"Alida, don't be such a prude!" Her mother stood before her, a blinding vision of incredible exposure, with long, stringy tits and a huge ebony triangle of pubic hair between wide alabaster hips. Alida shielded her eyes.

"Harlot!" she yelled.

The silence that fell seemed to encompass even a stricken forest. Nobody uttered a word. Nobody urged her anymore to disrobe. Nobody spoke to her on the long walk back to the road. Nor was the subject mentioned thereafter. Her father came to her room that night to talk to her, but before he had said a word, she burst into such a passion of tears that he departed in silence. Perhaps he had decided that she had suffered enough. She had said something so unspeakable that neither of her parents knew how to cope with it, so the episode was treated as something that had not happened. But Alida knew that her relations with her family had taken a new turn. She began to wonder if she was not even respected. She had been left with her defenses intact, and she would know how to use them in the future.

Had she found the headmistress repentant, Alida might have been content to let the incident at the Delamar Academy pass with a vote of censure from the board, but finding her defiant and quite ready to charge her critic with encroaching on the prerogatives of the principal, Alida declared war. Returning to New York, she called a special meeting of the board and demanded that Miss Delamar be discharged. The opposition was clamorous: a good proportion of the board insisted that Alida was making a mountain out of a molehill, and nobody knew what the outcome would have been, had not a newspaper reporter got wind of the fray and printed the whole story, whereupon the headmistress, humiliated and disgusted, resigned her post.

Alida had won what she boldly called a victory, but it was certainly a Pyrrhic one. She had broken her own rule of fighting only when she was sure of an easy win, and she had gained the reputation of being too willing to "throw her weight around." Assessing her damages and regrouping her forces, she decided to avoid the limelight for a period.

It was many years after this long forgotten (except by

her) episode, that, in late middle age, she encountered her first troubles with her husband.

Sam Carnochan had always been inclined to drink too heartily, though with a strong head for it, he rarely embarrassed the company he kept, but in his fifties this tendency notably increased. A muscular problem in his left arm reduced his golf score from the high seventies to the low nineties, he endured painful attacks of gout, and the old age that he had always dreaded began to loom. The Great Depression had reduced his fortune by half, and his business was decreased — consolation was more and more sought in the shining hour before dinner devoted to the martini.

Alida had never been such a fool as to suppose that she could, with subtle female flattery, lead her husband by the nose; she knew that, however unintellectual and unimaginative, he possessed a brain and a wit as sharp as her own. She was sure that any appeal to him to cut down his drinking on the grounds of morality or character would be fruitless; she had to concentrate on the danger to his health and on the increase it boded to his already considerable weight. This for a while had an effect, but she soon became aware that he was reducing only his home consumption and making up for it in his clubs. She decided on a more drastic method. One morning when he was donning his overcoat to go to the office, with his chauffeur and car at the front door, she swept into the hall and told him abruptly that she had to confer with him.

"What is it, dear?" he demanded impatiently.

She pointed firmly to a small room off the front hall that was hardly ever used. Its lonely severity would give a proper gravity to their little talk. Sam, seated uncomfortably on a stiff little gilt chair, his removed overcoat folded in his lap, listened unhappily as she related, relentlessly, the remarks she had garnered from her friends, and from his own children, showing how visible the occasional effects of his bibulousness had become.

When he responded at last, it was in a much gentler tone than she had anticipated. She had expected the usual defenses of the accused alcoholic: that the charges were absurdly exaggerated, that he was already cutting down, that if she thought *he* was bad, she should see some of his friends at the Hone Club. But no, his answer was startlingly different.

"I don't deny anything you've said, my dear, and I realize that you've shown the patience of an angel. But I want you to know that for sometime now I've been very much aware of what I've been doing to myself, and I've been determined to find a way out of my trouble. In the past two months I think I've really made some headway. Of course, I've been meaning all along to tell you about it, but I didn't want to get your hopes up before I was sure. Maybe even now isn't quite the time, but so long as you've chosen this moment to speak to me seriously, I guess that's my signal to do likewise. You know my old pal Sidney Wagstaff. I know you've never liked him and probably even blame him for leading me into what let's call my excesses. And there may be some truth in that, though I daresay his wife thinks it's the other way around. But anyway, all that's more or less in the past. What Sidney may be leading me into today is what I'm beginning not to be ashamed of calling my salvation."

Alida stared at him in astonishment. "Is it some kind of religious experience that you're referring to?"

"It is." His tone was sturdy, even a bit defiant. "You're surprised, of course. You know how little I've ever been a churchgoer. And how I've always sneered at the family for deserting the old black Presbyterianism of their forebears

for the more fashionable Episcopalianism of society. Looking for God, I used to call it, in the Social Register. But it
could be that I've found something I may have been uncon-
sciously waiting for. Or that's been waiting for me. In the
sense that it's been waiting for all human souls."

"Sam, what on earth are you talking about?"

"The Society of Reborn Christians. Have you heard
of it?"

"Of course, I've heard of it. It started in Newport,
didn't it? A rather opulent Bethlehem. Peggy Tulliver belongs to it."

"She does. And so does Sidney. Who's stopped drinking, believe it or not. He persuaded me to go to one of their
meetings, which I reluctantly agreed to do. But I was elec-
trified! I really was. And since then I've been to several
more. Oh, I know what you're thinking, of course. Lots of
our smart friends laugh at it. But those who see don't laugh.
And I think I'm going to be one who sees. Oh, Alida, if we
could be in this thing together!"

Alida could not deny that she had laughed at the Society. It was not a new religion but an intensification of religious feeling; its members were culled largely from Protestant sects, notably Episcopalians, for it had a distinctly
fashionable following and its conventions were apt to be
held in such summer communities as Newport, Bar Harbor,
and Nahant. It had no temples of its own, though it spon-
sored several elegant rural centers, usually donated mansions of the rich, for retreat and meditation. Its primary
focus was in congresses of the faithful where public avow-
als of sin and repentance were cheerfully and fervently proclaimed. Alida had amused a lunch table at the Martha
Washington Club by pointing out how neatly it reversed the
Christian story. It was as if, she maintained, the early fathers

had started at the peak rather than the nadir of their fortunes: in the court of Constantine rather than in a manger.

"Would you object terribly, Alida, if I invited Dr. Forman to come and dine with us? He's dying to meet you."

Well, of course she did object, but she was too wise to say so, and she agreed that the bid should be given. She had heard Forman lecture at her club and had deplored him. He was a small, dry, plump sexagenarian with thick steely gray hair, a rodent-like face, and a soft, mellifluous voice surprisingly capable of rising to a ringing tone when he came to a climax in his address. He was reputed to have been a dentist, somewhere in the northern Middle West, and to have abandoned his profession — and some said his family — to answer the call of God and rekindle the ebbing faith of dwellers on the Atlantic coast. He had enjoyed an extraordinary success, as astounding to his critics as it seemed natural, or even of divine origin, to his converts, who opened their ears to his purring persuasion and their purses to his ever-reaching hand.

Alida wondered how even a woman as intelligent as Peggy Tulliver could believe that any deity would have chosen such an emissary. But she was resolved to keep an open mind until she had thoroughly examined the field.

She broke down, however, on her first meeting with the new evangelist. His unctuousness undid her. She could sense his glee at the hope of winning over such a prize as the former Alida Livingston, and his chatter was strewn with honeyed references to the distinguished lady converts whom he had reason to believe, did he not, were among his hostess's friends.

"I know plenty of people, Dr. Forman," she was at last provoked to retort, "but I'm not in a mood tonight to tell you who they are."

But this, she saw at once, was a sad mistake. Forman, of course, knew just how to parry such a blow.

"Ah, dear lady, I had no intention of invading your privacy. I know well from your dear husband how you cherish the inviolability of the wonderful home you have created for him and your beautiful children."

After that, and under Sam's admonishing stare, she had to spend the balance of the evening being gracious to the odious little man.

In the months that followed, Alida failed in her every effort to persuade her husband to take the Society less seriously. He met all her objections to it with the bland and cheerful stubborn rebuttals of the convert on the road to Damascus. What was even more irritating was his serene assurance that time was bound eventually to bring around as goodhearted a listener as his spouse to a cause so shiningly true. Their son Pierre and younger daughter, Eliza, were tolerantly amused by his new enthusiasm, which they regarded as one of those understandable if mildly pathetic refuges for the aging (which, thank God, they were not yet) against the fear of approaching death. Alberta, however, took the matter more seriously. She found the Society the potential answer to her father's biggest problem.

"Ma, have you seen Mr. Wagstaff recently?" she asked Alida. "No? Well, you'd find him a changed man. He claims he hasn't had a drink in six months, and I believe him. He looks ten years younger. And he's already persuaded Dad to cut down his drinks to one before lunch and two before dinner."

"But that's still a long way from curing an incipient alcoholic. Everyone knows that going cold turkey is the only real answer."

"True, but it's still a start. And Dad would never have

done even that much without Dr. Forman's help. I know you look upon the man as a vulgar fraud, and I'm not saying you're entirely wrong, but Mr. Wagstaff told me that Forman believes strongly that if you could only bring yourself to take a little more interest in the Society and go to the meetings with Dad, he could get Dad off the booze entirely."

"No, Alberta! Attend those idiotic gatherings! Why, I'd be the laughingstock of all my friends."

"Not of all of them. Not by a long shot. What about Mrs. Tulliver?"

"Peggy Tulliver, Alberta, is the ass of asses."

"You didn't always think so. Couldn't you just try, Ma? For Dad's sake? For all our sakes?"

"But, child, you don't know what you're asking! Your father would not be in the least affected unless he believed in my absolute sincerity. He's nobody's fool, Alberta. And to convince him of that I'd have to be a better actress than I could ever imagine myself being."

"Mother, we all know you have the willpower to do anything you set your mind on. I know it's a great deal to ask of you. But, as the French say: *Pour les grands maux les grands remèdes*. However, if you can't, you can't."

Alida didn't like her conclusion. That same day she called on her brother-in-law at his office. She had a great respect for David's perception, and besides, he was the family counsel. He listened to her carefully as she told him of Alberta's suggestion. Of course, he knew of his brother's interest in the Society.

"I think Alberta's quite right," he said at last. "It might well be the saving of Sam. And it shouldn't be too hard to convince him of your sincerity. Violent converts like himself are prone to believe in other violent conversions. And there's something else to be gained besides getting him off the sauce."

"Surely you don't mean *my* salvation!"

"Please, Alida, I'm not the village idiot. I know how phony the whole Society is. What I'm referring to is the way this man Forman manages to extract fortunes from his converts. I'm not going so far as to say they go into his pocket, but we know whose pockets they come out of. And let's not let one of them be Sam's. Once you're in the organization with him, you'll have much more say in what he gives or doesn't give."

"I doubt we have to worry much about that. A Carnochan is not Scottish for nothing."

"There can be strange exceptions to that rule."

THE NEXT YEAR was an onerous one for Alida. She attended all the Society's meetings with an exultant husband who, as predicted by his brother, seemed not in the least surprised that the scales had fallen from her eyes. No doubt he attributed it to divine intervention, and why should it be surprising that the All Powerful should be able to turn the spirit of even the most reluctant mortal? He even boasted about it to his fellow reborns. The hardest part in the whole business for Alida was the necessity of keeping up the appearance of her supposed change of heart to the former dentist and his rapt followers. But it helped her that she feared that any apprehension on Sam's part that she was playing a game would probably put an end to his cure, and he had now given up drinking entirely. Her success might have been precarious, but so far it was complete.

No more complete, however, than her inner dejection. To appear before the world — *her* world, anyway — as an apostle of a ridiculous sect was a humiliation such as she had

never conceived she could endure. Pierre and Eliza, who
had not been told of the stratagem — Alida had not trusted
their discretion — treated their mother's new "hobby" with
the same condescending approval that they had accorded
their father's, and Alberta, awestruck at her mother's skill
and resolution at taking on so taxing a role, had to confine
her admiration to applauding glances. But Alida's women
friends, at her boards and clubs, were relentless in their acid
comments.

"Is it true, Alida, that you've fallen for this mounte-
bank?"

"Can one really have Forman for dinner?"

"What kind of magic did he pull on you?"

"You, Alida! Of all people! A priestess of the life of
reason!"

And all she could do was to shake her head sadly, as if in
sorrow at this demonstration of souls so benighted, and imply that she was waiting for the day to come when they, too,
would comprehend the truth and the light. But it was torture, and she could only pray for the time when Sam might
be pronounced cured and she could confess to a relapse to
her old agnosticism.

But the worst had not yet come. The worst was what
David had predicted. Sam, one night when they were dining alone, outlined to her gravely Dr. Forman's project for
a splendid new retreat and meetinghouse in Westchester
County, complete with a library of edifying works, a theater
for spiritual dramas, a museum of religious art, and exten-
sive gardens and walks for meditation and *recueillement*. Forman already had several pledges of "major gifts," and of
course, he was looking to Sam for one.

"How much are you thinking of?" Alida's tone was
very dry.

"Well, what would you say to half a million?"

She gasped. It was more than a quarter of what he was worth. "I'd say it was twenty times too much! What are you thinking of, Sam? How can you possibly contemplate taking such a hunk out of what we can leave the children?"

"But, Alida, my dear, if God tells us to do it?"

"He hasn't told me!"

"Perhaps you haven't been listening."

"Well, let us wait, then, till I've had a chance to. No, that is all I can say about this now, Sam." She had seen that he was about to protest vigorously. "I'll have to think it over. I'll need time. And I'll thank you in the meanwhile to make no commitments! I think you owe me that much, don't you?"

He bowed his head. "Of course."

She had gained a pause, only that. Sam would be patient for weeks, perhaps for months, but the day would come when Forman would put the necessary pressure on him, and when it came to choosing between God and his wife as to the disposition of funds earned by himself, it was easy to foretell whom he would select.

And now something new and ominous was beginning to simmer in her mind and heart. If Sam was turning himself into a different man from the one she had married, from the one she had loved and who had sired her children, if he had chosen, at the behest of an invented deity, to become the bland and fatuous factotum of a grinning parvenu whose greasy palm was outstretched for the family capital, was it not the remedy of his cheated spouse to play every card in her hand to reverse a losing game?

He had repeatedly and publicly given the Society full credit for his victory over alcohol; it was evident that in his mind he closely associated the two. It could not but occur to her that any lapse in his abstemiousness might be accompanied by a corresponding lapse in his fidelity to the God of Dr. Forman. If the Society failed him in his battle with the bottle, might it not fail him in other things? And might it not be better for her to be married to a sot than to a bigoted fanatic? Plus the fact that she might be saving her children's inheritance? For Forman would not be content with half a million. The pocket that had produced it would be deep enough for other grabs. She had to act.

But she could not do so until her anger had reached a boiling point. She would have almost to hate Sam. This, however, was not a state that it was hopeless to envision. Already her lip was curling with disdain as she watched him gloat over the long newsletters with which the indefatigable ex-dentist showered his faithful. He might consider himself reborn, he might see himself as a phoenix rising from the ashes of his former self, but what did he care for the charred remains of his spouse? Could she not see the degradation into which he had plunged her in the new attitude of her friends at the club? For they no longer jeered at her now; they had come to accept her as a sad lost cause and refrained from any reference to her religious affiliation in the same way that they avoided any reference to what they regarded as the "Roman superstition" in the hearing of their Irish maidservants. Useful inferiors should not be offended.

It had been her habit, in helping her husband to avoid temptation, to have her evening cocktail alone in her dressing room upstairs before joining Sam in the parlor before dinner and sharing his preprandial libation of tomato juice. But one night now, when the butler appeared in her retreat armed with his tray and the shaker, she directed him to take it below.

"I'll have it in the parlor tonight, Smithers."

In the presence of her keenly observing spouse she not only drank her usual glassful but poured herself a dividend from the shaker.

"Isn't this a change?" he asked her.

"You can take it as a sign that I regard you as cured," she responded briskly. "I don't have to tank up in secret anymore."

The following night she not only repeated the process before him but instructed the butler that she would take a glass of wine with her dinner.

It was only a week later that Sam told Smithers that he, too, would need a wineglass at his place. "I guess a sip of Burgundy isn't going to be fatal," he added, with a jovial wink, to the placid but evidently disapproving servitor. "I want to drink to my lady's health. Isn't it somebody's birthday?"

"Not that I know of" was Alida's dry response.

"Well, let's pretend it is."

Alberta, of course, noted just what was going on the first night that she dined with her parents. She was the only person to know, not only of her mother's pretended conversion, but of her father's threat to her own inheritance. Her situation in life, however, had been very much altered in the previous year. She was engaged to be married to a fine young doctor, whose last dollar had been swallowed in the expenses of his medical education and whom she proposed to support until he had finished his internship and started what everyone assumed would be a profitable practice. Money had for the first time occupied an important spot in her planning, and Alida suspected that her daughter was quite shrewd enough to sense what her mother was up to. But she guessed that Alberta was also shrewd enough to say not a word about it. There were things that would not bear even being thought of.

Anyway, it was working. Sam had started to miss meetings of the Society. He spent more of his evenings at his club. There were even times when he came home in such a condition that Alida had to awaken the faithful butler to help put him to bed. And then one early spring night, when they had moved to the Long Island house and Sam had attended a rather riotous bachelors' dinner at the Glenville Country Club for the son of an old friend who was to be married the following week, he took a stroll, perhaps to sober up before going home, on the terrace overlooking the golf course and stumbled over the edge, dropping a precipitous dozen feet to the ground below.

The accident should not have been fatal, but he broke two ribs, and the jagged point of one penetrated a lung. Pneumonia developed, and ten days later he was dead.

David Carnochan produced an old will, executed several years earlier, but a young lawyer whom Sam must have recently met at one of his New York clubs unexpectedly came forward with a much more recent one. It contained the bequest of a million dollars to the Society of Reborn Christians.

Alberta was with her mother in her Uncle David's office when they received this news. She had turned very white and insisted that Alida accompany her to another chamber where they could be alone.

"Dad *knew*!" she almost wailed. "He knew what you were doing to him! He had lost his faith in the Society. And his faith in you! He had nothing left but his revenge. And this is it!"

"Alberta, pull yourself together! You're making no sense."

"I'm making only too much! Oh, why didn't I stop you?"

"Will you please get up and go home. I must go back to

David. We have much to discuss. But of this you may be sure. You and I will never mention this topic again!"

Nor did they. And with David's great firm behind her, Alida successfully challenged her husband's will on the grounds of undue influence. Her case was not a strong one, but Dr. Forman dreaded the publicity that a drawn-out trial would give to his fund-raising techniques, and he settled for a mere hundred g's.

8

DAVID

IN THE TWO YEARS that followed the Japanese surrender in 1945, the fortunes of the Carnochans in the city might be said to have reached their peak. Their very visible presence in town was owed in some part to two factors: one, that their offspring were predominately males, which gave their name considerable currency, and, two, that none of them emigrated to other parts of the nation. The six stalwart sons of James and Louisa formed the most noted of the clan. Except for Andy, all had married to social advantage, and they occupied substantial residences on Manhattan's East Side. They were large-sized men, and their wives were for the most part of comparable build, sometimes plain enough but always self-assured; the ladies could be seen stepping briskly in and out of their chauffeur-driven motors as they entered or left the Colony or Cosmopolitan Club before or after a lunch between meetings of their charitable boards. Sam's widow occupied a red-brick mansion on lower Park Avenue; Ted, who headed an accounting firm, had built a small Beaux Arts palazzo on Seventieth Street, and Alex, a noted dealer in odd lots who had chosen as his bride a granddaughter of the late Mayor Peter Cooper Hewitt, resided in a double brownstone on Madison Avenue.

David had aspired to be the first of the six, and in his middle fifties, he had certainly come close, as the number two partner of one of the great law firms of New York. Indeed, by some of his partners he was considered the true head, for his father-in-law, Adam Carter, was now aged well over eighty and left all the administrative details of their association to his second in command. But that was not the way the clients or the general public viewed it. Carter, who had been a conspicuous solicitor general, a colorful ambassador, the revered adviser to Republican Presidents, and a giant of corporate law, stood high in the popular gaze, like some modern Colossus of Rhodes, a seventh wonder of the world of today. David, who had hoped to grow in his shadow, thought he might have reason to recall the old saying that some great men were like plane trees: nothing flourished under their broad boughs.

Of course, David could not claim that he had not flourished; the question was whether he had flourished as much as he ought. He enjoyed a large income; he was listened to respectfully by captains of industry; he had served both as president of the New York State Bar Association and the Association of the Bar of the City of New York; he was a man who was appointed almost automatically to the boards of his corporate clients, his clubs, his favored charities. And he lived well, too: he and his wife, Janetta, entertained extensively in their elegant little French pavilion, with its gleaming marble front and delicate grillwork, in a mews on Eighty-sixth Street, and in their high-gabled Louis XIII château in Westbury, Long Island. Yet he had never been summoned to take any part in the administration of his great nation, either as an attorney, a diplomat, or a cabinet officer. And he was beginning to wonder if his seemingly immortal father-in-law had not been an actual hindrance to his ambitions rather than the great booster he had originally hoped.

Of course, he was fair enough to recognize that, insofar

as federal advancement was concerned, the recent years had been against both of them. Carter's federal glories had been under past Republican regimes — Coolidge and Hoover — while his son-in-law was still too young to do anything but plod away to establish his basis on Wall Street. And in the years of the Great Depression and the New Deal, Carter's famed appearances before the United States Supreme Court to attack savagely and often successfully the constitutionality of F.D.R.'s social legislation had created a breach between Washington and Wall Street that rendered out of the question any political bid to a partner of the thundering attorney who had made himself the symbol of what was reactionary in America.

Indeed, David had come to question, entirely aside from his own future, whether Carter's reputation was altogether a good thing for the firm. Granted that it had brought in plenty of rich clients, would it, looking ahead, as the clear-minded David always did, be ultimately attractive to the brightest law students, whom the firm always hoped to attract? For David, who took sides in his own actions but rarely in his own mind, and who never honored his prejudices with any unnecessary loyalty, saw that the New Deal was more the wave of the future than the laissez-faire of its opponents, and bent his mind to ways of making his father-in-law a continuing asset rather than a liability to the firm.

It was thus that he concocted the plan of making use of the government's arbitrary imprisonment of Japanese immigrants in the beginning of the war. Although he was not personally much concerned with what was done to the poor souls who were thus roughly rounded up and incarcerated, despite their American citizenship and utter blamelessness, and although he quite took in the hopelessness of defending them against the war fever that swept the nation, the government, and even the courts, he had the wit to see that when times changed, as they inevitably would, this blatant disregard of the most fundamental rights would be seen as a scandal and that those who had opposed it would be deemed heroic.

It was with this in mind that he approached Carter with the proposal that he take a brief in the defense of the incarcerated. The senior partner, as always, honored him with his full attention. Carter was a small man, wiry and tense, whose slightly ominous stare was hard to interpret. His heavy concentration as he listened seemed to promise a heavy response, but David was only too aware of the older man's unpredictability and knew that he might answer with either a hearty guffaw or even an off-color joke. Carter was equally aware of his reputation for the unexpected and reveled in it. As a young man he had been known to make fun of T.R. to his face and get away with it!

This time, however, he neither smiled nor joked.

"Surely, David, the war powers of a President suffice to justify the measures that the Squire of the Hudson (you needn't rise) has taken to safeguard our Western coast from the dangers of invasion?"

"Even if those dangers are remote? Even if they may not exist? If we should ever find ourselves at war with Great Britain, and an arbitrary chief of state should decide to lock up all citizens of Anglo-Saxon heritage, where would you and I find ourselves, sir?"

"In the majority, my friend. And we wouldn't put up with it!"

"But how long will that majority last, sir? You know how the demographic charts predict that—"

"Yes, yes, yes," Carter interrupted impatiently. This was not something he cared to think about. "Get to the point, David. What do you want me to do?"

David knew his man. He knew that Carter's somewhat eighteenth-century conception of the Constitution was balanced with deep humanitarian convictions. If Carter believed in an almost total freedom of action for the great corporation leaders in whose capable hands, as he saw it, the economic destiny of our nation had been fortunately placed, he was also seized with a Jeffersonian passion for the dignity and freedom of the individual man. Carter had no use for kings or despots, and in religion he was at least a deist. His vision of the ideal republic was one where no man need fear repression of his body or his tongue, and where any man of brains and ability and determination, no matter how humbly born, might rise to take hold of any business that would cover the land with rails, pump oil from the bowels of the earth, and smelt ore into steel.

With this kind of libertarian argument David had been able to induce Carter to argue case after case on behalf of the unfortunate Japanese, and as he had foreseen, when the war was over, his father-in-law was hailed by law reviews, honored at testimonial dinners, and his name enshrined among the great defenders of civil rights. Fortunately, it did not come to the attention of the liberal circles of the bar that David had a good deal of trouble keeping his senior from taking a brief defending the continued segregation of public schools in the South. Some of the old man's ideas of liberty did not jibe with the times, and nothing could persuade him that "separate but equal" was not the same as equal.

But that was just David's gripe: that everything he, David, did redounded to the credit of his father-in-law, never to himself. The world seemed to smell out any lack of burning conviction and to honor only those who felt such. How was it possible that people somehow suspected that he, David, did not give much of a hoot about Japanese internment and that Carter did? Yet it was he, David, who brought about the briefs in their favor! Carter on his own would never have done a thing for them. It was the same way with the firm's German clients before the war. David had come to the reluctant conclusion, persuaded by his son, that the Nazi taint and the firm's public relations required that the firm cease its representation of Hitler-dominated businesses, and when he finally convinced Carter of this, and the old man took fire and enthusiastically shed them, Carter got all the credit. Because he cared, although it took David to get him to care! And David, who had acted purely out of policy, was sneered at. How did people *know* what he was thinking? And why did they care? Wasn't it the action and not the inner motivation — or inner fantasy (for that was what it often was) — that mattered? Evidently not.

It was not thus that he had visualized what his relationship with the great man would ultimately become when he had courted Carter's daughter Janetta in the winter of 1917. He had dared to predict it as an evolving partnership in which, with the march of ineluctable time, senior and junior would gradually and painlessly change places, all in the natural order of things. He now saw that he should have foreseen that his spouse's parent would be as solid and enduring an urban fixture as Grant's tomb.

In that early winter that saw our entry into the First World War, Adam Carter had been free of federal duties and was repairing a fortune depleted by the lesser pay of government service, as the all-powerful head of a small but brilliantly successful litigating firm. True to his never-failing confidence in his own future, no matter what years flew by, Carter had used a large percentage of his remaining capital to erect a freestanding Georgian town house, the long side of whose oblong shape faced not on a less tax-expensive side street but boldly on Park Avenue. There at night he worked with foreign experts on a secret bipartisan committee designated by President Wilson to work out a peace plan to be presented to the victors when an armistice should come. David, who had once impressed Carter when he had argued a brief against him — the attorney-statesman had always an eye out for young forensic talent — and who, though already commissioned, could be exempted from army service at Carter's wish, had been requested by the latter for his peace-plan staff, and had actually been asked to move into Carter's great house to be available for work at all times.

Of course the appointment had not come without maneuvering on David's part. He had carefully cultivated the first good impression he had made on Carter in court, following it up with respectful calls at the latter's home and letters with bright comments on many of the older man's law review articles or public addresses. The reward of his appointment had been beyond his wildest dreams, and he was intent on taking full advantage of it, including the courtship of Carter's big, blond, self-assured elder daughter.

David was anxious for a just peace, because any but a just one would reflect badly on its designers. It was obvious to him that Germany, fatally overextended, was doomed to lose, but he had never wasted much time being incensed by Hun atrocity tales or being inspired by Wilsonian dreams of a world made safe for democracy. He rarely expressed himself on the emotional aspects of the conflict or, at most, signified an adequate agreement with majority-held views. Mr. Carter allowed himself to be dramatically eloquent on the subject of Kraut brutality and Yankee idealism, but David was to note, three years later, when Carter, reversing himself, decided with his friend Senator Lodge that the League of Nations was a trap and fought it, that he used the same eloquence. And David once more assisted him, keeping to himself the low mark that he assigned to his senior's supposed sincerity.

Janetta, large and fair and strong, had played a kind of dumb Brunhilde to her father's wily Wotan. Papa always came first, particularly as she had lost her mother early and, as the elder daughter, had sought to take her place with a widower who had chosen to remain that, but she saw no difficulty or conflict in her attitude even should she marry, for she took it blithely for granted that everyone else, including any husband-to-be, would feel the same way. Marriage was an expected rite, even for a Valkyrie; David was pleasant, attentive, clever, and approved by Papa — what else could a daughter want? And when David, duly wed, after the war had prevailed upon her father to assume the leadership of the larger firm of which he was a junior partner and which had been temporarily crippled by a pair of senior demises, Janetta had felt that it was only fitting that her father should rule in the office as he had always ruled in the home.

Their marriage, which some observers called tepid, though both got out of it pretty much what they had sought and expected, was mightily assisted by the distraction of hard work. David's labors at the law accounted for the bulk of his time and partially satisfied both his ambition and his imagination, while Janetta's indefatigable energy in fundraising for charitable causes went far beyond the usual fashionable requirements: she enjoyed every minute of her highly successful drives. But the precariousness of the marriage's basis was ultimately made sadly clear by the wife's catastrophic menopause, followed by a near-fatal hysterectomy. Janetta, who had never been seriously ill in her life, suffered a nervous breakdown, and emerged from it only with the aid of a High Church Episcopal priest who transformed her formerly conventional religious observances into something much more fervid. This might have been an adequate salve to her apprehensive disposition had she not, for the first time in their union, turned the full lights of her attention on her husband in what began as a pleading and ended as an angry resolution to make him share her new faith.

David had always before been quite willing to give lip service, which cost him nothing, to all her expressed enthusiasms. After all, little more than a smirk or a nod had been needed to satisfy a woman who assumed that the world around her held all her little values. But now that she wanted him to say prayers with her and go to church with her, he waxed at first restless, then impatient, then irritated, and at last explosive. "I'm goddamned if I'll let you turn me into a Tartuffe!" he finally shouted at her, and the shocked silence that followed this outburst marked a profound change in their relationship. It was the reverse of what had earlier happened to his brother Sam and Alida.

Janetta was now forced to face the fact that David had sides to his nature that had not been revealed to her in the twenty years of their marriage. She was at a loss as to how to handle it, and when she went to her father (who else was there for her to go to?), it was only to be cruelly rebuffed.

"Hasn't David seen things your way for three decades?" he cried with a high cackle of laughter. "Can you expect more of a man? Good God, you women are insatiable!"

The souring of his dealings with his wife brought an odd but significant alteration to David's emotional needs. In all his life thus far he had been stalwartly independent of the usual human craving for love, both given and received. So long as his relationships with family, friends, and associates had been formally correct and outwardly cordial, he had not minded if they were tepid. His best friend, his most congenial companion, had been himself. Life was the clay, he the potter. His younger sister Estelle, whom he had lost while he was just starting out as a lawyer, had been a rare exception. Her intelligence had penetrated to the depths of his egotism, and her understanding had taught her that this quality in her brother might be used as well for good as for bad. In short, she had both *seen* him and loved him, the only combination that could undermine the walls he had built around his prickly personality. He might have been a different person had she lived.

What he found difficult now to face was hostility in the home. It was, of course, what he expected in the marketplace; indeed, that was what the struggle of life was all about. But the presence of domestic opposition bred in him the need for something else, something warmer and more gladdening when he opened his front door back from work, some gentle massage for a weary brow. And David began to be aware that if this was ever going to be offered him, it would only be by his son, Ronald, the sole issue of his marriage, an awareness that soon blossomed into a conviction.

The boy even looked like Estelle. He had her soft brown eyes, her delicately sculpted features, her pallor. He had been a beautiful child, and he was turning into a beautiful man. Slight of build but seamlessly put together, suggesting a poet, he was nonetheless sturdy and had a loud laugh of almost vulgar enthusiasm. His goodwill and good humor were infectious, and he had the gift of immediately reconciling his parents if a quarrel was threatened in his presence. People found it hard to be disagreeable when Ronny was around. Nor was it because he was naïve or innocent. In fact, he was very shrewd, though, like his late aunt, he made every kind of charitable allowance for those he loved. And wonderfully, indisputably, he loved his father. He even seemed to want to protect David from David, as if he had some mysterious mission to guide his father through the sloughs of despond. To his mother he was blandly affectionate, charmingly considerate, but it was as if he sensed that there was not much he could do about her. She was what she was.

His life was a succession of successes. He was a popular student at Chelton, Yale, and Yale Law School, a gallant naval officer in World War II, and a brilliant and industrious associate in his father's law firm. He had wanted to go into politics, but David had persuaded him to follow the example of such great leaders of the New York bar as Elihu Root, Henry L. Stimson, and Adam Carter, and first establish the firm and profitable base of a law partnership from which he could take a leave of absence if called by a President to fulfill some cabinet or ambassadorial position. At the time of what David came to think of as the "Krantz crisis," Ronny had been an associate for two years and was doing very well.

There was only one aspect of his son's personality to which David took private exception — private because there was certainly nothing that he could reasonably complain about and even less that he could do about it. It was the young man's unqualified worship of his maternal grandfather. To him Adam Carter was the symbol of the great American lawyer-statesman at his finest and best, whose genius oiled the wheels of the nation's business and whose wisdom guided Presidents in times of war and world crises. And how could David, himself one of the embellishers of the legend, even hint that there might be another side to his sainted father-in-law? Still, there were times when it was bitter tea to swallow.

The worst of these sprang from the issue with Joel Krantz over the firm name. Krantz had long been the thorn in David's side that made his troubles with his wife seem a harmless itch. Krantz headed the important litigation department of the firm. He was a big bulldog of a man, handsome enough in his own rough way, with high-rising gray-brown hair parted in the middle, a broad brow, massive chin, and steely eyes, usually garbed in well-pressed black with a scarlet necktie, who made no pretense of hiding his humble Brooklyn background and sneered openly at the amenities of social life, which he lumped under the term "fancy pants." But he was no bull in a china shop; nothing crumbled before his stealthy but steady advance except his adversaries in the courtroom. A great trial lawyer, he could thunder or purr as the occasion demanded, and he instilled in his clients the pleasing conviction that God was on their side. Adam Carter had spotted him years before as a coming force in the courts and had lured him away from a rival firm with an offer that had then seemed to David extravagant. But it had worked, as even David had to concede.

So long as Carter's grip was firmly on the firm's tiller, a comparative peace reigned over the partnership. But when age began to relax the old man's hold — at least to the eyes of his intimates, if not to those of the public — and he seemed to be retaining, like Lear, "only . . . the name and all the additions to a king," Krantz began suggesting to any partner with whom he happened to be lunching the possible desirability of raising himself to equality with David in the number two spot of the firm and even changing its letterhead from Carter & Carnochan to Carter, Carnochan & Krantz. When he had enlisted what he considered an adequate number in his favor, he approached David directly in the latter's office.

"We're living in a new world, Carnochan," he began, in a near-hectoring tone. It was his habit to call his partners, with a few chosen exceptions, by their last name, a ploy that seemed designed to keep them at a discreet distance, or at least to warn them to look out for themselves. "These young fellas of ours returning from war service have had a rougher time than they ever anticipated. If a man's been through the hell of the Normandy beaches or Iwo Jima, he's not ready to sit quietly by while some old geezer who never saw a shot fired in anger gobbles the firm profits that younger guys have earned. He's lost four years in uniform, and he wants a slice of the here and now."

"Are you and I, Joel, among these old geezers?" David asked acidly. "Are you suggesting that we surrender our undeserved share of the take to these young Turks?"

"I'm talking about changes in the general atmosphere. Not of anyone in particular."

"And not of the nonparticipation of our age bracket in the recent conflict? Forgive me if I misunderstood you. Perhaps the point you wanted to make is that the new spirit of which you speak is contagious. That it affects even those of us who fought only the home battle."

"I sent a son to the Pacific."

"And so did I."

"We all know that, Carnochan. I even thought it might make you more understanding of the young men's point of view."

"Isn't it the old men's of which you are thinking?"

"How do you mean?"

"My dear Joel, you can't think that I am so much out of touch with firm matters that I have not learned of your interesting proposals for changes both in our name and in our percentages?"

Krantz glowered at him. "Very well, then. What are you going to do about it?"

"First of all, I must talk to Mr. Carter. I must see how he views your ideas. Particularly as to the change in the firm name."

"Is it his decision alone?"

"Isn't it?"

"Funny. I thought it was yours. Well, speak to me after you've talked to him."

Saying which, Krantz turned abruptly on his heel — he had not chosen to sit during the short interview — and marched (there was no other word) out of the room.

Carter, as no one knew better than his son-in-law, was never to be totally relied on. There was nothing more likely to elicit his negative response than the least assumption of a favorable one; he hated the idea of being predictable. Added to this was his fear, or at least his apprehension, as he aged, that the next generation might "gang up" on him, so that he derived a certain relish from any falling-out among his younger partners. He didn't even mind outraging Janetta's younger sister when she was divorcing a notoriously philandering husband by muttering about middle-aging wives who put on weight with their wrinkles yet expected their husbands to be saints.

"Well, I don't know but that our Joel may have a point." Adam Carter leaned back as he drawled this proposition in the Louis XIV armchair by the great boule Renaissance table that served him for a desk. Black-and-white Piranesi prints of old Roman forts and prisons looked down on him and David from the paneled walls, interspersed with silver-framed autographed photos of kings and presidents. "Carter, Carnochan & Krantz strikes me as perhaps more in keeping with the ethnic widening of our day. Krantz. What exactly is Krantz? Probably shortened from something else. Krantzberg? Krantzstein? Is it Jewish? It might be. At any rate, it leaves the door comfortably ajar for a minority member to speculate that it might be his own. And it's certainly not Wasp. There was no Krantz on the *Mayflower.* Mightn't it be even better to put the monosyllabic name in the middle? Carter, Krantz & Carnochan, how does that strike you? Of course, people would abbreviate it to Carter Krantz."

"Why not Carter & Krantz?" David queried bitterly. "Mightn't that be best of all? Or just Krantz. Krantz et al. Alone and magnificent."

"Now, dear David, let's not be silly about this."

"It's the man's pushiness I object to, sir. The way he barges into my office and expects me to bow to his every demand. A gentleman should at least give the appearance of waiting till he's asked."

"But Joel doesn't claim to be a gentleman. He probably despises gentlemen. And I must say, he's never asked anything of me."

"He knows better ways of getting around you, sir."

"You mean by channeling it through you, David? Well, think it over, my friend. Think it over. I haven't given it my blessing. As yet."

David had reached the point where he shared his deepest concerns with his son, who had converted one floor of the Carnochan town house to a temporary bachelor's flat. It was almost as if he needed concerns to justify the serious sessions where Ronny would sit with him over a nightcap after his mother had taken herself to bed with a rather cross "You two night owls can sit up till dawn if you like."

The night when he told Ronny of his grandfather's enigmatic reaction to Krantz's proposal, the latter was silent for a couple of reflective moments before he had a comment.

"Don't you think you and Mr. Krantz could hit it off?

He might be easier to deal with if he got the recognition he thinks he's earned."

David looked at him carefully. Of course, he was well aware that Ronny belonged to a tight little social group that included Elly Krantz, the monster's daughter, who, damn her, was blond and pretty. David had hugged to his heart the wishful thought that his son had befriended her with the object of easing the tension that he knew to exist between their fathers, but he couldn't blind himself to the possibility that, even if such had been the origin of his interest in the young woman, the girl's strong sex appeal might well give it another emphasis.

His tone in replying to his son was dry. "I'm not really sure I could stay in a firm where I had to check every major decision with Joel Krantz."

"Is that really the case, Dad?"

"I'm afraid so. Do you think that's petty of me?"

"I'm not so much interested in assessing it as I am in facing it. But if it's a case of you or Mr. Krantz leaving the firm, I think it would be better for both of you if it were he."

"Why for both?"

"Because the firm is more your life than his. He could be just as happy doing something else. You couldn't."

"How do you know what would make Joel Krantz happy or unhappy?" David's tone had an edge of jealousy.

"Because I know him. And because I've discussed him with his daughter. Mr. Krantz would love above all things to be a federal judge. He yearns to wear a black robe and rule men from the bench. He says he's practiced law enough. Now he wants to *be* the law."

"He's never told me that. And he must be aware that I'm on Senator Clark's panel to advise on potential judicial appointees."

"But that's just it! He thinks you'd blackball him if his name ever came up."

"Instead of which, suppose he owed his appointment to me?" David was dazzled at such an easy solution to his problem. To rid himself of Krantz without a rift in the firm, to do it, on the contrary, to the applause of the firm, which would be gratified by the elevation of a member to the bench, and to the everlasting gratitude of Krantz himself — what a panacea! "But wait a second, my boy. Wait a second." Of course, it was all too good to be true. "What has prompted you in all this? What is between you and that young woman? Are you conspiring together?"

"Conspiring what?" Ronny seemed in no way to resent the implication. He merely smiled.

"Conspiring to put the whole world on your side! So that if you marry Miss Eleanor Krantz, you'll have a father-in-law who loves the father he now detests and a fool of a father who's happy to fancy himself the power behind the throne of the firm still called Carter & Carnochan!"

"Everyone doesn't have a mind as devious as yours, Dad."

"I know one young man who has."

"With that I'm going to bed. Good night."

They did not discuss the question again, nor did David tell him, a week later, that he had made a luncheon date at the Downtown Association with Senator Clark. When they met it did not take the white-haired, black-eyebrowed, stout, gruff Republican boss of Long Island long to get to what he naturally suspected would be the object of their meeting.

"Joel Krantz? Well, of course, David, the name of so prominent a litigator as he has come up before. Several times in fact. Krantz has every qualification but one. What sticks in my craw is that old case of Judge Blackburn in New Jersey. You remember that one, I'm sure."

"Don't we all!" Blackburn, a federal district judge, had been convicted of bribery. It had created a famous scandal a decade earlier. "And I assume you're referring to the Jekyll Steamship Line case. But there was never any evidence that Krantz had any notion that the judge had been fixed when he argued the case before him. Or that he had anything to do with the bribe our client — our very *ex*-client, I should add — had paid the judge. It was just a lot of loose gossip, the kind that a mess like that is bound to engender."

"I grant it was never proved. But it was believed by your ex-client's opponents in the case, who were badly damaged by the corrupt ruling, even though it was ultimately vacated. They made a big stink at the time about Krantz knowing that Blackburn was on the take and telling his client about it. Of course, they were bitter and prejudiced, and they never came up with any convincing evidence, but some of that mud stuck."

"But do *you* believe it?"

"I don't believe it or disbelieve it, David. That's not my job, as I see it. But when I'm faced with a choice between two equally eligible judicial nominees, one with a question like that behind him, no matter how unfairly, and one without it, you know which one I'm going to pick. That's politics. You don't buy even an easy fight to win if you don't have to. And there are plenty of candidates with records as clean as this napkin." And here the senator took up the still-unused linen by his plate and shook it at his luncheon companion.

That afternoon David sat alone in his office, his door closed and his secretary instructed that he would take no calls. He had to give the deepest thought to the news that the senator had imparted to him. Or rather to what purpose, if any, he might use it. Suppose he should go quietly to Krantz and lay before him, entirely as a matter concerning the welfare of the firm, the possibility of injuring its reputation in the Street by adding to its title the name of a lawyer even unjustly tainted with an ancient scandal? Of course, Krantz would angrily reply that nobody credited such mildewed and malicious gossip. But David would have the additional ammunition, as yet unknown to Krantz, that the mildewed gossip was still fetid enough to stay the appointing hand of a powerful senator. If that did not work with Krantz, might it not work with some of the other partners, into whose ears this item could be discreetly deposited? And could David not add the clinching point that the senator had hinted that he, for one, believed there might be some basis for the rumor? Had Clark not so hinted that? Or in words that could rationally be so construed? And David could add to his argument that not only would the proposed new firm name carry a whiff of scandal but its alteration would open the partners up to an annual fight with other aspiring members who thought their work entitled them to greater publicity on the letterhead.

David rehearsed in his mind how the discussion at the ultimate firm lunch might go. Joel would, of course, be away, arguing a case somewhere. That could easily be arranged.

"But surely, David, you put no credit in this old wives' tale yourself?" someone would be bound to ask.

"None whatsoever" would be his firm response. "I've never harbored the slightest suspicion that our Joel was anything but true blue. But what I can't get away from is the fact that here we have an important lawgiver who is unwilling to raise him to the judiciary."

"But isn't that just a politician's super caution and fear of the yellow press? You don't suppose that Senator Clark really believes that crap?"

David's shrug would be monumental. "Who knows what a senator believes. A senator believes what it is politic for him to believe. And it seems to be politic for Clark to believe that Joel's name is something less than shiningly clear."

"But did he say that he thought there was anything in the allegations against Joel?"

David would be ready for this. "He certainly didn't deny it."

Yes, it might work. It might well work. And Krantz would probably not walk out of the firm. Where could even such a talent as his command a larger income?

David had resolved to speak no word of his plan to anyone, even Ronny, until he had definitely decided whether or not to execute it, but it was so weightily on his mind that he broke down on the first evening that he found himself alone with him in his dark, leathery, book-lined study after dinner on a night when Janetta was absent at a governors' dinner of her club. Ronny had been the one to bring up the subject by asking him if he had done anything about the judicial appointment. David then told him all.

After a thoughtful pause he asked, "What do *you* think about Mr. Krantz, Daddy? Do you believe he bribed that judge? Or that he even knew about it when he argued the case?"

"Good heavens, dear boy, what has that to do with the price of eggs? I'm concerned with the reputation of the firm and what might hurt it."

"Then it doesn't matter to you that Mr. Krantz might be made to suffer for something he hasn't done?"

"Not having his name in the firm title is hardly suffering."

"It might be. For him. He's a very proud man. I know about his ego and all that. But Elly maintains he'd have cut his hand off rather than pay a judge."

"Oh, so you've discussed that matter with Miss Krantz?"

"I have indeed. Which is why it concerns me now to know what you really think about her father. In your heart of hearts, I mean. Was he guilty or not?"

In the heavy pause that followed, David felt he was perspiring. "I just don't know."

"You don't know? You mean you don't care about having a crook for a partner? It's just his being named a partner that you mind?"

David felt he could no longer stand the gravity of Ronny's stare. "How is one to tell what to do in such cases? How can one read another's mind? Any lawyer might think or not think that the judge before whom he's appearing might be fixed. I've had enough of this. I'm going to bed!"

Ronny at this arose without a word, kissed him on the brow, and left the room.

Alone, David refilled his glass from the decanter on the little sideboard. Alone he felt, indeed, and as never before. Or was it really as ever before? Ronny with his terrible question had removed himself, as with a flash of lightning, from the tiny group of humans who had understood him — his old nurse in childhood, his sister Estelle, a boy at Chelton School, all long dead. The world that had always looked askance at him, the world that hated him because it feared — and rightly so — that it was basically like him, was a world of sin, and he and that world were both in it together, however much they might deny and dislike it. Did he be-

lieve that Krantz was guilty? Could anything be more irrelevant? Had he even bothered to consider it? How could a
thing that was past be worth considering except in how to
deal with it?

But he found himself now considering it; he owed at
least that much to his son, even if that son was blatantly deserting his cause. With a conscious effort he tried to divorce
himself from the mental picture of him and Krantz and to
see Krantz alone. Could Krantz have bribed a judge? he
asked himself. Never. He was much too smart, too cautious.
Could he have advised a client that the judge was bribable?
Probably not. Again, he would have been too aware of the
risk. Had Krantz known, when he argued that case, that the
judge he was endeavoring to convince had already been convinced? Quite possibly. But wasn't it a crazy world that cared
to get into the recesses of Krantz's mind or into those of David Carnochan? What earthly difference did it make what
went on in one's own private thoughts? Wasn't that indeed
the essence of freedom? But there it was. The world *was*
crazy. He had always known it; he still knew it, and he could
only act on it and accept a crazy universe. Ronny would no
longer be with him in soul, only in body. For Ronny had
joined the world.

The next morning at breakfast he found his son smiling, alert. They were alone, as Janetta always had the first
meal of the day in bed.

"I've thought things over," David announced flatly.
"I've decided that Joel Krantz is pure as driven snow and
that I shall no longer oppose his desire for more public notice in the firm."

Ronny actually clapped his hands. "Oh, Daddy, I'm so
glad! And now I can tell you *my* news."

"Oh, I think I've guessed that. Indeed, I wonder if I
haven't known it subconsciously for some time."

"Has it been so obvious?"

"I think to everyone but me. Does your mother know?"

"Oh, yes, and she thoroughly approves."

"Well, the girl's a charmer. When will you marry?"

"Right after I get my first raise. On New Year's Day. You'll see that I do, won't you?"

"Oh, I'm quite broken, my boy. Do with me what you will."

"Well, I'm going to make it a condition with my future father-in-law that you and he will be the best of friends and the most cooperative of partners."

David made a little face at this. "We shall try, anyway. And I shall endeavor to see an alliance with the Krantzes of the Gowanus Canal as the acme of our long social clamber!"

Ronny jumped up to give him a hug. "Try not to be any nastier than you can help!" he exclaimed with a laugh.

Alone again in his study before going downtown, David reflected that to face defeat with assumed equanimity was the nearest thing to a victory that such a man as himself could expect. Ronny had even looked like his grandfather at the breakfast table. The Carters had won again. No doubt they always would.

9

JAIME

THOSE WHO DECRIED the morals and character of Jaime Carnochan, son of Andy and nephew of David, of whom there were many, and branded him a heartless Don Juan for whose long-merited punishment the statued Commendatore had not yet descended from his pedestal, might at least have had some insight into the origin of his ceaseless philandering had they been able to read the senior thesis that he had submitted to his English professor at Yale in the winter of 1934. His mother, Tetine, possessed the only copy of this singular document; she had preserved it with care, because she alone knew what it was: not the whimsical expression of a sexual philosophy of total permissiveness designed more to amuse than instruct a reader, but the promulgation of what the writer believed to be an absolute truth. It would have been difficult for the world, Tetine's world at least, to credit anyone, even Jaime, with a sincere faith in so godless a creed, but Tetine could very well believe it. Indeed, she knew it as the only explanation of her adored son and heir.

The subject of the thesis was English Restoration comedy, as exemplified in the plays of Congreve, Wycherley, and Vanbrugh. The following quotation expresses the kernel of Jaime's thought:

> It was an age of true enlightenment. The religions of
> the world, before and after it, have shrouded the natural

joys of sexual gratification, granted us perhaps by a remorseful demiurge to compensate us for the manifold errors of creation, in a dark mist of fear and sin. Tragedians have written eloquently of the agonies associated with great passions; dramatists have used jealousy as the basis of half their plots, and ultimately Proust equated it with love itself. But for a brief era of glittering sunlight the immortal Congreve and his fellows had the genius to assign all this to the dustbin. His heroes, those superb, utterly self-confident, magnificently strutting bucks, are intent on gratifying each passing fancy that assails them. To them the rantings of a pantaloon husband or the snivelings of an abandoned mistress are simply comic. Is that heartlessness? The pantaloon had no right to expect fidelity from his much younger spouse, and the reproachful mistress would soon enough console herself. Too much, far too much has been made through the ages to justify, or even to glorify, the greedy possessiveness of men and women who should be grateful for even the temporary affection of their more attractive mates. Congreve taught us that if you take the gravity out of sex, you may also take the pain. So what have we lost?

Tetine, born Smiley, the daughter of a reasonably prosperous dentist whose patients had been largely fellow residents of the affluent but unfashionable Riverside Drive section of Manhattan, had entered the Carnochan clan more through her own seeking than theirs. Not that they didn't like her, but they certainly hadn't gone after her, and had any male member other than the amiable but hardly promising Andy courted her, there might have been some sharp objection. Who were the Smileys, anyway? The West Side and a dentist? Really! Weren't they probably Jewish? And had changed the name from Smilkstein?

Actually they weren't and hadn't. Tetine from the start had known exactly what her in-laws might surmise and how to handle them. She was the essence of tact. Though not endowed with beauty — she was slight of build, with an oval face and a nose a touch too long — she had wonderfully expressive, greenish-brown eyes and a wit that could put a man gently in his place without hurting. From childhood she had been, as her family and all the neighbors had put it, "bright as a button," and her father had not hesitated to send her to Barnard College in 1910, a time when many parents still regarded a daughter's education concluded at eighteen. Graduating, she had worked for a spell on a fashion magazine, but once she had taken in the new world around her, she had decided that marriage was still the surest path for a woman's advancement.

But the young Tetine was never charged with the lack of heart that so many would later ascribe to her firstborn, nor was she ever crudely ambitious. She always made a point of this in her silent sessions of self-appraisal. To attract the sort of man she wanted she might have been a bit short on sexual allure, but she knew well how to use the equal asset of a lively and resourceful mind. Always an astute observer, she had noted in her magazine work the difference between fashionable society and her own family's milieu, and she had modeled herself successfully on the more restrained and disciplined ladies of the former, as exemplified by her charming and capable editor in chief. She was very clear in her own mind about the environment in which she would choose to live.

All of which did not have to entail any condescension toward her own home. She was perfectly aware, for example, that her mother, quite unlike her modest, hardworking, and docile father, was too stout, too dressy, too trivial, too pushy; in short, that she was patently vulgar and a hindrance to a daughter's entry into any society more select than her own. Yet she still loved her mother, and chose to think of herself as an Elizabeth Bennet in *Pride and Prejudice*, seeing her female parent through Darcy's gimlet eyes but never wavering in her family loyalty and support. And so it would be with any man she was lucky enough to catch as a mate. The husband who pulled her up would be pulled up himself. She would work to make the best of any male material she had to hand.

Her chance came when an aunt, a sister of her father who had made a fortunate match with the owner of a large hotel, took her on a lavish summer tour of Europe, partly for her amusing company and partly to act as a friend and companion for the aunt's crippled daughter, a polio victim. They crossed the Atlantic on the White Star liner *Boadicea*, of course first class, and Tetine and the cousin, who was both charming and lovable in her pitiable state, found themselves widely cultivated by sympathetic passengers. The ocean was a great mixer, and the two flanking sides of Central Park, the untouchable West and the snooty East, aided by the brisk sea air and the tumbling billows, came together in a third world where apparently the twain could meet.

Coming up from cabin class, where even rich young bachelors were apt to be quartered, knowing full well that they would be always welcomed above, were three young Carnochans, two brothers and a cousin, traveling together for a bicycle tour of France. Two were law students, David and Gordon, the third, Andy, a broker, and the trio were soon the center of the younger set on board and regular guests for cocktails in Tetine's aunt's commodious suite.

She found Gordon the most attractive of the three; he was the handsomest and quietest, and his shy good manners had considerable charm. But it did not take her long to elicit from his franker and noisier cousin Andy that his heart was wholly possessed by a young lady in New York. David, the evident leader of the group, she instantly assessed as a snob who would never take seriously a girl who lived on Riverside Drive, however much his rather aggressive twinkling might open the door to less binding attachments. There remained Andy, to whom she turned her principal attention.

Large, portly, very friendly and gregarious, merrily loud and rather too much the "life of the party," Andy, with his blond hair and laughing blue eyes, might have been almost handsome had he lost thirty pounds. He was certainly the intellectual inferior of his brother and cousin, and Tetine gathered that he had not been able to get into Harvard Law, but he was nobody's fool, and she suspected early that he knew more about what was going on around him than he cared to let on. If he was dominated by his brother David, it was in part because he chose to be. He recognized the elder's superior brain, but saw no reason to be humbled by it. On the contrary, he probably expected to profit by it. Andy, for all his joking self-depreciation, was somebody in his own right.

He liked to circle the great vessel on her top deck every morning for some twenty rounds, and he invited Tetine to accompany him, to which she cheerfully agreed. With his hearty male egotism he would regale her with stories about himself and his doings, providing so much of his own laughter that she hadn't to do more than smile in return, and rarely intruding on any province of her own presumably less interesting life. But she found herself enjoying his buoyancy in the shining sunlight and against the infinite blue of a benign Atlantic. And at last he did favor her with a few personal inquiries and showed himself frankly amused at the information of her place of residence and her father's profession.

"A dentist!" he exclaimed in mock dismay. "And a West Side dentist at that! Tell it not in Gath! At least not while King David is within earshot."

"He'd disapprove?"

"Oh, David rolls up the windows of his car if he's driving on the West Side, north of Central Park. The air, as he puts it, is *malsain*. And as for the noble medical practice of your revered sire, to him your old man might as well be an undertaker."

"Do East Siders have no teeth? And can they compare the paltry stream that abuts their shore with the mighty Hudson?"

"Don't get me wrong, dear girl," he hastened to reassure her. "I have no such idiotic hang-ups. We're speaking now of my more elegant sibling. To David the number of places where a so-called gentleman can reside and the number of professions in which he may engage are strictly limited."

"And you're not ashamed to be seen on deck with a dentist's daughter? Or is that the reason you take me to this less-frequented one?"

"On the contrary, it is to spare you from being seen on such cozy terms with a cabin-class passenger," he retorted with a broad smile, and actually put an arm around her waist. "But to be serious for a moment, Tetine," he continued as she gently disengaged herself, "the only reason I couldn't be a dentist is that I'm not smart enough. People make fools of themselves over what is fashionable and what isn't. Have you ever been to Newport? We go there for a week every summer to stay with Granny Carnochan, who has a quaint old house on Washington Street overlooking the harbor in a dear old district that is no longer fashionable. So to swim we go all the way to Bailey's Beach to get our noses full of the smell of garbage dumped from passing barges and our toes nipped by crabs in the most miserable stretch of sand on the East Coast. But would we be seen dead on the public beach, not only more available and less crowded, but boasting clean sand and pure water? Never! Perish the thought."

"And these arbitrary standards are carried over to New York?"

"Of course. How can anyone compare the splendid sweep of the West Side and the glory of the Hudson with a neighborhood huddled by the smelly East River? No, as the French say, *Il faut souffrir pour être belle*, and *belle* to my family means the least attractive area of Manhattan. Yes, I note your moue. My Gallic accent leaves something to be desired."

"Your accent is just fine by me," she assured him, and did not resist the hug with which he now encircled her. "And I'm glad that you're not governed by your brother's strictures."

"Oh, David's all right," he conceded, releasing her. "David has a few quirks, but he's always someone to be reckoned with. David is going places in this life."

"And aren't you?"

"Well, maybe not quite the same ones. Not as grand, perhaps."

"Oh, you'll be all right."

And indeed, she was beginning to see that he really would. She thought she could already make out the kind of man he would be: one who knew instinctively how to use his social contacts and his easy popularity so as to minimize his lack of drive or ingenuity. She saw him holding forth cheerily to a group of amused men in club bars, in locker rooms, at dining-room tables after the ladies had retreated, and, downtown, rising to some trusted post in a bank or broker-age house, never the top, but generating a good income. Quite as important, she fancied that she could discern, be-hind the bluff of his off-color jokes and the barely concealed lubricity of his views on the relationship of the sexes, a fun-damental kindness and decency. Andy, she decided, would not make a bad husband at all, certainly as good a one as she would be a wife. For although she didn't go so far as to think she could "civilize" him, she could certainly help him by keeping him under control as he grew older, fatter, and cruder. Which men like him were only too apt to do.

The crossing of the Atlantic took only six days, but by the time they docked in Le Havre, Andy was showing her serious attention. He had evidently the rare sense to see that this smart and vivacious young woman might have just the qualities needed to complement his own, so that between them they should be able to tackle just about any problem that was apt to confront them in the kind of life they were presumably destined to lead.

Nothing more committing was said on this trip, but when they found themselves back in New York, Andy be-came a regular caller on Riverside Drive, and in the fol-lowing spring they became engaged. Louisa Carnochan ac-cepted this new daughter-in-law with tempered enthusiasm; she had hardly anticipated that the rollicking Andy would choose so sober and intellectual a bride and had been appre-hensive of one of a decidedly different nature. The family was quickly unanimous in its decision to make the best of her. The only relative whose welcome was a bit distasteful to Tetine was David. She hardly relished the obvious inference that she was probably the best that he could expect poor Andy to do.

Their marriage turned out a good deal as she supposed

it would. But not entirely. Andy was a kind and faithful husband, and for a long time he earned a sufficient income on Wall Street as a stockbroker. And Tetine fitted easily enough into the fashionable East Side social life that she had wanted to join; to the faultlessly behaving member of a solidly established clan all doors were open. But there was one thing she had not counted on. She found that she was bored. She was careful not to show it, but there it was. The life that seemed so completely to satisfy her sisters-in-law was not enough for her. She had hoped that maternity might distract her, but for three years it didn't come. When it did, however, with Jaime, another life began for her, and she was determined to make the most of it.

He was very much her child from the start. He had her oval face and longish nose, and his eyes had that quizzical appraising stare that was apt to be followed by a little hoot of infectious laughter. He was witty at an early age, acutely sharp, but not malicious; the world to him seemed a joke that never ceased to amuse. But where she divined their difference was that he had much more charm, an irresistible charm, particularly, as he grew older, to women. He was not handsome, at least in a silent-movie-star way, but his pointed features and tangled auburn hair had the curious attraction of an oddly beneficent and slightly ruffled sparrow hawk whose beak and claws offered no threat. Above all, he was bright, bright as that proverbial button to which she herself had been compared.

He was everything to her, and he knew it, and she knew that this was not altogether a good thing. He had captivated and rendered impotent the parent who should have been his guide. In somewhat the same way he handled resistant forces in the highway of life: governesses, schoolteachers, rival boys, and, as he matured, critics of his lighthearted epicureanism. No name-calling could shatter the steel wall of his stubborn amiability. He seemed always to get his way, to succeed in doing the thing he most wanted to do. And, most baffling of all, he gave her the impression of knowing that nobody really understood him but herself, which might have been why he kept even their most intimate talks on a keel of light persiflage, as if they both understood that anything more serious might open the door to disconcerting disclosures. There were things, evidently, that even he was not anxious to face.

That he also thoroughly understood his father was shown in how deftly he handled the latter. He would roar with seemingly genuine laughter at oft-repeated paternal jokes and cap them with better ones that would elicit genuine roars from the delighted Andy, who could deny him nothing and spoiled him outrageously. Jaime flattered him to death by treating him as a totally congenial contemporary whose company he preferred to that of his schoolmates. They would plan little ruses together, as when, at Chelton School, Jaime, then a fifth-former and chapel usher, handed the collection plate to his father seated by the aisle and the latter calmly placed it in his lap, removed a number of bills, and solemnly returned the platter to his impassive son. The astonished and scandalized witnesses would learn later, of course, that the bills had been duly returned.

Yale and girls brought complications to Jaime's life, for his idea of a "date" was a good deal more sophisticated in the early 1930s than it would later become. It was only because the outraged parents of one impregnated debutante dreaded an open scandal that they held their tongues and consented to a secret abortion. Tetine, to whom an at last temporarily troubled son made a full confession — his father never knew — gave him what his old Irish nurse used to call "the length

and breadth of her tongue" for the first time in their relationship, but she had little hope that he would reform his
ways.

She pinned her feeble hopes for a less tumultuous life
on his making an early marriage, which he did. Graduating
from Yale, he took a job with the famous advertising agency
Ross and Codman, which seemed the ideal opening for one
of his facile and ingenious talents, and he was soon courting
the beautiful Lila, daughter of the powerful head of the firm,
Alton Ross.

"You're planning to marry her, I hope?" Tetine demanded of Jaime when he stopped by, as he often did after
work, to share a cocktail with her. He had his own apartment now, and she knew only too well why.

"Well, I guess I'll have to, won't I?"

"Not, I hope, because of anything you've done."

"Of course not. Mothers have dirty minds, I'm afraid.
No, it's because of what I want to do."

"You relieve me."

"Mother! You don't think I'd seduce the boss's daughter, do you? It would cost me my job!"

"Or get you a promotion. Isn't the son-in-law the natural heir of the American tycoon? The son too often goes to
the dogs."

"Will you be pleased if I bring you a princess for a
daughter-in-law? A commercial princess, anyway."

"Only if you promise to be a good and faithful prince."

"You do ask rather a lot. What do you give in return?"

"My blessing."

"And I, poor fool, thought I could count on that in any
event! But I see that a mother crossed may become the
wicked fairy godmother. Had you known what I might become, would you have tossed a curse into my cradle?"

"Much good it would have done me. Or anyone else, for that matter."

"And what does that mean?"

"What it means, dear heart, is that I'm very much afraid that whatever you do, you'll get away with."

"That's my lucky card, is it?"

"You beg the question."

Jaime married Lila Ross at a big church wedding, followed by a bigger reception on the St. Regis Roof, to the plaudits of all concerned. Two children were born to the couple in the first three years of their union, and Jaime's first adultery, or at least the first of which anyone had any notice, did not occur until their fourth anniversary. He then had an affair with the wife of a Yale classmate who had been best man at his wedding, Gilbert Warren, a sober, serious, high-minded lawyer who deemed it his duty to think the best of all his friends, even Jaime. When his wife, Eugenie, exasperated at the fatuity of his seemingly willful blindness, actually threw her guilt in his face, he solemnly suggested a conference between the two couples to discuss the situation and its possible solutions in a thoroughly modern and scientific fashion. Lila and Eugenie reluctantly and resentfully agreed, but the meeting came to an explosive finale when Jaime, straight-faced, calmly put on the table the suggestion that the air might be cleared of its thunder if his wife and Gilbert would first conduct an affair of their own.

"And then we'd be able to talk without the hang-up of outmoded tribal myths," he concluded with a brisk nod, as if disposing of the whole question.

An outraged Lila appealed to her even more outraged father, who at once fired Jaime from his office. Through the loud denunciations of Alton Ross his son-in-law's suggestion of an open marriage which might otherwise have re-

mained in the dark became the talk of the town. Like everyone else, the whole Carnochan clan was scandalized. Even
Andy, prone to excuse, or at least snicker at, the most fla-
grant sexual excesses, thought his son had gone too far.
Meeting his wife and Jaime at noon at his lunch club in
a private glass alcove commanding a dazzling view of the
wicked city, he reverted for an odd moment to the harshness
of an old Presbyterian divine.

"What you suggested, Jaime Carnochan, struck at the
very roots of our church and our faith. It is hard even for a
loving father to condone what you have done and, perhaps
even worse, what you have said. I can reluctantly understand
why your unhappy wife has chosen to sue you for divorce
here in New York on the one ground allowed. The only
thing I can suggest, sirrah, is that you disappear for a considerable time. Time enough so that the town, or some of it,
anyway, may forget this wretched business."

"Forget what, Pater?" demanded his obviously unre-
pentant son. "My offering a simple proposition that might
have turned an ugly row into a pleasant roll in the hay? Is
everybody crazy?"

"Somebody is!" Andy's cheeks were turning a beet red.
"At least that's the only excuse I can make for you. Speak to
him, Tetine, will you please!"

"Oh, leave me out of this, I beg of you."

"But it's just this sort of talk that's making his father-in-
law badmouth us all over town! He's asking everyone what
sort of bringing up you and I could have given our son."

"Well, I'm a big girl now. I can stand up to it."

"Mr. Ross takes that position publicly, does he?" Jaime
swooped on the idea with a laugh that was actually cheerful.
"I love it! The mighty Ross, who's covered his great nation
with ads to make the smelly multitude dream that it can cure

its natural stink. Or to delude the victims of halitosis with the lure of sweeter breath. And for what purpose? That they may aspire to attract sexual predators! What else, in the name of a puritan heaven? Why, Ross's whole business is founded on sex! Does he care if it's priest-approved? A fat lot he does."

Tetine sighed as she listened to him. She knew now what she had known but tried to repress before: that her son was hopelessly and irredeemably amoral, certainly in all matters relating to sex, and probably in a goodly number of others.

"I think, anyway, my dear," she responded in a milder tone, "that what your father suggests about a trip is a good idea. Also, it might be wise for you and Eugenie Warren not to see each other for a bit. Anything else might look as if you were flaunting your affair in the face of society."

"I think that's good advice, Ma. *Very* good advice."

"Oh? Why is it so good as that?"

"Because the minute Lila obtains her decree, I become vulnerable."

"Vulnerable to what?"

"To husband seekers. Who else?"

"And you think Eugenie, when she gets *her* decree, might fit into that category?"

"I *know* she would fit into it."

"And that is so much to be avoided? We thought you two were so close."

"Mother! Can you imagine your Jaime boy wed to a woman who thinks that going to two nightclubs after the theater is twice as much fun as going to one?"

"And three times, three times as much?"

"Precisely. For Eugenie there is no law of diminishing returns. She'd be an exhausting spouse."

"But she is good, I gather, for other things."

"She is very good for other things."

Which Jaime indeed proved, for he broke off his liaison with Eugenie Warren, took an extended trip to South America, and resumed the affair when he returned to New York with his second wife, Estella, whom he had met in Rio.

This second match was already on the rocks when Jaime joined the army in 1941. As a first lieutenant he was sent to London at an early date to join the staff there planning the ultimate invasion of the Continent. He engaged in a regular and detailed correspondence with his mother, in which he offered to her bemused but resigned eye lighthearted descriptions of the new fields for gallantry that the dislocations of war had brought to a formerly more ordered society.

Tetine knew that she would never be able to change his nature; all she could hope to accomplish was somehow to keep him within the borders of respectability. She had made it her business to study his nature to the bottom, and she thought that she now understood the extraordinary attraction that he exercised over her sex. It was not that he was so handsome, though there was more than a smitch of the Byronic in his pale intensity which made so intriguing a background to his mocking wit. Plenty of men less successful with women were better looking and had heftier builds. It was more the lightness of his touch that did the trick. He stripped the ancient mystery of sex of all its formidability; he made it seem as harmless and noncommittal as a picnic or a day at the races. He made a girl feel a fool to have taken for a mountain what nobody had taught her was only a molehill. And at the end of the affair, if the girl reverted, as they often did, to the old theory of the mountain, where was Jaime? He was gone. Tetine wondered at times if he was a scamp or a prophet. Was the so-called sexual revolution of the postwar world not perhaps a confirmation of his theory?

Andy had lost a good percentage of his capital by holding on too long to his shares in businesses only temporarily enriched by the war, and Tetine, partly to supplement their reduced income and partly simply to conquer her boredom, had joined with a woman friend to form a business partnership that would plan and organize private entertainments: debutante dances, anniversary dinners, charity balls. She found that she had a definite flair for the job, particularly for parties in the last-named category, and would ultimately write a bestseller, a memoir entitled: *Who Pays for Elsa Maxwell's Ticket?*, but her real reward came with her discovery that her firm provided just the niche that Jaime had always needed.

He had returned from the war jobless and penniless, with a reputation for philandering that hardly endeared him to the business and banking world of men. He was delighted to go to work for his mother, and soon proved adept at the job beyond her most extreme hopes. He delighted prospective hostesses with his enthusiasm and his imaginative ideas. If his underlying principle was that life was — or at least could be — a party, why should a lady not use her money, her talent, her very soul, to make it a good one?

"What is a party, after all, but a prelude to love?" he asked his mother.

"To your kind of love, maybe" was her rather dry response. But she saw that her plan was working.

IN THE TWO DECADES that followed, Jaime expanded the business to a point where his name was known throughout Gotham. His fame did much to mitigate the severity with which his philandering had formerly been condemned.

The eye of criticism is misted by success, and Jaime's affairs were treated by society as the minor warts on the amiable countenance of a popular and accepted celebrity. Any mistress of his — or wife, for he married four times — who complained of betrayal was deemed a fool for not having anticipated what everyone knew would happen — everyone at least who had any doings with the "great world."

He had progressed far beyond the debutante party. He had seen early with his mother that the charity ball would become the regular and indispensable staple of social entertainment. The rich, both old and new, bowing to the fashionable liberalism that had sprinkled the surface of the economy ever since the New Deal, found it better for their public relations and easier on their consciences, when they had any, if they could identify their quest for festivity with the alleviation of human misery or the fostering of the arts. They danced for hospitals and medical research; they wined and dined for museums and schools. Charity excused their show of diamonds; humanity justified their mirth. Jaime used his agile inventiveness to conceive of ever-newer divertissements; he reveled in creating a world that more and more seemed to resemble the world as he had originally imagined it.

At a dinner party in the 1960s for the older generation of the Carnochans, given by David and Janetta, and attended by Tetine and Andy, their aging but still very alert host, David, held forth on a favorite theme of his.

"The old Presbyterians in our family used to preach at great length of the joys of heaven and the pains of hell. They feared that you couldn't expect even decent behavior from mankind without a promised reward or a threatened punishment. And, as it was obvious that in this world the wicked often prospered and the good suffered, they had to invent another life where the score was more justly kept. But do we really need that today? Don't we largely get our comeuppance in this mortal life? By 'we,' mind you, I don't refer to the poverty-stricken masses of the globe who die wretchedly of hunger and disease. I'm talking about the people we know, our own kind, who are born with the luck of a decent affluence and at least the opportunity of a decent career. Look about you at your relatives, your friends, your business associates, even your enemies, if you have any. Don't the good ones, on the whole, have a pretty good life, and don't the bad ones generally end up in some sort of trouble? Do they have to die to get what's coming to them?"

This was followed by a rather noisy round of general chatter as the table, amused as always by David's theory, discussed it. Names were offered as examples, pro and con, sometimes eliciting hoots of laughter. Someone suggested about an apparently successful evildoer that a secret guilt might be his punishment, and was answered by another who jeered that in that case a secret self-satisfaction might be an adequate reward for a virtuous sufferer. A good time was had by all.

Until Andy introduced a jarring note. As he aged, he not only had become more portly; he was more inclined to refresh his thirst with whiskey. With a flushed resentment perhaps sparked by a lifelong jealousy of his "Irish twin" now at last beginning to break through its long cover, he seemed willing to sacrifice his own son to rebut David's assumptions.

"What about Jaime?" he demanded, and the table fell silent. No one had seen fit to use a family member as an example. Tetine looked down at her plate as one who knew that any remonstrance would only make matters worse. "I guess everyone here knows what a merry life my Jaime has led," Andy continued heartily, grinning around at the table. "We have little doubt as to what our emigrating ancestor would have thought of him. He would have sternly pointed to the yawning gates of hell! Yet what has happened to the sinning Jaime in this mortal vale of tears? He has built a prosperous business. He has had his pick of the beauties of the land. His children, left largely to the care of their abandoned mothers, have not only succeeded in their chosen careers but made happy and lasting marriages. And what has happened to your own offspring, oh, ye virtuous folk?" Here he almost leered as he glanced about. "Aren't half of them on drugs? Don't you curse the fatal sixties? While Jaime goes from prize to prize down the primrose path! To what? Perhaps to a restful oblivion."

David was clearly irked by the sour turn that his brother had given to a topic designed to amuse. He smiled, but his smile was a wry one. "Jaime may still get his comeuppance. And in this life, too. And all the worse for being delayed!"

A nervous titter from his audience was the only response to this. The family sensed the grimness in David's tone and thought best to make light of it. Then Tetine, with her customary tact, put an end to any further discussion of her adored son.

"The Commendatore has not yet descended from his pedestal," she observed. "And I for one hope he will remain perched on it. Hadn't we better let it go at that?"

10

RONNY

Ronny Carnochan "celebrated," or rather deplored, his fifty-second birthday alone during the hot summer of 1970 in his red-brick colonial rented Georgetown house in the District of Columbia. His wife, Elly, had gone to New York to be with her ailing mother. A strict and loving observer of anniversaries, she had wanted to stay with him, even at the cost of discomforting an invalid parent, but he had insisted on her not doing so, asserting, quite truthfully, that he saw no occasion for festivity on reaching the age that he had. Particularly as neither of their two children would be present: Tom having hidden away (shamefully, as Ronny had originally seen it) from the draft in Denmark and Elsa being in Chicago to organize another of her protest marches against the war in Vietnam. Certainly neither of them would have cared to raise a glass to toast a father who, as a special assistant to the Secretary of State, was toiling night and day to support a war which they abominated.

So Ronny welcomed the chance for an evening alone to reflect, over a modestly refilled whiskey-and-soda, on the vicissitudes of a life that had brought him to this pass. For if he had initially greeted the prospect of war in Asia as a crusade for the containment of Communism, he had subsequently incurred grave doubts not only as to its wisdom but as to its morality. And if he had deplored what he had deemed at first a lack of patriotism in his offspring, he was now not so sure that their national loyalty was not deeper than his own. And if he had once seen the assemblage of his brightest contemporaries around the shining star of Jack Kennedy as the advent of a golden age, he now found himself wondering if "Camelot" had not been as fictional as King Arthur's round table.

What he himself had once seemed and what he had wanted to be was symbolized by his portrait as a naval lieutenant in World War II, which had been hung over the mantel in the parlor by a loyal wife determined to give it the most prominent place. It had been painted on one of his home leaves in that earlier war, commissioned by his adoring father, David, who had had likenesses of his only son taken at every stage of the latter's life. The picture, embarrassingly flattering, showed a young officer adorned with ribbons and battle stars whose pale, delicate features, high brow, rich curly hair, and far-gazing eyes seemed to unite a poet and a warrior, an idealist and a man of action. Time of course had altered the model, but the present Ronny had at least retained the hair, the figure, and the almost lineless physiognomy of the man in the portrait. Oh, yes, he was vain enough to acknowledge that he had worn well enough, at least outwardly, but he was also still able to recognize that he was, and always had been, a bit too small in stature to quite justify the air of importance that emanated from the canvas. Indeed, from boyhood he had been haunted by the sense that his modest physical dimensions just missed living up to the expectations that his facial beauty aroused. Was it nature's warning to him to temper the elation evoked in him by the admiring glances of others with a judicious modesty?

For he had been undeniably the pet of his family, of his school and college mates, of his fellow officers and law associates. All his life he had been blessed and burdened with charm. His mother, Janetta, large, bland, practical, and preoccupied by the exact performance of her daily tasks, had been a trifle baffled as to how to handle this prince in the family and had ended by giving in to him in everything, but her attitude had almost smacked of indifference in contrast to Daddy's total absorption in him. And Daddy was the one who counted, whose rule was absolute over the Louis XIII château in Long Island and the small but elegant marble-fronted town house in New York.

Indeed, Ronny's relationship with his father raised all the principal questions in his life. His tall, bald, gleaming-eyed, enigmatically smiling parent, great lawyer and associate of the great, was unlike the fathers of Ronny's friends in that he could never seem to have enough of his son's company and liked to have him with him on all kinds of occasions in which fathers and sons were usually apart. David would sometimes, for example, even take Ronny with him on business trips or to his law firm's outings. Ronny had the opportunity to see his father from more angles than did other sons, and he came to note that some people were a bit afraid of him, however much they may have admired his legal or diplomatic skills, and that there were even some who manifestly disliked him. But what he noted in particular was that his father, despite his barrage of outer friendliness and habit of broad smiles, seemed to have little real warmth in his feeling for people. Even with Janetta there was a certain coolness in his approach. But there was no mistaking David's feeling for his son; his voice in addressing the boy took on the same tone that it did when he spoke of a favorite sister who had died young.

All of which had given the young Ronny a curious sense of responsibility for his seemingly impregnable sire, as if, by some quirk of fate, he should be the one person in the world with the capacity of hurting his father. And the fear of ever doing so, of setting off a fire in the too dry interior of this fortress of a man, engendered a deep devotion to him. For Ronny began to realize that if his father was vulnerable to anyone as weak as a young son, he might not be so impregnable, after all, as that son had imagined, and it might be Ronny's mission to protect him, not only from the effect of his exaggerated love for his son, but from the hostility that his personality indubitably sometimes aroused.

When Ronny was only twelve, he actually intervened in a dispute between his father and his maternal grandfather at a Sunday family lunch. Grandpa Carter was the only person who could prevail over David even in the latter's own home. The issue discussed was David's plan to send Ronny the following fall to Chelton, the Massachusetts boarding school that he and his cousins had attended and which was still under the administration of the same veteran headmaster, Dr. Nickerson, who had taught them.

Mr. Carter was in the habit of taking positions opposed to those of his family, sometimes in order to stimulate them to new ideas and sometimes simply to irritate them, but in neither case did it keep him from waxing violent.

"Of course, we all know that the only real value of the New England private schools is what they can do for a stupid student. With their big endowments and fancy faculties they are in a unique position to pay attention to backward boys. The glory of Chelton is that it was probably the only academy that could have got my friend Cabot Storey's moron grandson into Harvard. But they can hardly boast about that, can they? And why does Ronny here need Chelton? Isn't he already at the top of his class at Buckley?"

"Isn't it a proper thing, Mr. Carter," David demanded, a bit testily, "for me to want the best education going for my son?"

"Pooh. Boys like Ronny educate themselves. I know I did, and I believe you did. All we needed was the books. The good teachers know that. They know that boys like Ronny are the sort out of whose way you have to get. The odd thing is that all those expensive private schools are hell-bent to get just the students who don't need them. They want to exclude the only ones they can really help. But then, we know it's a cockeyed world."

"How do you explain, then, that practically everyone you know is doing their damnedest to get their sons into schools like Chelton?"

"Very easily. Because they're all after another thing those schools *do* offer, and that is not just education. How many fathers in Wall Street give a hoot in hell about cultivation? Not many, as I'm sure you'll admit, David. They want to send their sons to the schools and colleges where they will make the friends most valuable to them in the financial world of the future. That's the system, and it works, too. You and I, my dear David, have seen many examples of just how smoothly it works. But Ronny's already in that world, thanks to your efforts. Thanks even a bit to my own."

"I think you grossly underestimate, sir, the effect on a fine mind like Ronny's of really first-class teachers."

Ronny could see now that his father was becoming really upset. He knew how carefully his parent had laid all his plans for his son's future, and that it was truly painful for him to hear Mr. Carter disillusioning his child. Ronny felt it suddenly incumbent on himself to reassure his sire.

"But, Grandpa," he interposed tactfully, "if I don't go to Chelton, I'll have to change to another school in the city. Buckley doesn't take us through to college. And many of my friends are going to Chelton. I should miss them."

"Oh, Chelton isn't going to do you any *harm*, my boy," Carter said with a sarcastic smile. "I know old Nickerson. He's not what I'd call an intellectual man, and he thinks he talks to Jesus, but he means very well. As they say in England, a gentleman needn't know Latin, but he must have forgotten it. Your son is quite safe, David. Even if he doesn't go to Chelton, everyone will think he has."

"Oh, Father, you're hopeless," Ronny's mother now exclaimed. "You make fun of everything."

And with this, the little dispute was terminated, but Ronny appreciated his father's grateful glance. It marked the beginning, not of their mutual love, which had existed all along, but of an alliance in which the son was beginning to realize that he was destined to play an important supporting role, and that his whole heart would go into playing it. For nobody understood his father as he did!

Ronny's entry into the life of Chelton School was eased by his being accompanied by so many of his pals from their day school in New York. They even formed a little clique in which they could stand together against the trials of being "new kids." And then the school itself was a kind of extension of the family; more than half his form mates were the sons of graduates who were even more in awe of the headmaster than their parents were. The panels in the main hall listing the alumni bore the names of several Carnochans. And the shining red brick and white columns of the buildings gracefully spaced around the emerald green of the circular lawn opening on the full beauty of a New England rustic fall lent a welcome even to the boy least sensitive to scenery. Add to this that Ronny's father was an active trustee of the institution, often consulted by the headmaster himself.

Ronny, as he grew into his teens, was too smart not to be aware that all the world did not see Chelton as he and his father did. The father of Tony Gates, his closest friend there, though a graduate and classmate of Ronny's father, had been the *enfant terrible* of an ancient Boston family, and he still enjoyed being blasphemous about his alma mater when he came up to visit his son and took him and Ronny out to supper at a local inn. His diatribes would go something like this:

"If Dr. Nickerson had been the governor of the Massachusetts Bay Colony, he wouldn't merely have exiled the sainted Anne Hutchinson for her antinomian views, he'd probably have hanged her! Like John Winthrop, he'd have fled religious intolerance at home to establish his own version of it on the rocky coast of New England. Is there a single Jewish boy in Chelton? And how many Catholics?"

"But we're a church school, Mr. Gates," Ronny pointed out. "Jews have their own, don't they?"

"What about the many who have converted?"

"Dr. Nickerson says they did so for social reasons. Which doesn't make them true Christians."

Mr. Gates's laugh was as big and noisy as himself. "I love it! Nickerson wouldn't have even let in Saint Paul!"

"And we have several Catholic boys, sir."

"Yes, but not many. And they still have to attend the chapel services, do they not?"

"Yes, but they can go to early Mass in the village."

"With the chambermaids in the school bus! I remember that from my own days. Oh, my dear young Ronald, I see you've been brainwashed. That's why I come here so often to visit my Tony." Here he gripped his son's shoulder. "To see that he gets at least a glimmer of other points of view. After all, no matter what walls we raise around our precious youngsters, they're bound one day to have some contact with the great unwashed."

But Ronny was far from being brainwashed. He saw perfectly that, for all his free thinking, Mr. Gates had taken care to send all his three sons to Chelton. Whatever it was that the school offered, it was evidently something that made up in Mr. Gates's mind for religious intolerance.

Ronny also saw that Chelton and its headmaster stood sincerely for the principal virtues: honesty, courage, chastity, industry, cleanliness, patriotism, moderation in satisfying natural appetites, and gentlemanly good conduct. What was wrong with that? The school might draw its students from a limited social stratum, but that was because the headmaster had cared deeply for the small group of families that, fifty years before, had helped him create his then exiguous academy, and he had ever since favored the sons of his graduates. And if fewer of his boys went into the church or public service than he had hoped, was it not because, as President Coolidge had stated, the main business of America was business?

When Ronny's father came to the school — and his fiduciary duties as well as his paternal concern made such visits frequent — Ronny asked him how best to answer Mr. Gates's onslaughts.

"Ted Gates has always made a thing out of being a rebel against the status quo. It's jealousy, pure and simple. Even at school he was bitter about not being made a prefect. And he's never succeeded in anything. He may take potshots at old Boston, but he hasn't rejected the comfortable trust fund that keeps him, and you won't find him spending a summer in any place less fashionable than Nahant. He's the kind of liberal who is concerned only with tearing down those above him, never with raising up those below. You'll find a lot of men like that in life, I'm afraid, my boy. Ignore them."

Ronny took this advice very much to heart. He tended now to see critics of his school, like those of his father's great law firm, as wantonly destructive agents, gnawing away at pillars that were just strong enough to keep society from the ever-present danger of crumbling to pieces. The few boys in his form who sneered openly at such evangelical hymns as "Onward, Christian Soldiers" were apt, he suspected, to

contain a nasty streak in their nature; he compared them to
the Red Soviet guards who had butchered the lovely young
grand duchesses in that cellar in Ekaterinburg. There wasn't
enough good in the world to permit the smearing of what
little there was. Life would be a fight to preserve that good.
But it would be a brave fight. He even began to wonder if
brave fights were not what life was all about.

   He lacked the physical bulk to be a star at football, but
he was adequate at other sports, and he became editor in
chief of the school magazine, a prefect, and president of the
Dramatic Society. Shakespeare's *Henry V* was chosen for the
annual school play in his last year, and he learned by heart
every one of the ringing orations of the warrior king, im-
ploring the master who directed the drama not to cut a line
of them. It was generally agreed among the boys, faculty,
and visiting parents that his performance was a sterling one.

   Certainly he had put his whole heart into the part. The
spirit of the conquering monarch thrilled him.

> And Crispin Crispian shall ne'er go by,
> From this day to the ending of the world,
> But we in it shall be remembered,
> We few, we happy few, we band of brothers;
> For he, today that sheds his blood with me
> Shall be my brother; be he ne'er so vile,
> This day shall gentle his condition:
> And gentlemen in England now abed
> Shall think themselves accurs'd they were not here,
> And hold their manhoods cheap while any speaks
> That fought with us upon St. Crispin's day.

   When Tony Gates's critical sire had come up from Boston to watch his boy play Fluellen at a rehearsal and had
taken him and Ronny out for supper, he offered the argument that the play contained Shakespeare's hidden pacifism

and that King Henry's seizing on an abstruse dynastic claim for the French crown had been only the bald excuse for his arrant imperialism.

"But he sincerely believed in his claim," Ronny had protested, almost passionately. "However abstruse later commentators may have deemed it, he was truly convinced that God wanted him to become King of France and that the war was sanctioned from heaven! And anyway, the play contains some of the greatest poetry ever written about man's courage to fight for what he deems right!"

"Let's hope, then, that life will give *you* such a chance, my boy" was Mr. Gates's rather grim answer to this.

"Amen, sir."

Ronny became something of a favorite of the aging headmaster, and Dr. Nickerson actually consulted him from time to time on matters of discipline. On one occasion, Nickerson summoned him to his study to ask him why more boys did not attend holy communion, which, of course, unlike other chapel services, was strictly optional.

"I haven't really heard it discussed, sir," he answered gravely. "But I do know that one boy's mother objected to his drinking from the same cup used by others."

The headmaster shook his great bald head with equal gravity. "But doesn't she know that it's optional to dip the wafer in the cup and consume the wine that way?"

"Perhaps she doesn't think that's quite enough."

"Anyway, I always give the edge of the cup a good strong wipe with the napkin after each use."

Ronny might have pointed out that this might be less than the sterilization required by a worried mother, but respect sealed his lips. And something else. For he knew that the "strong wipe" was only a concession to the weak in faith. Dr. Nickerson had not the slightest doubt that no germ could be transmitted in the celebration of a sacrament. His faith was the rock on which his school and his life had been founded. Whatever doubts might assail so frail a vessel as Ronald Carnochan, it was not his function to shake that rock. And, anyway, it could not be shaken.

Ronny's transition to Yale was even easier than his transition to Chelton. One half of the Chelton graduating class went with him to New Haven; the other half, minus one to Princeton, matriculated at Harvard. But Ronny was at first determined not to be sheltered in a "prep-school crowd"; he dreaded the aridity of social snobbery which he knew infected the Ivy League colleges. Snobbery had existed, it was true, at Chelton: rich boys for poor ones, athletes for the unathletic, even bright students for the stupid, but there had been no "class" distinctions. The millionaire father of one boy might have been the college roommate of another's bankrupt parent, and the mothers of both might have been debutantes together. Yale offered Ronny the opportunity of meeting men from all over the country and from widely varying backgrounds, and in his first two years there he made some successful efforts to extend the circle of his acquaintance, but the prep-school men who dominated his class and who included some of its most attractive members welcomed him so warmly that it was hard indeed to resist their encompassing embrace.

Yet even as late as Tap Day in the spring of his junior year Ronny was not sure that he would accept the bid from Bulldog which it had been strongly hinted that he would receive. He wanted to make *one* gesture of protest against the enveloping mold. It was his roommate, Tony Gates, whose own essential conservatism had received its one and only blow in his having chosen, to irritate a too pushy father, Yale over the ancestral Harvard, who argued him out of it. They had sat up late on the eve of Tap Day discussing their options.

"The whole white Protestant Anglo-Saxon world is going to disappear," Tony observed complacently. "Our rule is over. The gentleman will become as extinct as the dodo. The private clubs and schools, the restricted summer resorts, the stock exchange, even the debutante parties will be taken over by Jews and Catholics and Irish and Latins, to leave not a wrack behind. But, God, are we going to be missed! A world without Scott Fitzgerald or Noël Coward or even Hemingway! A world without Cary Grant! But let us at least go out in a splendid twilight of the gods. Let us show that our Ivy League still has ivy! Let us make it a great year for Bulldog!"

"Really, Tony, you sound too utterly 1918. Wasn't that all said about Rupert Brooke and his sacrificed generation?"

"It is true that the mortal wound was given us in the Somme and the Marne. We can only play the last act with style."

"You're being trivial, my friend. We're not nearly done for. There's plenty of leadership and courage and honesty still in Wall Street. You'll see! Men like my father and his law partners not only still stand for something. They're willing to fight for it!"

Tony's silence might have betrayed a somewhat different view of what his roommate's father stood for. When he spoke, however, it was to use the name of David Carnochan to back his essential point.

"What your father really stands for is Bulldog. He will simply expire if you reject their bid."

And Ronny had reluctantly to admit that this was true. His hands were tied. He went to bed for a sleepless night, and the following afternoon he and Tony stood in the Branford Quadrangle to receive the shoulder taps from Bulldog and run obediently to their room to be initiated.

Furthermore, they both had a happy senior year.

Ronny, however, had been utterly sincere in his stated belief that the world in which he had been raised contained vital elements of public leadership, and he was quick to note that in the rising public feeling against the Nazi rule in Germany the sentiment of his family and their friends and associates was very much ahead of popular opinion in its opposition to the British policy of appeasement. Indeed, he found himself more and more absorbed by the dark drama of what Hitler was bringing to Europe. He read every article he could find on the suppression of human decency in Germany and Italy. But it was not entirely with a dirge in his heart that he read of each new horror, each new violation of the most basic principles of humanity. It seemed to him that matters were bound to come to an issue, and to a global issue at that, and that it would be a glorious thing to fight, even to perish, in the final struggle against the forces of evil. If the kind of society to which he belonged was really doomed, how fine it would be to go down, not in foolish merriment such as his friend Tony had seemed to suggest, but heroically!

Ronny had always felt at ease with his father's first cousin, Gordon Carnochan, whose mind he found congenial and whose gentle character, attractive. It was Cousin Gordon who, visiting New Haven for a Bulldog dinner, had alerted Ronny to the criticism his father was incurring in downtown New York for not giving up certain German corporate clients who importantly supported the Nazi regime.

"Our younger partners are particularly disturbed by it," Gordon told him. "I've spoken to your pa about it, of course, but I can get nowhere with him. He might listen to you."

Ronny did not wait. On the very next day, a Sunday, he took the train for New York, and on Monday he lunched with his father at the Downtown Association. He went straight to the point. His father gave vent to his irritation.

"Gordon's been after you, hasn't he?"

"Daddy, it doesn't matter who's been after me. The point is that I've heard that you continue to represent these evil men. If you don't, please relieve my mind."

"I represent the two firms you have mentioned, yes. That is, I represent them insofar as they have business relations with American companies. I have nothing to do with what they do or don't do abroad or in Germany. I do not regard it as my duty to inquire as to what may be their politics at home. And I can assure you that working on their contracts in New York does not align me in any way with supporting how they may be violating human rights or persecuting Jews in Europe. I mind my own business, my boy, and I advise you to mind yours."

"But what is my business, Dad? And what is yours? Will your ghost, like Marley's, wail, 'Mankind was my business!'?"

"Ronald, I must ask you to change the subject. You are making an ass of yourself, and I can't bear to listen to it."

And indeed Ronny took in the flash of true pain in his father's eyes. It even appalled him.

"I'm sorry, Dad, but I can't talk of anything else. It's too awful to see you put yourself in the same boat with these butchers."

"Ronald!"

"Sorry, Dad, but I can't!"

Ronny rose abruptly, left the table and the club, and returned to New Haven. Two days later he received a telegram from Cousin Gordon informing him that the German clients had been dropped.

His desire to take a military part in the war that broke out in Europe in 1939, while he was in Yale Law School, cooled a bit during the long winter months of 1940 when so little action occurred, but it flared again to a frenzy with the fall of France and the desperate Battle of Britain. He wanted to go to Canada and enlist in the air force, and was restrained only by his father, who, distraught at the notion, finally persuaded him that it was his duty to stay home until he could serve with his own countrymen in a war that was bound to involve the United States. Ronny controlled his impatience and trained for the navy aboard the U.S.S. *Prairie State* in New York, becoming what was called a "ninety-day wonder," an ensign, just before Pearl Harbor.

After two years of convoy duty on a destroyer in the Atlantic, hearing that trained officers were needed for the new amphibious craft, he volunteered for that service and became the skipper of a Landing Ship Tank destined for the invasion of Normandy. The landing in France was followed by months of channel crossings carrying troops and supplies for the fighting front and bringing back the wounded and prisoners of war to England. It was toward the end of this duty that a serious crisis occurred in Ronny's life.

While his vessel, high and dry on the Normandy beach, was receiving prisoners through the open bow doors to its tank deck, he strode down the shore to visit other skippers of landing craft who were standing about smoking, not being needed for the business of loading. He found they were discussing a large band of ragged-looking young men who were being assembled to be marched away from the scene and not transported to Britain. He asked who they were.

"It's the damnedest thing," an officer told him. "Apparently, they're Russians. They were fighting on the Eastern Front and captured by the Huns, stuffed into German uniforms, and sent to France as cannon fodder. They're mostly dumb peasants who've no idea where they are. Some have never heard of France or England. They're young, too, sixteen or seventeen, and some have turned out to be women. But Russia wants them back, and Ike is sending them. Poor bastards, they'll probably all be shot for being in German uniforms. How can you be a good Red after that's happened to you?"

Later Ronny learned that that had indeed been their fate, thousands of them.

In the weeks that followed, on the bridge in the tossing channel, or in the wardroom playing cards, or in his bunk, he could not free his mind from the image of those strange, round-faced, bewildered young men (and some women!) in their ragged, ill-fitting uniforms, huddled before a machine gun and mowed down. He seemed to see their facial expressions as blankly accepting their fate, as if it were no more than what had always been meted out to them from the start of their wretched and unwanted lives. God knew how much he had heard of the slaughter of innocents (who wasn't innocent?) since the start of the war, but somehow his having actually seen this last batch made it permanently real and permanently ghastly to him.

In Portland harbor, on a dark stormy day, when his LST was waiting in a long line for its turn to discharge on the crowded docks, a cargo of wounded American soldiers lying on stretchers on the tank deck, an army doctor pushed his way onto the bridge and shouted at him about the need immediately to disembark patients dying of the pitching and rolling of the vessel. Ronny tried to explain to him that he had to await his turn, that the ships in front of him had their own share of desperately wounded men. The doctor continued his now near-hysterical appeals, until Ronny had to have him forcibly removed from the bridge.

The incident angered him. How could an officer, even if a medical one, be so unreasonable? Had the war not taken its toll on millions? And then, as the image of the Russian peasants surged again in his mind, his heart flamed with wrath against the Soviet regime. For what were the Communists doing but stripping the whole horrible struggle of its only possible excuse, which was the glory of putting down evil in the world? He vowed never to forget or forgive it.

Later he was transferred to the Pacific, to be the executive officer to an LST flotilla commander, then in Ulithi. After the Japanese surrender, the flotilla went briefly to Sasebo Harbor in Japan, bearing troops for the occupation. He and his chief took a day off to drive a jeep to neighboring Nagasaki and view the devastation of that unfortunate city. They started at the crater of the bomb and drove in circles to the outer perimeter of its damage. The god of battles had indeed avenged the rape of Manchuria and China and the treachery of Pearl Harbor, and Ronny, for all the horror of what he saw, could not resist the elation of total victory. It was indeed Saint Crispin's Day. If only it didn't have to be shared with the Reds!

R O N N Y, retracing the principal emotional crises of the two decades that elapsed between the end of World War II and the beginning of the one in Vietnam, had to admit the fact, often, even irritably, pointed out by his all-observing and sometimes critical, though always loving, wife: that the vision of the slaughtered Russian prisoners never altogether deserted him.

"Why," she would want to know, "is that bit of barbarity always so poignant to you? Haven't we lived in a world of unspeakable atrocities?"

"It's because we had those people and *gave* them to the Russians! It stained our victory!"

"But things like that are necessary between allies. We needed the Russians to lick Hitler. We couldn't have done it without them."

Ronny at such moments was reminded that Elly was the daughter of a great trial lawyer. She had been reared to believe that compromise was never to be disdained. "I maintain we could have!" he declared stoutly. "And then America would have been the shining light of the world! After all, we saved civilization twice in my lifetime. And we didn't have to!"

"Pooh. We fought because we were attacked."

"Attacked by evil forces, yes. And we're being attacked again by them. By Communism, all over the world."

"Oh, of course, we're all against Communism," she retorted with a shrug.

"Perhaps not enough."

Ronny himself took as active a part in resisting the spread of Marxism as a busy and successful corporate lawyer could. He took a leading role in the Council on Foreign Relations; he chaired debates on international law; he rejoined the navy and worked in Washington during the Korean conflict; he took a year's leave of absence from his firm to act as assistant counsel to the CIA, and finally, under L.B.J., he accepted a post as special assistant to the Secretary of State in Indochinese affairs. His closest friends, from Chelton, Yale, and the downtown New York law firms, were almost to a man in enthusiastic accord with him; they, too, took time out to perform government functions and were constantly meeting to promote their common cause.

Even the ever-skeptical Elly had to admit that the society into which her husband had introduced her was an amiable and admirable one, however much a privileged background may have formed its greatest common denominator. The men all had good war records and important jobs; their wives were all engaged in serious charitable works; their opinions were attractively liberal and their marriages, most remarkable of all in an era of myriad divorces, were happy. They loved their work and their parties, and though exclusive so far as intimate friendships were concerned, they somehow managed not to be or to seem snobbish. They were content with themselves as a social group, and why not? What more did they need? What did they lack?

Elly thought she might have found the answer to the last question at a cocktail party in Washington in the 1950s while Ronny was with the CIA. The talk revealed the dismay of the group at a report of socializing between Jack Kennedy, much admired by all, and the nefarious Joseph McCarthy.

"But they're both senators," Elly had protested. "Senators always talk to each other. Isn't that what they're for?"

"It may be the Irish in Jack," someone observed. "They call it realism."

"And they're both Catholics," another remarked, but the room booed him. Religion was taboo.

"Do you know something?" Elly exclaimed, as a bright thought struck her. "Do you know the real reason you all hate McCarthy so?"

"Because he's made a travesty of justice!"

"Because he's made bum wad of the Bill of Rights!"

"Because he's the shit of shits!"

"All that, of course," she replied. "But there's something else. Because he's made it seem villainous to be anti-Red. He's so godawful that some decent folk feel they have to be against him in *everything* he stands for. He makes the whole struggle against Marxism seem ridiculous."

"You're not, I trust, darling, implying that it *is*," her husband asked, with some concern in his tone.

"No, but I think it's exaggerated. Yes, I really do,

Ronny. You needn't look at me that way. Is there a single Communist Party member in the House or the Senate? Just tell that to a Frenchman or an Italian and then try to convince him that this country is in any real danger of revolution. The trouble with all of you is that you never knew a Communist in your fancy backgrounds, so you don't know how easily the thing can be dropped. You didn't, as I did, go to public school in Brooklyn during the Depression and before my father made good in the law. Why, half my friends were Red! And none of them are today."

The discussion ended on a more or less friendly note, but the evening was important in Ronny and Elly's married life, as it marked the beginning of a definite rift in their political thinking that steadily widened with the passing years. Elly was a resolute isolationist who believed that one went to war only when directly attacked, but she was determined not to allow foreign affairs to effect a dent in her marriage. She became more and more silent in discussions of foreign policy, and when Ronny undertook his State Department job during the fury of the Vietnam War, and her children rebelled, home life became almost unendurable for her.

"I will not discuss the war with you, Ronny. It's the only way we can live together."

"But, darling, when I live, breathe, and eat it every hour of my day, how can I shut it off?"

"I don't know, but you'll have to try. I'm just about at the end of my rope."

Alone with his whiskey now, he stared balefully into the fire in the grate. Had Elly really gone to New York to be with her mother? Hadn't the last news from the Krantzes been that she was definitely on the mend? Bereft of wife, son, and daughter and beset with doubts over the appalling and seemingly endless continuation of the war, he had the sick feeling that his whole life had been a farce. There had been a mob of young protesters in front of the White House that very morning, howling obscenities about men who were only doing their duty as they had always been taught to do it. Had everything been in vain?

The front doorbell rang, and he jumped up in surprise. A wild hope sprang up in him that it might be Elly unexpectedly returning from New York. But to his shock the figure that greeted him on the threshold was his father.

"I'm just off the train from New York. Can you put me up?"

"Dad! Of course. But what good wind brings you here?"

"Not all that good a one." David Carnochan, now eighty, used a cane as he entered the hall. Ronny grabbed his suitcase. "I'll tell you all, my son. But first let me wash up while you get me a drink."

Seated some minutes later by a relogged fire, David took a long sip of his Scotch-and-soda. "I came down to bring you this news myself. Elly has flown to Denmark to be with your son over Christmas. She knew how upset you'd be at her going without you, and that you would try to stop her, so she wanted me to tell you. I was going to telephone you, but I thought I'd rather come down here and be with you."

Ronny said nothing for a few long moments. "But she'll be coming back?"

"Oh, good Lord, yes. There was no question of her leaving you. You couldn't have thought that, could you?"

"Oh, but I could. She's had a lot to put up with."

Another silence followed this, and then David seemed to have gathered courage to bring up another topic. But it was another sore one.

"Look, Ron. Why don't you quit this thing? Resign your post. You and I have both begun to see this war as a mistake. We were both for it at first, but it's tearing the nation apart. I've always been a realist. There have been times in the past when you thought I was being too much of one, and you may have been right, and I appreciate your having guided me. But now let *me* guide you. It's never too late to change one's mind. And with one's mind, one's position, one's stand."

"But not one's President."

"Unfortunately not."

"Dad, I see your point all too clearly." Ronny had a sudden odd memory of an air raid in London while his ship had been at dock there. A buzz bomb, called a V-1, had hurtled overhead rattling ominously, but while it rattled one was safe. It was when the rattling stopped that one ducked, for that meant it was coming down. And now he visualized it exploding on the very roof of this house in Georgetown, but noiselessly, and his home dissolved to ashes, but harmlessly, leaving him and his father sitting together in a void. "We must not lose the war, Dad. I must not leave my team."

"Ron! You talk as if you were back at Chelton! This isn't a football game."

"Perhaps Chelton is where I belong."

David always knew when he was licked. His only consolation was that a son with an alienated family would be closer to a loving and faithful parent. It was not a bad consolation, either.

11

PIERRE

PIERRE AND RONALD Carnochan were first cousins and contemporaries, both born in 1918, but in looks and character they were strongly contrasted. Ronald, the shorter and slenderer of the two, had some of the appearance of a romantic poet, while Pierre, tall, blond, and rangy, had the easy, slightly supercilious air of an English peer's son at Oxford. Yet most of the time, and except for one bitter quarrel in their last year at Chelton School, they managed to get on fairly well together. Each felt that the other had something that he himself lacked, and however much he might try to depreciate it, he couldn't help suspecting that this missing quality might be just what he should one day most need. The issue between them might be summed up in Talleyrand's principle: *Surtout, point de zèle.* Ronald was full of zeal; Pierre had none. Or if he did, he would have died rather than show it.

Pierre was his mother's darling. Alida Livingston Carnochan thought him the fine flower of her Hudson River heritage, the best type of American colonial aristocrat. She saw him, even as a boy, adequately equipped to handle one day the financial tangles of Wall Street, while at the same time preserving the standards and manners of a more elegant past. In short, she deemed him her equal, if not her superior, in not only resisting but actually repelling the intrusion of modern vulgarity into the citadel of good taste. But in one important respect, which she utterly failed to perceive, her son was very much unlike her. Where she took for granted that the standards in which she had been raised were based on a Christian — and hence to be accepted — order of creation, Pierre had no belief in anything but himself. His sole duty in life, as he conceived it, was to make of Pierre Carnochan a perfect gentleman, not only in poise, appearance, and social grace, but in wealth, power, and social status. When a man had done that, and only then, could he chant his *Nunc Dimittis*.

But Pierre had been born with a shrewdness that made him early aware that a failure to believe that human events were ordered by a higher power was regarded by many in the highest positions as obnoxious and even sinful, and as nothing was to be gained by exciting such hostility, it was better to give a silent or even smiling assent to the fatuous idealism to which, particularly in youth, one was so relentlessly exposed. Besides, it was easy to do. Alida had no idea that the boy who knelt beside her in church on Sundays in Rhinebeck saw the Gospels as only novels, and bad ones at that. It was true that she never gave a thought to her own God outside the church, and even inside He had to compete in her thoughts with her plans for the week, but she never doubted His existence.

There were, of course, moments in his life, however rare, when Pierre felt the need of crying out, like Puck, "What fools these mortals be!," but he knew that life in due course was bound to supply him with fellow cynics, and in the meantime, he could get some relief by baiting his cousin Ron, whose naïve enthusiasms created a china shop that would have aroused the most listless bull. And the great thing about Ron was that, however shocked he might be, he would never give one away.

Chelton School was the subject of their most important falling-out. Pierre had quite taken in, by the time he was seventeen, the glaring dichotomy between the high principles on which the institution was built and the lives of its average graduates. The latter Pierre had had ample opportunity to observe, as they included his father and his uncles. They all professed what could only be called an ardent admiration for the veteran headmaster who had also been theirs, and highly approved the way he united his students in a hearty "school spirit" which made a kind of jumbled sense out of the heavy emphasis on athletics, chapel, and the classic tongues. But Chelton to them was entirely a part of their past and seemed to have had very little effect on their business and social lives. Yet Pierre was quick to see that to have been to Chelton was still an asset in the 1930s, and he was not one to denigrate assets. It was well to do well at Chelton, and besides, it was not difficult.

Pierre was good at sports and enjoyed them. He liked football, though he gave it up, as allowed in his last year, concentrating on crew, where he stroked the school eight. He was popular with the other leaders of his form, as was Ron, but unlike Ron, he was less so with the boys who did not stand out or who did not fit into what was called the "Manhattan crowd," and these gave him the nickname of "Captain O'Haughty." But these were not the fellows whom he expected to see much of when the blissful, long-awaited days of college at last dawned.

And they very much dawned in the late fall of his last school year, when Pierre had already relegated Chelton to the back of his mind and was looking eagerly forward to what he could do with the next step in his life. He carried this to the point where, on a Saturday afternoon, the day of an important football game with a principal rival academy, he did not even bother to watch the play but reclined on the couch of the study that he shared with Ron, reading the latest Galsworthy novel.

When Ron came in at last, wearing the darkest countenance, and flung himself gloomily down in a chair, Pierre looked up from his book with a smile.

"I take it we lost."

"And you didn't even go!" Ron almost shouted. "You've been sitting here on your ass all afternoon while Chelton lost the big game of the year!"

"Why should I give a tinker's damn about the silly match? Really, Ron, you look as if you'd actually been crying."

"I have! And I'm not ashamed of it! It's better than being a snot bag like you!"

"You don't think it's time you grew up? just a little, anyway?"

"Grow up! Is that all you care about Chelton?"

"Look, Ron. We'll be out of here for good, come spring. You ought to be thinking about Yale and what you'll be crying about there. If you're still crying, which I devoutly hope you won't be."

"You think they don't care about football at Yale and who wins a game? Well, ask your old man. Uncle Sam is one of the greatest boola-boolas of all!"

"I concede that about Dad. In fact, I concede it about all the Carnochans. Maybe that's just what's wrong with Yale. I'm thinking myself of applying for Harvard. Uncle Timmy Van Rensselaer says that no Eli is ever quite a gentleman."

"Who the hell is Uncle Timmy? And who cares what an old snob like that thinks!"

"Uncle Timmy is on my mother's side of the family, no kin to you," retorted Pierre, with a semicomic affectation of loftiness. "He married Mummy's sister. A Van Rensselaer wed to a Livingston. Makes your mouth water, doesn't it?"

"I seem to find it still dry. You're not serious, though, Pierre, about going to Harvard? You wouldn't break with a family tradition just to please some stuffy old relative of your ma's?"

"No, but to become a gentleman I might."

"I don't know what's happened to you, Pierre. But I know I don't even want to go on sharing this study with you!"

Which resolve Ron actually proceeded to implement, finding a classmate who was glad to change his own study mate for the more amusing Pierre. But Pierre saw that he had let things go too far, and he took pains to make things up with his cousin, which the latter's open and generous nature soon made possible.

As Pierre carried out his plan to go to Harvard, and as Ron, like his forebears, matriculated at Yale, the cousins saw less of each other in the next four years. Pierre's father, Sam, always a stout Eli, had objected at first to his son's rejection of his alma mater, but his wife's firm endorsement of the decision had weakened his opposition, and when Pierre was elected to the Porcellian Club, deemed by many of Sam's downtown circle to be the *ne plus ultra* of college societies, all was forgiven, even Uncle Timmy's muttered remark that one Carnochan had at last "made the grade."

Pierre at Harvard considered that he had finally come into his own. He dressed well, dined well, and cultivated those whom he considered the leaders of his class — mostly members of fashionable families in Boston, New York, and Philadelphia. His weekends were rarely spent in Cambridge: there were debutante balls in the cities mentioned, rural house parties, and even fox hunts. He was careful, however, to achieve respectable grades in all his courses — a gentleman should not, of course, be a "greasy grind," but on the other hand, he must never fail in anything he undertook. Hard work could be properly postponed until one had adopted one's life career, and then it was fully countenanced. Pierre was under no illusion that the material success on which he counted could be attained without labor and dedication.

For a time he had debated entering Harvard Law School, whither Ron was bound, and the cousins discussed this during a Christmas vacation in New York. Ron pointed out that there would undoubtedly be a good opening for both in his father's law firm. Far from seeing a hurdle in nepotism, David Carnochan, in the still-accepted European fashion, believed in the kind of solidarity that a united family could give to a continuing organization.

"Yes, but isn't the question whether you'd rather be the client than the client's counsel?" Pierre wanted to know. "Of course, I know that argument doesn't always fit the bill. I'd rather, for example, be the patient than his dentist. On the other hand, I'd rather be the undertaker than the corpse. But take a gander at your father's principal clients. Aren't they all a dozen times richer than he?"

"Oh, at least. They head big companies. But they haven't the joy and interest of a learned profession."

"They have the joy, anyway, of being rich and famous."

"Oh, Pierre, be serious."

"I've never been more so. You'll be nodding yourself to sleep over some old casebook while I'll be strutting up and down my private art gallery, admiring my fake Rembrandts and genuine Picassos, or whatever junk I happen to want to buy."

Pierre opted to go into his father's small but very successful investment banking firm, determined to learn everything he could about the stock market. He combined long days of hard work with evenings at parties, some dull and some almost brilliant, yet always apt to be written up in the social columns of the evening papers, where his name made a frequent appearance. But he saw the war coming in Europe, and he studied how to make the best of what was bound to be an interruption of his career.

That he would have to be an officer was obvious, and it was equally clear that combat would make a more dashing entry in his record than desk or headquarters service, so he chose the navy, partly because sea spray was more picturesque than mud and partly because most of his Porcellian pals had elected it, too. Shortly before Pearl Harbor he had received his training and his commission as an ensign, and when war broke out he did not hesitate to induce his father to use such pull as he had in Washington to get him assigned to a destroyer. The image of himself on the bridge of so sleek a warship attracted him, and it was an image not difficult to make real.

He served on the U.S.S. *Barclay* for three years, on convoy duty in the Atlantic, and in two atoll landings in the Pacific. He performed his tasks efficiently, as assistant gunnery officer, then gunnery officer, and ultimately as first lieutenant, was liked by the men, and became something of a favorite of the captain. Some of the junior officers, particularly those from small towns and lesser-known colleges, found him a bit standoffish, but nobody disliked him, even though his ardent cultivation of senior army brass and naval braid at officers' clubs was noted and commented on. In the last year of the war, at such a club in Pearl Harbor, he ran into Ron, now skipper of an LST, and they sat at the bar together.

"Just like you to end up in the amphibious navy," Pierre remarked with family candor. "How did it happen? Couldn't your dad have done something? Oh, no, of course, your conscience wouldn't allow you to use anything like pull, would it?"

"Pierre, I volunteered for amphibious."

"Why, in God's name? Didn't you know the regular navy regards it as second class? Or even third? I'm surprised they even let you use this club."

"They probably wouldn't if they didn't have to," Ron replied with a grin. "Our flotilla commander is USN, and he's supposed to have been assigned to us as punishment for some gaffe he made in the Pentagon. But I heard they needed officers with sea experience, so I thought I'd give it a whirl. You may call us sea trucks, but it seems sea trucks are needed to win the war."

"And we'll probably both be blown up anyway, invading Japan," Pierre conceded, to finish the argument. "But if we survive, what'll you do? Finish law school?"

"Oh, yes. And you? Back to the money mine? Will that sort of thing go on as before, do you think?"

"Even more so! The war may have bust the world, but it will have made America rich. And I plan to share the wealth." Here he allowed himself a wink. "Even if I have to marry it."

Ron ignored the qualification as typical Pierre. "Speaking of marriage, do you realize that more than half our Chelton classmates are already wed? The war at least has speeded that up."

Pierre shrugged. "Let us not be in a hurry, my friend. Let our friends plunge into wedlock as they choose. Half of them will live to regret it. A good marriage takes time and patience and careful observation, and I intend to have a very good marriage indeed. A wife can be a great asset, or a great liability. My bride shall be beautiful, or at least very handsome, with the kind of looks, anyway, that people notice and admire. She shall be poised, gracious, and cultivated. Not a *bas bleu*, mind you, but well-read and up-to-date on things. She shall be every inch a lady, if not by birth, at least by training. She will conform to the decorative tolerance of the highest society, where prejudice against color, religion, or sexual preference is deemed small-town or middle-class. She need not be an heiress, but I rather assume that she will come of a background that will supply her with at least a competent dowry."

"You describe a paragon."

"She shall be a paragon."

THE ATOM BOMB aborted the invasion about which Pierre had been so dark and accelerated the future about which he had been so hopeful, and he found himself back on Wall Street and happily at work in his father's firm, of which he was now promoted to partnership. He made a fortunate choice when he induced his parent to make a substantial investment in a new company that produced novel and imaginative children's toys (and one, incidentally, run by a young ex-army colonel he had met at an officers' club in Leyte), and now a millionaire in his early thirties, he was heralded in the press as one of the most eligible bachelors in town.

His cousin Ron was also on the rise, a promising associate in his father's law firm, a position solidified — if such were needed — by his marriage to the daughter of the number two partner. At one of their biweekly lunches, he reminded Pierre of the peerless bride whose existence he had predicted at that officers' club in Pearl Harbor.

"I think I can assure you that you won't have to wait much longer," Pierre informed him, with a superior and confident smile. "And what may surprise you is that you already know her."

And know her Ron certainly did, though not well, as she was more than a decade younger than the two cousins. Isabel Grantley was a stepcousin of theirs, being the daughter by her first husband of Letitia Carnochan, widow of Benson Carnochan, cousin of Sam and David, and son of the late Bruce and the still-living Ada, the oil heiress. And as Benson had left no children of his own, and his mother regarded her stepgranddaughter with a favorable eye, Isabel might find herself one day possessed of more than the "competent dowry" that Pierre had once taken for granted in his envisioned consort.

Isabel had dazzled the world as a much-publicized debutante, with her large, mysteriously smiling dark eyes, her smooth pale skin, and her raven black hair. Her dress was impeccably expensive, her motion graceful and flowing, and she radiated a mild, oddly shy friendliness. Her smiles went everywhere, like those of Browning's last duchess, the envious commented, and she was bound to arouse envy, particularly, of course, among those of her own sex. These would also point out that, though she had the undoubted gift of making a striking opening remark, she could never seem to follow it up. But who cared? Her silence was charming.

To Pierre, anyway, she seemed the epitome of all he had been looking for. And the bluebird, as Maeterlinck had predicted in his play, had been found at home, in a Carnochan nest! Early in their relationship, though after it had graduated from cousinly chats at family gatherings to dating, but still prior to the birth of sentiment, Pierre had introduced her to a playful conversational game in which they discussed what they would do if they were married.

"I believe in disciplining children," he told her once with mock severity. "Sternness tempered with love. Never threaten a punishment which you fail to impose if the occa-

sion calls for it. And never allow children to pass the hors
d'oeuvres at a cocktail party, shoving plates every minute at
the poor guests and expecting to be cajoled. And never talk
about your children when you go out. Only bores do that."

"I was never allowed to attend one of Mother's parties,
much less pass anything," Isabel responded, with a definite
wistfulness.

"Do you know something, Isabel? I don't think your
mother really likes children. More mothers don't than you
might suspect."

"Oh, I can suspect it."

"Of course, I didn't mean to imply that your mother
doesn't like *you*. Don't misunderstand me."

"I don't think I do."

"Everyone likes you, naturally. How can they help it?"

"Well, they seem to."

"Certainly, Aunt Ada does. She raves about you."

"Oh, Granny's all right."

The girl had certainly her baffling side. She seemed
perfectly content to go out with him, but it was as if she
somehow felt that the family connection guarded her from
any alteration of the tempo of their relationship and as if
she derived a certain comfort from this security. Nor did
she go out, so far as he could make out, with other men, despite every opportunity, with the exception of a few old
boy friends whom she had known from childhood and with
whom she seemed to enjoy a joking and apparently sexless
congeniality. He had a curious sense that neither the future
nor the past had much meaning to her; she could only just
cope with the present.

What he had not known and was only gradually beginning to suspect was that Isabel had grown up without parental love. Her father, an amiable and irresponsible alcoholic,

married for such money as she had mistakenly thought he had by the icy Letitia, had been early shed and disappeared to the Orient. Her mother had finally found the money and security she craved in her marriage to the bland and dull Benson Carnochan, who was too stubborn to be dominated by her and too inwardly directed to be more than numbly conscious of her bad temper, and the match had more or less worked out, each learning to leave the other alone as much as possible.

A handsome woman herself, Letitia had been gratified by Isabel's beauty, and had used her excellent taste to see that her daughter was well turned out and put forward, but she had little heart and saw Isabel as she saw the interiors of her houses, as something to be "done up." She didn't even try to conceal her disappointment that Isabel lacked her own biting intelligence and constantly threw her impatience at what she regarded as the poor girl's stupidity in her face. She saw that marriage was the only way to dispose of her and deplored Isabel's lack of interest in beaux. Finally, she decided that what struck her as Pierre's "God-given" interest in her was what might save the day.

"For heaven's sake, can't you perk up a bit when you go out with him?" she cautioned Isabel. "Anyone can see that you have him hooked, though God knows why. A girl with your looks doesn't have to do much, but she has to do *something*."

"But I'm not sure I even want to get married."

"I'd like to know what else you think you can do with yourself."

"Maybe I can get a job or something. Lots of girls do."

"Lots of girls are trained for something. What are you trained for? You can't even count your trumps in a bridge game."

"Oh, Mummy, please! You're hurting my feelings."

"It's for your own good, my girl. I know what I'm doing. Didn't I marry a Carnochan myself? It wasn't a bad solution, even with Benson, and with Pierre it could possibly be brilliant. And if you don't mess things up with my old bitch of a mother-in-law, she may do handsomely by you. I know men like Pierre. They may be hard to live with if they don't get what they want, but they're fine enough husbands when they do. And he will get you, if you'll only play your cards right. You and he can go to the top of the world together. My God, when I think what I could have done with your opportunities! I guess it's true that God sends manna to those who have no teeth."

"But, Mummy, suppose I don't want to go to the top of the world!"

Letitia sighed deeply. "Then you're a fool."

The only person in the family whom Isabel could talk to heart to heart was her stepfather's mother, Ada Carnochan. This small, plain, dignified, and outspoken old lady, who despite her kindness would put up with no nonsense and was inclined to sniff at the oily manners excited by her large fortune, had early sensed that Isabel used her beauty to shield herself from people's discovering what she feared was her lack of other assets. To cope with her stepgranddaughter's problem, she spent more time with the girl than with her actual grandchildren, who, however affectionate, needed her less. Isabel, indeed, had become her favorite.

"But how do you yourself really feel about Pierre?" she wanted to know, when Isabel told her of her mother's bludgeoning. "Do you love him? Or could you love him? If we're going to talk about this at all, we may as well get down to basics."

"Well, he's nice to be with, you know. Really very nice. He's so smart and funny."

"Oh, I know that, of course. He rather makes up to his old great-aunt. He may put it on a bit, but I like it. He has charm. We can start by admitting that."

"And he has interesting ideas. Not like other people's at all. And I think he's kind. At least he seems so."

"My dear, I asked you about love."

"Well, I think maybe I could love him if he loved me."

"And he doesn't?"

"No. Though I think he'd like to."

"Because he thinks you'd make him a good wife? And wouldn't you?"

"But not a useful one, Gran. That's what worries me. I have this impression that he's looking for a wife who'll be so-cially useful to him. I don't mean moneywise. He's very well off himself."

"Humph. That doesn't mean he doesn't want more. These men! Don't tell me. But I'm far from viewing a mer-cenary motive as prohibitive, unless it's the only one. I was married in part for my fortune, and I always knew it. But un-like you, my dear, I was small and plain, and in the worldly society in which I grew up, I soon learned that money was my chief magnet. The thing to do was to pick the right man among the swains looking for it. And Bruce Carnochan was just that. He proved an admirable husband and father. But I agree with you that Pierre is not primarily interested in money. To begin with, he's very knowledgeable and is quite aware, I'm sure, that what you will have depends largely on myself and that I have a considerable progeny to share my estate. And second, as you say, he's a big earner himself. Pierre, my dear, is a better man than many consider him. He puts people off with his airs. But he has brains and character.

He's what they call a catch. That doesn't mean for a minute that you ought to marry him. But it's something you ought to think about. A life with Pierre could be an interesting life."

"And now it's my turn, Gran, to ask *you* about love."

"Not all men are capable of great love. And those who are, are often prone to feel it for more than one woman in their lives. I suspect that the temperature of Pierre's heart is nearer cool than boiling. But that's not always a bad thing in a husband."

"Oh, Gran, that sounds so cynical!"

"I'm a realist, child. Or try to be. I've seen a lot of things in a long life, and Pierre is not a man to be underestimated. I know what some of the family think of him. That he's worldly and snobbish. That's so like a family. They skip over the fact that he was a wonderful son to his father and is still one to his mother, that he was a brave and competent officer in war, and that he's successful downtown. Furthermore, he's never been known, to my knowledge, anyway, to have been mean or malicious. So what do they have against him? Simply that he allows people to know that he thinks well of himself and that he wants to get on in the world."

"Gran, you're telling me that I should marry him!"

"I am not! I'm telling you that he'd make a good husband. Whatever he does, he'll do well."

"But would I be the wife he needs?"

"You can leave that decision to him. But, anyway, why shouldn't you be?"

"Because I'm stupid about so many things. Mother says I can't even count trumps."

"That's only because you don't like bridge. If you ever got to like it — and there's no reason you should — you'd count them soon enough."

"But I'm so slow!"

"My dear, you're quite capable of doing anything you really set your mind on."

"Oh, do you really think that?"

"I do. And if you think you *could* be in love with Pierre, doesn't that mean you are? A little bit, anyway?"

LETITIA CARNOCHAN saw to it that her daughter's wedding was a principal event of the social season. And when the bride and groom returned from a honeymoon in Barbados, where a beautiful Palladian villa had been lent them by a client of Pierre's, they moved into a charming little Park Avenue duplex, which the bride's mother had tastefully decorated. It seemed to everyone that the lucky couple had a life opening before them as elegant as an issue of *Vogue* or *Town and Country*.

Nor was it all outwardly seeming. Isabel, even in her moments of greatest apprehension, had to admit to herself that she had married a man of imaginative goodwill and kindness. He was always supportive, never impatient. When he instructed her in the details of how to manage a dinner party for a difficult client or what not to mention to a sensitive weekend hostess, he was never bossy or overdetailed and always appreciative of her efforts. But the instruction was there; that was the rub. She was not only a spouse; she was a pupil. She was being fitted, she could only surmise, for her role as a partner in what to him was evidently a noble enterprise. It was true that he was always careful not to overdo it. After one of their entertainments he would always congratulate her on how well she had done things, and only after that would he drop a gentle hint on how she should always check the guest list in advance to be sure of the names and how she could tactfully change a subject if it was arousing an argument too violent. Yet these gentle hints always suggested to her that she had failed him in one or another respect.

For some months their satisfactory lovemaking at night made her hope that at least she was not failing him in this very basic aspect of marriage, but eventually her gratification at her success in bed paled before the realization that any attractive woman could have given him that. Was she improving herself in the arts of social life, where his needs could only be supplied by a wife? Alas, she was increasingly convinced that she was not. She was getting worse, not better, at remembering names, and at table now she would sometimes sit in utter silence, unable to conjure up a word to say to the embarrassed and soon bored gentlemen on either side of her. And with her fear of further failure she became worse.

In time she began to excuse herself from dining out with the invention of a migraine. The third time this happened, Pierre insisted on staying home with her. He was all solicitude. She begged him desperately to leave her and go to his party, but he refused. Then she actually heard herself tell him that she might be pregnant. This, of course, would excuse everything. Pierre was elated.

"Darling, why didn't you tell me before? At the very first hint of it? Of course, we won't go out at all now until you are feeling absolutely fit."

"Oh, but you must!" she protested in dismay. "I'll be perfectly all right alone in bed with a book. You can't just isolate yourself because of me!"

"But I'll be glad to! And I'll read to you. Anything you like. Even one of your detective stories. After all, it'll only be till you give birth to a bouncing boy."

"Boy?"

"Our second will be a girl."

To her surprise, and almost as if some hidden fate was determined to spare her a lie, she discovered that she *was* pregnant. She was briefly delighted. Here at last was something she *could* do for him, and something that would fit in perfectly with all his plans for the future. And besides, it would give her a blessed intermission in the long and tedious drama of her social life; she could stay at home, in bed or on a couch, reading mysteries, as much as she liked. She shamelessly exaggerated the discomforts of her condition and treated herself to the isolation of what she fantasized as a luxurious Oriental harem maintained for the benefit of a single inhabitant. Pierre was constantly attentive and spent many of his evenings reading aloud to her from Jane Austen or the Brontës. She was content, but of course she always knew it couldn't last.

It ended abruptly and painfully with a dangerous miscarriage, and her doctor recommended that she should put off starting another pregnancy for at least a year, and possibly two. For some weeks she was plunged into a deep depression, and it was not until she began to show signs of emerging from this dark period that Pierre urged her to take the first steps toward picking up the old strings of her life. And one of these, of course, was going out to dinner parties.

Little by little they resumed the old pattern of their existence. But there was a difference now. Isabel had discovered the anaesthetic of alcohol. A swig of gin before Pierre came home, from the tiny Burgundian chapel of a bar that her mother had designed off the living room, fortified her if they had to go out, and the swig soon became two.

It did not take Pierre long to perceive what was going on. He had already unsuccessfully tried to free her from smoking; now he undertook to tackle her drinking. He never reproached her, never scolded her, never even asked her if she had been imbibing. He would simply gravely warn her.

"Smoking, my dear, may kill you, but drinking is worse. It can ruin your life."

She swore to him that she would give it up, and would do so for a time, but she always returned to it, and when he removed the bottles from the little bar, telling her, of course, just what he was doing, she bought her supplies on the sly and hid them about her room, though she knew he never searched it. Of course, she did not fool him, and he insisted finally that she consult a psychiatrist, for he seemed to shudder at the publicity of Alcoholics Anonymous. Isabel went dutifully to this new doctor and undutifully shunned his advice. Her fuzzy condition at dinner parties was now widely noticed, and at first she tried to persuade herself that people thought each occurrence was a rare rather than a habitual thing, but it was soon evident even to her that their friends had classed her as a "case." Pierre mostly refrained from comment. At a social gathering, when he detected across the room (for he always had an eye on her) that she was beginning to look hazy, he would rise, get her coat, and approach her with a quiet: "Darling, I think you're looking tired. It's time we went home." And at home he would help her undress and put her to bed without a word. It agonized her to think that people were praising him as the perfect gentleman in dealing with a "sousy spouse." Was he even putting it on, she thought once with a stab of terror, to salvage what little gain he could from a lost cause?

The end, or what she hoped might be the end, came at a glittering dinner party given by old Mrs. Townsend Martin to bid farewell to her Gothic mansion on Fifth Avenue, now to be replaced by an apartment house in which a part of her

EAST SIDE STORY

purchase price would be the penthouse. At the long dining-room table, with its glittering gold service and centerpiece of Neptune on a craft driven by dolphins, before the splendid tapestry of Louis XV at a hunt, Isabel, who had been feeling unusually queasy, leaned suddenly forward and vomited all over the place in front of her.

The next morning she stole out of her apartment while Pierre was still asleep and went to her stepgrandmother's. Ada, who had already heard of the disaster from Mrs. Martin herself, took her in without a word and put her to bed. She sent a note to Pierre immediately by her butler, stating briefly: "She's here safe and sound. You'd best leave her to me for a day or so."

The following day, Isabel sent her husband a letter offering him a divorce without alimony and volunteering to go herself to Reno to obtain a decree on neutral grounds without legal cost to him. "The least I can do for you," she ended, "is to put you back as nearly as possible to the happy state you were in before I wrecked your life."

She could hardly refuse to see him when he called, only an hour after receiving her letter. He was grave, almost solemn. He stated his proposition briefly and very clearly, asked her please to give it her closest attention, raised a hand to indicate that he wanted no immediate answer, and took his departure.

What he proposed was that she should return to him and resume their wedded life as if nothing had happened, except that they would both give up alcohol permanently, and also give up all social life, barring family gatherings and meals with intimate friends, until such time, if ever, when she felt ready and willing to greet the world with pleasure. He even ended on a lighter note, saying that they would turn the Burgundian bar into a powder room. She burst into tears as he closed the door behind him.

210

"Think of it, Gran!" she exclaimed to Ada afterward. "Think of his behaving so kindly after seeing what he had hoped would be the perfect wife make that unspeakable mess at the dinner table."

"It can't have been pleasant for him. But it gave him the chance to be what he has always wanted to be: the perfect gentleman."

"But that sounds so artificial!"

"It doesn't have to be. When I say gentleman, I'm using the term in its best and truest old-fashioned sense. That's what so many of the family haven't the sense to see about Pierre. But I have, God bless me. He's an idealist. And he knows that looking and acting like something you want to be may help you to become it. Theodore Roosevelt, whom so many young people tend to deride today, used to say that by pretending to be brave, you could cast out fear. I think you married a good man, Isabel."

"But if he wants me back just to be good, is that enough?"

"Enough for whom?"

"For *me!*"

"I see." Ada nodded ruefully. "Like so many sillies you want love. Or some big red smothering thing you call love. Has it never occurred to you that this may be Pierre's way of loving?"

"And you think I should make do with it?"

"I think you should certainly try. And if you try, you'll very likely succeed. As the old hymn says: 'Only God's free gifts abuse not, light refuse not.' "

Ada wisely declined to say more. She was sure that she had won her little battle. And she knew something else, but that was something she was most certainly not going to say. She knew that the brilliant Pierre had chosen just the right way to create the "perfect wife" at last.

12

LOULOU

Louisa, "loulou," Carnochan had more than ample time, since her retirement as a trained nurse in 1955, to contemplate the early steps she had taken in the initial mismanagement of her life. Of course, the real fault, or at least so she liked to tell herself, had been in the date of her birth. She should have been a doctor; that would have made all the difference. Some girls, like herself born in 1890, had indeed become that, but very few, and none at all in the walk of life in which she had been raised. It was a shocking fact, in view of the general enlightenment that had come later, that after her coming-out party, neither she nor her family had even considered her going to college. It had been taken quite for granted by all that marriage would be her career unless she elected to stay at home and ease the long exit from life of aging and seemingly immortal parents.

Yet the hand that had been dealt her, as such hands went, had not been a bad one. In looks, it was true, she was a bit on the diminutive and plain side, unlike her older sister, Betty, who was the "beauty" of the family, though this was something of a relative term, but she had bright eyes, high spirits, and a modicum of wit, and was considered a "sport" by her contemporaries. Unfortunately, however, she tended to accept the unspoken but obviously felt verdict of her so dignified parents and sister that if she was a dear little thing she was also something of a social liability. Her brother didn't share this opinion, but Gordon as a boy didn't count, and Loulou shielded herself in the role of the tomboy, the clown, the family jester, someone to be coddled, even loved, but not basically an integral part of serious living. Not anyway a girl whom, when they grew up, the boys who now genially played with her would marry. No, they would marry sticks like Betty.

Loulou, however, was to know what love was, and at its most cruel. The tennis pro at the Bar Harbor Swimming Club, Harvey Glenn, was a sturdy brown god of a youth, and Loulou took as many lessons from him as her mother would allow, which was not many after Julie had caught on to the real reason for her younger daughter's sudden interest in the sport. Many other girls at the club had noisy crushes on the handsome Harvey, but Loulou's worship was cultivated in absolute silence. She knew it was futile, and she knew, too, for her eyes were sharp, that Harvey had a low nature and was hunting for an heiress, and indeed, he eloped with one, but not to any avail, for the heiress's father was one of the few parents on Mount Desert Island who really meant it when he said he would disinherit any child of his who married against his wishes. Loulou would have been happy to console her tennis pro when he coolly ditched the bride he had impoverished, but needless to say, there was no job for him now at the club, and he disappeared from her life forever.

Elwood Atkins had presented a more practical problem for her. He wanted to marry her and actually proposed. He was a bit on the stout side, dull and honest as the day was long, but that day was very long indeed, and he had a solid job in a small automobile company, where he was the right-hand man of an eccentric executive who was rumored to be something of a mechanical genius. Loulou's family and friends tended to look somewhat down on the socially awkward Elwood, despite his gentle and kindly manners and upright character; only her brother, Gordon, insisted that there was more to him "than meets the eye."

Loulou liked Elwood; she liked him very much, but she did not love him and doubted that she ever could. But he was persistent, and time was passing, and it was evident to her that her parents were of the opinion that this was very likely the best she could ever do. Eventually they became engaged, but secretly, at least outside the family, and on a tentative basis — she could withdraw anytime she felt the least doubt. Loulou, however, began to be tortured by the idea that she might be doing *him* a wrong. Did she feel for him, for example, anything like what she had felt for the tennis pro? No!

She told her mother: "I'm going to write Elwood and break our engagement."

"Well, don't use the best notepaper" was Julie's dry rejoinder. She knew how often that letter would be rewritten.

Loulou was angered. She wrote the letter only once and mailed it herself before she could change her mind. Elwood left the island and neither returned nor replied. He took her decision as final and six months later married another girl. Evidently he had been determined that the time had come — if, indeed, it was not overdue — for wedlock. Loulou was bitterly disappointed, but she knew she had no one but herself to blame. She began to realize that she might have learned to love him.

Of course, he later made a fortune in automobiles.

Loulou assumed that another lover would come into her life, and indeed one might have, had she not so violently regretted the one she had lost. His business success, following so rapidly upon the act of marriage that he had apparently counted to get him really started, seemed to fling in her face the deserved consequences of a folly that proved her to be a born old maid. At any rate, she found herself more and more resigned to sharing the regular and mind-numbing brownstone existence of her aging parents, reading at night, working in the daytime with the very young and the very senile at a settlement house, and occasionally on weekends visting at the houses of her fewer and fewer unmarried woman friends.

And then one evening as she was reading Anatole France's wonderful story "The Procurator of Judea," she came upon these words: "It was amid such peaceful occupations and meditations on Epicurus that, with surprise and a faint chagrin, he met the advent of old age." Of course, with her it was not senescence; it was worse — it was middle age. She was in her thirties, early thirties, it was true, but still . . . what could she do to give her life some shred of meaning? A friend in the management of her settlement house had spoken of the city's urgent need of more trained nurses, and the idea lit a sudden fire in her head. She talked to her brother, Gordon, her only true intimate in the family, and he gave her instant and enthusiastic encouragement. He looked into the possibility of her enrolling in the Bellevue Training School and brought her the needed forms to fill out.

Of course, there was initial opposition. Her mother took the position that a "lady" could never be a nurse and that it had taken a major war to make Florence Nightingale reacceptable to the good society into which she had been born. But the younger members of the family thought it very sporting of Loulou, whose warm and cheerful personality had made her a popular figure, to strike for her own thing, and Julie Carnochan was induced at last to withdraw her veto, practical woman as she always was, insisting only that Loulou should confine herself to hospital work and never serve in a patient's home, where she might find herself treated as a kind of upper servant.

Loulou did not find it always easy to train with much younger women, most of whom came from very different backgrounds, but she had brains and determination, and she achieved not only high grades but the ultimate admiration of classmates who were impressed that a woman of her age and class should undertake so many humble and often distasteful tasks. And in the two decades that followed, she rose to be a head floor nurse in the private patients' wing of a famous New York hospital. Even the older Carnochans were now actually proud of her and cited her as an example of the contrary if some young radical son of a friend was so brash and bold as to suggest that the family belonged to a bypassed society that had not kept up with the times.

Loulou's career as a nurse was cut short at sixty-five, when she developed cancer and had half a lung removed. She decided to retire while recovering from the operation in a private room on her own floor of the hospital, where, needless to say, she was receiving the best of care. But an incident with a new young intern who did not know who she was or her connection with the hospital put her on notice of how much her old background still clung to the modernized professional woman.

The intern had asked her, as part of a routine questionnaire, if she had ever given birth. She pointed to the name on her door, which was slanted inward.

"If you'll look at that card, Doctor, you'll see it reads *Miss* Carnochan."

The young man glanced at the card, shrugged, and repeated his question.

Loulou felt immediately a fool at her old-fashioned assumption that virginity had to be assumed in an unwed lady and answered his question in the negative. But it weighed on her mind that even two decades of medical service had not made more of a dent in the Carnochan way of viewing the world. And when she left the hospital and took up her life as an unoccupied lady of small means, she began to wonder if it had been anything but a disadvantage to have been born and raised as she had been.

The principal fact in her new life was that she was poor. The term, of course, was relative, but it was certainly applicable to her — indeed dramatically applicable — in contrast to her siblings and cousins. Her father had been nearly ruined in the Great Depression, and his situation had not been ameliorated by his wife's refusal to recognize it, with the result that Loulou's one third of his estate enabled her to maintain only a two-room flat in a respectable East Side Manhattan apartment house and escape the hottest part of the summer only in a modest seaside hotel in Maine. The difference of her daily life, deprived now of the busy work of the hospital, from that of her sister, Betty, who had married a man of considerable means, and that of her brother who was a successful lawyer, was only too painfully evident. Gordon, it was true, helped her out from time to time with welcome checks, but she still found it in her heart to criticize a family that had raised her in such luxury only to leave her in such poor straits.

She had nonetheless found a kind of occupation in her jobless days in putting together the history of her family, at least of its American chapters, which were all that were known of it, and speculating on what motivated, or failed to motivate, each generation of the Carnochans. She noted one particular characteristic that seemed to attach itself to most of the members, and perhaps to account for why so large a percentage of them succeeded either in retaining the social status to which they were born or in improving it. The males, and there was an unusual predominance of them, were all able either to make money or to marry it. There were none of the social dropouts or exiled remittance men that plagued so many families listed in the Social Register. The family instinct for survival was strong indeed. On the other hand, its contribution to the arts, to politics, to teaching, to any occupation that involved giving out rather than taking in, was minimal. If there were no criminals, neither were there any saints. The Carnochans seemed dedicated to their own permanence.

And why had Loulou ended up as she had? Because she had neither made money nor married. She might have done more, in her own small way, for people who had needed such services as she had been able to provide, than any other member of the family, but what did that avail her now? Resentment followed by curiosity began to turn her study of the clan into a kind of obsession. She started to fill albums with photographs and press cuttings, yellowing invitations and pages of old letters; she wrote to all her cousins asking for dates of births, deaths, marriages, and divorces, and she undertook to compile a book of the family tree, which Gordon promised to have printed. The family was becoming the occupation of her life.

She discovered, however, that she now had a value to her aging siblings and aging cousins quite other than that of historian. It was not, however, particularly gratifying to her. She found herself frequently invited to spend weekends or even weeks with relatives who in the past had found bids to dinner over Christmas or Easter a sufficient recognition of the connection. Of course, it was her nurse's training that elicited these bids. How comforting it was to have staying in one's house, and at no expense except for her meals, a competent medical practitioner whom one could consult at one's ease about one's back or hip or throat or heart, or whatever organ or limb the evening of life was eroding!

Worst of all was her sister, Betty, who considered Loulou only too well compensated by her presence in the big breezy villa on Long Island Sound, not only for her temperature takings and back rubbing, but for her secretarial assistance with bills and correspondence.

Though handsome enough as a young woman, Betty had broadened with the years, and her limited imagination and unlimited ego, plus her confirmed status as a *malade imaginaire*, had rendered her not only less easy to look at but less easy to live with. Yet Lionel Harrison still saw her as the "marble beauty" with whom he had fallen in love decades before, and her children, taken in by the claims of her self-esteem and shamed by her unjustified complaints of family neglect, hovered around her with constantly proffered love and sympathy. Loulou could never forget how, on a family trip to Europe in their younger days, the prurient Betty had flung her copy of *Anna Karenina* over the side of the ocean liner, outraged by its vision of adultery. There had been, however, no violation of the marriage vow in her own union. Life had filled Betty's lap with treasures: her husband's ample means as well as his blind devotion, healthy and obedient children, and doctors who catered to her every whim. Yet she persisted in believing that she had kept her head up under an avalanche of misfortune.

Loulou had been invited to Long Island for the Christmas season and had been asked to help with her sister's Yuletide greeting cards. Betty, in the grip of one of her periodic and pointless fits of economy, had decided that by using the

cards sent to her the previous year, cutting off the front flap
with the picture and scribbling her name and greeting on its
verso, she could save herself the trouble and expense of ac-
quiring new cards. She was even fatuous enough to assume
that such friends as might thus receive back their own muti-
lated card would appreciate so wise a saving.

Loulou at last drew the line. She threw down her pen.
"No, Betty, I'm not going to write another one for you. You
can't send this trash to the family. It's a disgrace."

"But we're saving our national forests!" Betty declared
grandly. "Recycling Christmas cards! Isn't that the kind of
thing you're always advocating? Take Lionel's office, for example. It has a hundred employees. If each one sends a card
to the other ninety-nine, that's ten thousand cards! To and
from people who see each other daily!"

"It's madness, I grant. But why not give it up altogether?"

"Oh, I couldn't do that. Everyone sends them. It's an
expected thing."

"Well, it's not expected to do it the way you do. I shan't
address another envelope."

"And of course I wouldn't dream of asking you to. But I
must say, Loulou, you don't show much gratitude for what
Lionel and I have done for you."

"Nor do I feel any. You're lucky I don't send you a bill."

"Loulou! How dare you say such a thing!"

"Well, that's it. I've said it, and I'm glad I said it. I think
I'll go back to town tomorrow."

"Loulou! You can't do that. You promised me you
would stay till after the New Year!"

"Well, I've decided to join David and Janetta on their
Mediterranean cruise."

"And when did you decide *that*?"

"Just now. I'm not going to be a free nurse anymore for a family that's too cheap to pay for one!"

But Betty was now ready to give as good as she got. "And what do you think Janetta wants you for?" she sneered.

"For her heart, of course. David is my one honest cousin. He makes no bones about why he's asking me. But he offers me a first-class cabin on a luxury cruise, and he sees to it that I'm free to take every expedition in every port in which we stop."

"David has always been one to get his money's worth," Betty retorted with a sniff.

"Damn right he is. Because he's willing to pay the price. You always know just where you stand with David."

A month later, steaming toward Sicily on a benign sea, Loulou reclined on a deck chair beside David Carnochan and told him of her encounter with Betty. Janetta was sleeping the sleep of the unjust in the cabin behind their chairs.

"It will make no difference in your relationship," he assured her. "Betty will always be willing to have you back. On her own terms."

"And I'll probably be fool enough to go. The Bettys of this world never seem to get their comeuppance."

"Don't be too sure of that. Old age approacheth."

"And for me, too, David. But I shan't need much of a comeuppance. I haven't made much of my life."

"As much as any of us."

"Oh, David, don't say that. Not anyway from the pinnacle of your success."

"Such as it is. And what is it? You know what my marriage is. And as for the great law firm I dreamt of running my own way, I've had to share it, first with a bossy father-in-law, and now with a bossy partner whom I detest. And with whom I've even had to share my beloved son."

"Oh, but you've had so much else. Your being able to take this cruise, for example. Whenever you like. And even being able to take a poor old cousin along. Who, incidentally, is enjoying it very much."

"Mind you, I'm not complaining, Loulou. It was you who brought the subject up."

"Fair enough. And, of course, anything bad that happens to any member of a family like ours is more or less that member's fault. For each of us started with a pack of advantages. It was up to each to use them as best he or she could."

"Except for my darling sister, Estelle, who was given only twenty-three years of life."

"Which she made the most of! I wonder if she wasn't the happiest of us all!"

"You know, in some ways I think she was."

Loulou thought they had now said enough on the subject, and she rested her head against the back of her chair to contemplate the blue infinity of the motionless sea. She thought of her young cousin Estelle, and a pleasant peace stole over her. She had been a few years younger than this lovely and popular relative, but the latter had always been particularly kind to her, insisting that Loulou had qualities just as fine as any possessed by her prettier sister, Betty. She recalled now Estelle's little cry: "Never forget, Loulou, that you're *somebody*!" And glancing now at the austere profile of David beside her, she felt a sudden impulse of real warmth toward him. He, too, had loved Estelle, though she had never had to convince him that he was somebody!

"Estelle would have been proud of you, David."

"Oh, my dear, you don't have to say that. Estelle saw me through and through."

"That's what I mean."

The next day they were anchored off Girgenti in Sicily, and David and Loulou went ashore with the group that was to visit the line of ancient temples looming over the harbor. Janetta, who was suffering from a cold, had chosen to remain on board and confine her acquaintance with the ancient world to what she could espy from her deck chair with field glasses.

As they ascended the rocky pathway that led to the largest and best preserved of the temples, David asked Loulou if she had not been there before.

"Oh, yes," she replied, "on a summer cruise, not unlike this one, with my parents when I was seventeen."

"Is it the same now?"

She looked up at the front columns of the temple they were approaching, and suddenly and startlingly, she felt again the thrill that had penetrated her whole body at her first visit to the scene. Where could it have come from, that long-forgotten sensation? That early visit had provided her with her first sight of an old Greek temple, and the dramatic surging of it before her eyes, in place of all the photographs and prints she had seen on schoolroom walls, had filled her with a strange ecstasy and a curious but elated conviction that she was going to have a wonderful life!

"It *is* just the same," she replied at last in answer to David's question. And then she added: "And this path is just the same."

"They might have fixed it up a bit in all those years."

But she ignored a comment that had nothing to do with what was happening to her. Looking ahead at the backs of the members of their group who were preceding them, she had become mysteriously conscious of quite other backs. What she saw now in her mind's eye, but just as clearly as if she had turned the page of an old family album, was the ascent of another group of tourists on the mild gradient of the same path to the edifice above. All the figures were familiar to her, though she viewed them only from behind. She recognized her mother, who seemed about to stumble, for her father had a hand on her elbow, and a boyish Gordon, who was hurrying ahead of them. She also recognized the stout outline of Mr. Talbot, the cruise lecturer, and the big ugly black hat and broad shoulders of Mrs. Otis T. Lanier (how in those days people used to stress the middle initial of familiar society names!) and the small bobbing figure of her paid (and probably underpaid) companion, Miss Trimble. And then the picture disappeared as abruptly as if someone behind her had reached over her shoulder to slam the album shut.

Yet she knew, she knew of a certainty, that what she had seen in her mind was a moment of the past preserved precisely as it had been on that particular Sicilian summer morning of 1907. She was familiar with all the scrapbooks that she herself had put together about family excursions, and there was no such photograph in any of them. But why had this particular and not very interesting vision been saved so carefully in the dark archives of her mind?

It was all very well for her to argue to herself that there didn't have to be a reason for one memory to be kept and another lost, that the mind contained a jumble of impressions that didn't have to make sense, but she could not deny the little flame of ecstasy that the vision had excited in her heart. All during their subsequent visit to the temples, she tried to put together this vision and her reaction to it in such a way as to tell her something about herself, and the only answer she could arrive at was that both were somehow twined about that strange prognostication inspired by the temples when she was a girl that she was going to have a wonderful life! Was it simply the irony of her existence that she had just been telling David that such a life was precisely what she hadn't had?

When, back on board that night, she told David of her experience, he nodded in some bewilderment, but made a conscientious effort to take her tale with at least some of the seriousness with which she endowed it.

"Well, there you are, Loulou. It's as I was saying. You *have* had a wonderful life."

"Is that what a wonderful life is?"

"It seems so. It doesn't necessarily follow that you have to *feel* you've had a wonderful life."

"And might that be true of you, too?"

"Very probably. We seem to be an ungrateful pair, you and I. But there is one thing, now I come to think of it, that strikes me about what you call your vision. What you saw was everyone's back. It was entirely a rear view, I take it?"

"Entirely. No one turned around."

"And haven't you yourself, as you have told me, spent a lot of time recently looking backward? All those family albums and charts?"

"You think it might be a warning to me to start looking forward? But to what?"

"No, it might be just the opposite. A hint that you should go on with what you're doing. Write a memoir about the family. Tell the whole truth, at least as you see it."

"Oh, I could never do that!"

"Why not? You don't have to publish it. Not in your lifetime, anyway."

Janetta now joined them, and they had to tell her of their excursion, carefully modifying the account so as not to make her feel that she had missed an important sight.

"We didn't really see anything that you couldn't see with your field glasses," David assured her. "The columns and pediments are really all that's left of the temples."

Loulou told herself that she wasn't capable of writing a

COOS BAY PUBLIC LIBRARY

book, but she didn't for a minute believe it. David's idea had so deeply excited her that she hardly dared dwell on it for fear that it might evaporate. For the rest of the cruise the concept of a family history kept jumping up and down in her mind, and when the cruise was over, and she found herself once again in her small apartment, a return that she had once dreaded, she was elated at the prospect of really starting the project.

But the calendar reminded her that the time had come around for her next chest X-ray, and when it was taken, it showed that her cancer was back — and fatally so.

WELL, HOW MUCH did it matter, she asked herself over and over in the dreary months that followed. Were not the albums, with all their monotonous contrast between the stately poses in the studio and the high jinks that people used to feel obliged to affect before the candid snapshot, and all the dates of births and deaths, even the tedious lists of favorite sports and recreations, the fatuous self-appraisals in reply to her ceaseless interrogatories, a sufficient record of the Carnochans?

Indeed, was there even such a thing as a family? With royalty the constant intermarriage of cousins preserved a certain physical resemblance, such as the Hapsburg lip, but was that such a good thing? Didn't she have to recognize that such impact as the Carnochans had made on the social scene had been largely through the multiplication of the name due to the unusual preponderance of male births? Hadn't she been planning a species of novel with what was at best a collection of short stories?

Her brother came to see her every evening at six, in the bedroom to which she was now largely confined. He was an angel of sympathy.

"You've done more than any of us," he kept assuring her. "You've assuaged an iota of the world's misery."

"And you've assuaged much of mine. Can one iota be greater than another?"

"Anyway, I can promise that I'll take good care of all your family records."

She didn't tell him that she thought he'd do as well to burn them. She knew how much he wanted to feel that he had done something for her. Maybe it would be an iota for both of them.